WOLF
AN EVIL DEAD MC STORY

NICOLE JAMES

WOLF
AN EVIL DEAD MC STORY

NICOLE JAMES

Published by Nicole James
Copyright 2015 Nicole James
All Rights Reserved
Cover Art by Viola Estrella
ISBN# 978-1532827990

CHAPTER ONE

Wolf sat in the dark in Crystal's bedroom, waiting for her to come home. He leaned back on the pink striped chair in the corner of a girly bedroom, so at odds with the tough tomboy she portrayed herself to be, that it made him smile. He knew better. He knew the Crystal who loved to fuck hard but kiss soft. She was a complicated contradiction. Tough and edgy on the outside with a soft side she only showed from time to time, maybe only to him.

On more than one occasion, he'd tried to figure out what it was about her that was so different, that affected him on such a primal level. And then it became clear.

She was the only one who understood the beast inside him, and that beast was hard for *anyone* to understand. The fact that he'd found her was truly rare. It wasn't something he could describe to other women he'd been with, not that he'd tried.

When he was a boy, he once saw a tiger at the zoo, stalking back and forth in its enclosure. It paced from one end to the other, a well-worn path along the bars, its haunches rolling with its gait. Back and forth it moved in agitation.

He knew what that agitation felt like. He often felt it growing inside of him, that feeling of a pacing cat, wanting out, wanting…*something.*

Whenever that feeling grew until it was clawing at his insides, there was only one thing that had ever satisfied it, one place he went to settle that pacing tiger inside him, one place he *always* went. Crystal. He'd find himself seeking her out. Every. Single. Time.

Women were all too easy to come by for a member of the Evil Dead MC. And so he'd tried satisfying that craving with other women—an endless stream of them. No one ever came close. All roads led him back to her. They always had. Hell, they probably always would.

He'd found something with her that he'd never found with any other woman. And fuck, it wasn't for lack of trying. But his sexual needs were a little darker than most. He liked to dominate and Crystal liked to be dominated. They clicked. Goddamn, did they ever click. She was the yin to his yang.

Maybe he was more like that big cat than he realized. He'd always heard when cats had sex, the male held the female in place by taking the scruff of her neck in his mouth and pinning her down. Wolf grinned at the thought. He understood that need to dominate.

His mind drifted back months ago to the party at the Evil Dead MC's clubhouse when everything had started to go wrong, *to the place where it all went off track…*

Misty, his flavor of the month, the latest in a long line of strippers from Sonny's, the strip club that the MC was invested in, had shown up. Crystal had gotten jealous and turned to that newbie, Shane, who was now prospecting for the club. And that had pissed Wolf off and gotten him jealous. Not one to have his face rubbed in it, Wolf had let them both know the power a full-patched member of the Evil Dead MC wielded. He'd taken Crystal away from Shane, and there wasn't a damn thing the man could do about it, not against a club member, not in his own damn clubhouse. He'd dragged Crystal upstairs, corralling her against the wall and showing her just who the hell she belonged to no matter what games they played with each other.

Their passion had always been explosive with all the fire they both stirred in each other. They fought. They loved. They often ended in a frustrating faceoff, neither giving an inch. Their relationship was a constant battle, a constant push and pull of wills.

He remembered growling down at her that night, "You push me away. I pull you back. That's our game. That's always been our game, baby. And what's more, it's a game *you like*. And you know it's a game *I love*."

Later that night, he'd started a fight with Shane, and his club brothers had broken it up. After the brawl, his President and VP had enough and ordered him to cut Crystal loose. He couldn't blame them. In their eyes he was just jerking her chain, leading her on and treating her like his personal fuck toy, and maybe he had. And it was starting to affect the club.

But they didn't understand the connection he and Crystal had, the intense draw they had to one another, the overwhelming, undeniable pull of animal attraction. The only problem was he wasn't looking for an ol' lady or to commit. And that's what Crystal would be—a commitment. She wouldn't be like all the other women he used and cast aside. He knew if he ever let himself get serious with her that would be it. It would all be over. Done deal. And that scared the shit out of him. He didn't know if he could do a real relationship, one where he had to live up to someone else's expectations.

And then fight night had come around. And Mack's glorious idea that he and their new prospect, Shane, work it out in the cage. Wolf grinned at the memory. He had beat the crap out of Shane that night, and hadn't that shown Crystal?

But his satisfaction had been short-lived. He and Crystal had lashed out at each other, and it had gotten them nowhere.

And now he was ordered to cut her loose. Impossible. No matter how hard he tried, he couldn't leave her be. For Wolf, it was all about the chase, had *always* been all about the chase. And maybe that fed into his sexual need to dominate. He didn't know, and he didn't give a fuck. Whatever the explanation was, it just *was*. Fuck trying to explain or understand it.

Wolf loved women. He was good with women. He understood them in a way most men did not. He could talk to them, and more importantly he listened. He observed. He picked shit up, shit most men missed. He could read women, knew what made them tick. He'd heard that saying…men were from Mars and women were from Venus. And damn if *that* wasn't the truth. They thought differently. They communicated differently. Women were emotional, verbal, and analytical. They thought shit through, analyzed the hell out of it, what every word meant, what every action meant. Men thought in terms of action. Men were problem solvers, not normally good listeners. Women liked closeness and men needed space. Women loved to give advice and men hated taking advice. It meant they weren't trusted to figure it out for themselves. A woman trusting a man to figure out problems and take care of her meant everything to a man. Why the hell was that so hard for women to fucking understand?

The sound of the door unlocking broke into his thoughts. Crystal was home. And fuck, she'd better be alone. If Shane was with her, he'd kill him. At the very least beat the shit out of him. Hell, if any man was with her…

He heard her footsteps coming down the hall and enter the room. She flipped the light switch. Nothing. A smile tugged at the corner of his mouth. He'd unscrewed the light bulbs.

He watched her shadowy figure move to the bedside table, and he heard the click as she turned the switch. Nothing.

Wolf smiled. He hadn't missed that one either.

"What the hell?" he heard her mumble, the only light in the room being the dim light coming from the hall. She moved to the walk-in closet and turned on that light. He'd left that one alone. She began stripping off her clothes, and his eyes slid down her body. She had on a pair of low slung jeans with a big brown belt, and a short, tight tank top that left about two inches of skin bare between them. Just enough to tease the hell out of a man. The tank came up and over her head, revealing a black lace bra. She kicked off her boots. Then her hands dropped to her belt and unbuckled it. He watched as she shimmied out of the jeans and put them in the hamper. Her panties matched her bra, and his eyes zeroed in on her ass. Crystal loved expensive lingerie, and they always matched—pretty little sets that were sometimes sexy and sometimes virginal, but always beautiful. He began to get aroused and shifted in the seat to adjust the growing erection in his jeans.

And the Goddamn chair creaked.

Shit.

She whirled around and gasped, her back slamming up against the wall as she stumbled into it. Her eyes widened as she took in his dark shape in the corner. He was out of the chair and moving toward her in a flash. She darted toward the door, but in two strides he beat her to it, his palm slamming it shut as she tried to escape. Grabbing her upper arm, he yanked her around and pushed her up against the wall, pinning her there.

She tried to scream, and his hand pressed over her mouth. Her wide eyes stared up at him.

"Shh. It's me, baby." Her breathing was coming fast with fear and panic, but slowly recognition flickered in her eyes, and she slumped against the wall as he felt the fight slide right out of her. He slowly removed his hand.

"Wolf," she hissed in a relieved voice.

***

One hour earlier...

Crystal wiped down the bar and glanced around the Evil Dead MC's clubhouse, a place she'd come to love. It was practically her home away from home. Mack, their president, and Red Dog sat at the end of the bar quietly talking and sipping on their drinks. Cole, their VP, and Crash sat at a table talking. Other than the four of them, the place was deserted. She glanced up at the clock behind the bar. Ten past midnight and things were winding down. Crystal was tired and ready to go home. She'd finished stocking the cooler with beer for tomorrow, washed all the glassware, and removed and cleaned all the liquor pourers. Not that the bottles ever lasted long enough for them to get dirty. One thing for certain, this bunch sure went through the booze. But Crystal had always been a bit of a neat freak, which was why she was so good at her job.

Walking over to the corner where Mack and Red Dog sat, she wiped the bar off and tossed some coasters their way.

"A coaster?" Red Dog snorted. "Those are for people who put their drink down." He flung it like a Frisbee back at her.

"Hey, watch it."

"Be a doll and hand me that bottle of vodka." Dog pointed to the shelf behind the bar. Crystal turned to look.

"Which one? Cherry, pineapple, coconut…?"

"Christ. Life was a lot simpler when there was only one flavor of vodka."

"Amen," Mack agreed.

Crystal grinned. "Pick a flavor, Dog. I want to go home

sometime tonight."

"I'm thinking. I'm thinking."

She picked a flavor and slammed the bottle down in front of him.

"Well aren't you just bein' the worm in my tequila tonight."

"Dog." Mack gave him a look.

"What? I don't try to annoy people; it's just a gift." Dog rose up, leaned over the bar and grabbed two shot glasses, and then he unscrewed the top and poured them. He slid one to Crystal. "Drink up, cupcake."

They lifted their shot glasses, drank, and made a face. Dog picked up the bottle and looked at the label. "What the hell flavor did you pick? Cotton Candy? What the…?" He turned to look at Mack. "What the hell are we stocking this shit for?"

Mack chuckled. "The girls like it."

Dog slid the bottle back at Crystal. "Pick another, shorty."

She laughed and handed him the cherry.

He grimaced and looked at Mack. "Bet this is gonna taste like cough syrup."

"Yum," Mack muttered sarcastically and watched as Red Dog poured himself and Crystal another shot.

"Dog, the way you drink, you're going to shorten your life by ten years," Crystal advised, picking up the shot.

"That's okay. I just want to live long enough to ride the scooter shopping cart at Walmart."

Mack spit his drink out, laughing. "Sorry. I just had a

visual of you trying to get your giant body in the scooter."

Crystal giggled, practically snorting her shot out her nose.

"Speaking of Walmart, does anyone else get road rage pushing a cart through that place? Or is it just me?" Mack asked.

Dog looked over at him. "That's 'cause you don't know when to go. The best time is the middle of the night."

"Is that right?"

"Yup. That's when you see all the best outfits. Just the other night I yelled at some guy, 'Hey, dipshit! Shoes do not turn pajamas into pants.'"

Mack chuckled. His phone went off and he pulled it out, looked at the screen, and put it to his ear. "Hey, baby."

Crystal rinsed her shot glass and then picked up her dishrag and moved around the end of the bar. Red Dog caught her around the waist as she moved past and pulled her against his side. Then he put her in a headlock and rubbed his knuckles on her head, giving her a classic noogie like big brothers had tormented kid sisters with for ages. "Come here, you little spitfire."

She shoved against him and teased back, "Let me go, you big brute."

He wrapped his arms around her and pulled her in for a bear hug. "You know I kid, baby girl. I love you like a sister."

When he released her, she bumped him with her hip. "I know it, Dog. I love you, too. Isn't it time you went home to your wife?"

Dog was married to a classic Asian beauty with a petite figure, gorgeous face, and long, silky dark hair that hung to her waist. She was the kind of girl most men could only fantasize about. She was also very intelligent and almost as much of a smartass as Crystal. The two of them made quite a striking pair—Red Dog with his big Viking warrior looks, complete with long reddish-golden hair and beard, and Mary the petite China doll.

He winked at her. "Yes, ma'am."

Mack tossed the phone on the bar top with an angry clatter and huffed a string of curses.

Dog grinned and murmured before tossing back another shot, "If our ol' ladies could hear the next five seconds after we hit end on a call, we'd never get any pussy."

Crystal rolled her eyes at Dog and looked over at Mack. "Everything okay?"

"What do women say when they actually *are* fine? Jesus Christ."

Red Dog grinned. "Yeah, they like to get inside your head and rearrange the furniture."

Crystal shook her head at Dog and asked Mack, "Trouble in paradise?"

"She called me a stubborn ass! I'm not stubborn. My way is just always better."

"You know, Mack, some things just go perfectly together, like *I told you so* and sleeping on the couch," Crystal informed him with a grin.

"Fuck."

"You finally figuring out that being right isn't nearly as

important as knowing when to shut up?" Dog grinned over at Mack.

"Christ. Just shoot me now."

Dog grunted. "With pleasure. No one wants to listen to you whine about your miserable life. Just shut up and become bitter and resentful like the rest of us."

Crystal looked over at Mack with his dark hair graying at the temples and his salt and pepper scruff. "Dog's going home to his wife. And what about you?"

"I ain't got a wife."

"No, but Natalie's probably waiting on your ass."

His eyes crinkled at the corner as he grinned, and she watched his brows rise as he replied, "She's a little pissed at me right now. But I guess that's what I get for falling for a damned redhead."

"Hey!" Red Dog protested. "What's wrong with redheads?"

Crystal shook her head. "You're so full of shit, Mack. Am I right, Dog? If she wasn't the firecracker she is, our 'fearless leader' here never would have looked twice." Natalie was in her late forties, but she still looked like a young Ann Margret. A redhead with the temper to match. Somehow, she and Mack worked. Him with his gruff I'm-in-charge-and-don't-you-fucking-forget-it attitude combined with her fiery straight-talking personality. She was classy and soft-spoken, but she also had a way with Mack that had him eating out of her hand. She was also the only one who called him on his bullshit, and apparently, that was exactly what he'd needed because he'd fallen for her hard.

"Firecracker. Yup. Just like you, darlin'," Mack agreed.

Crystal winked at him and started to walk off, but not before Mack reeled her in for a peck on her forehead. "Not that I don't appreciate how clean you keep this place, but go on home, kid."

She smiled as she pushed away. "You know what a type-A personality I am. I couldn't sleep if I went home before mopping this floor."

Mack chuckled. "You're crazy, girl. But have at it."

She moved off toward the tables and began upturning the chairs so she could mop. When she got to the table where Cole and Crash were kicked back, she moved behind Cole and slid her arms around his neck, leaning down with her head next to his blond one, her long dark hair falling over his shoulder and leather cut.

"Uh-oh," Crash murmured, grinning. "She wants something, boss."

Cole grinned back, one palm sliding over her forearm to rub back and forth. "Something I can do for you, darlin'?"

"Um-hmm," she purred in his ear.

His grin widened and he purred back, playing along with her game, "Name it, sweetheart."

"Move your ass, so I can mop."

He pulled her around his chair and down on his lap so fast she squealed as he captured her in his hold. "Move *my ass*?"

"You might need to spank *her ass* for talking to you like that, VP," Crash teased.

Crystal looked down at Cole's smiling face. "You

wouldn't."

His palm dropped from her waist to squeeze an ass cheek. "I might."

She squealed and struggled to break free, laughing.

"Settle down. I'm kidding."

Crash lifted his glass to his mouth, but spoke right before he downed the last of his drink. "She'd like it too much, anyway."

Crystal threw her dishrag at him, hitting him in the face. "Shut *up!*"

Both men laughed, but then Cole tightened his hold, squeezing the hand at her waist, his voice turning serious. "You doin' okay? Wolf been giving you anymore problems?"

Her smile faded at the reminder of the man who held her heart, yet continually broke it. A man she'd fallen for the minute she'd first laid eyes on him. The energy in the room would change when he'd walk in—at least for her. But Wolf wasn't looking for an ol' lady no matter how strong the connection was between them or how good the sex was. He'd made that clear from the beginning, and she had to come to terms with it. Any relationship they'd ever had was always on his terms.

Wolf had a bossy, demanding, not-to-be-denied way about him that drew her like honey. But Wolf was also a flirt who could woo and coax whatever he wanted from her. One minute the sweet-talking, cajoling charmer who could lure, tempt, entice, and persuade his way to anything he wanted. And the next minute, the bossy, demanding badass, who didn't hesitate in claiming, commanding, and *exacting* what he wanted. No asking—just taking.

It was the contradictions of these complexities that kept her on her toes.

Then had come the night several months ago when he'd rubbed his latest stripper in her face, and she'd attempted to make him jealous with Shane. She'd definitely gotten a reaction out of Wolf that night, just not exactly the one she'd been going for. After the men had stopped the fight, Mack and Cole had ordered Wolf to cut her loose.

"Crystal?" Cole nudged her out of her thoughts.

She focused back on his face, remembering his question. "Everything's fine."

"Fine, huh?"

She looked away. She could never get anything past Cole.

"You steer clear of him."

She nodded, but her expression must have given away the sadness that seeped into her with every mention of Wolf, because she felt Cole's hand pat her thigh.

"Consider it tough love, babe."

"I know."

Cole's brows rose. "And stay away from our new prospect, Shane. At least until he gets his patch." He grinned, softening his order. "Then you can have at him."

Crystal rolled her eyes. He was trying to get a smile, and she rewarded him with one.

Crash stood. "Well, I'm heading home to my ol' lady. Give me a hug, doll."

Crystal stood up and moved into his embrace. Crash wrapped his arms around her and rocked her from side to side, murmuring against the top of her head, "You deserve to be happy, Crystal. If Wolf's not gonna step up for you, you need to let it go."

She nodded against his chest.

He kissed the top of her head, gave her a final squeeze, and then released her.

She moved off to the old jukebox across the room and distracted herself from all thoughts of Wolf by searching through the songs for some music while she mopped.

***

Cole watched Crash look over his shoulder at Crystal before his eyes returned to him. "I don't think she's lettin' go."

Cole blew out a frustrated breath. "I don't think either of them are. And that's gonna end badly, 'cause one of them is going to end up leaving. And we all know it's not gonna be Wolf."

"Man that sucks. I like Crystal."

"We all do."

"Well, I'm takin' off."

"Set your alarm. We got business to take care of in the morning."

Crash grinned. "Why set my alarm when I can just wait until someone texts me *Where the hell are you?*"

Cole shook his head. "Get out of here, Brother."

As Crash walked out, Cole's gaze returned to Crystal. Wolf left about an hour ago, and Cole had a sneaking suspicion where he'd gone.

Fuck, he hoped he wasn't right.

***

Crystal stood with her head dipped, her face illuminated by the glow of the jukebox. She flipped through the choices, but her eyes didn't see the song titles. Instead, her mind drifted back to the first night she'd ever laid eyes on Wolf. The first time she'd ever even been on Dead property...

Six years ago...

Crystal was standing at the stove stirring the goulash in the skillet that she'd made for dinner when the back door opened and her man walked in. She turned to look, her eyes sweeping over him. His jeans and t-shirt were stained with grease, and his hands were almost black. Jason had converted the three car garage out back into an automotive repair business. He was good at it—a real gearhead.

He moved to the sink and hit the pump on the industrial strength orange hand cleaner, and then he began soaping his arms to the elbows. He sniffed the air.

"Goulash again?"

"Yes, Jason, goulash. Our grocery budget is pretty tight this month. You know tips down at the bar have been shit lately." Crystal bartended part time at a dive bar a few blocks from where they lived.

"Maybe it's your attitude." He looked over at her.

She gave him a death look and slammed the wooden spoon against the pan.

"Go get cleaned up. We're going out tonight." He dipped his arms under the faucet all the way to his elbows, and then grabbed up a dishtowel.

"Out? Where?" She frowned.

"Marnie says there's a party up at the clubhouse tonight. We're going."

Crystal didn't have to ask what clubhouse he was talking about. She knew he was referring to the clubhouse that belonged to the biggest, baddest biker club in town: the Evil Dead MC. They weren't some riding club. No, these guys were the real deal. Bikers. Outlaw bikers. The biggest club in San Jose, and one of the biggest in the state of California.

Marnie was Jason's sister, and she'd recently started seeing one of the members. Well, not just one of the members. Marnie didn't do anything halfway. No, she couldn't be content with one of the brothers; she had to go after the big fish—the MC's Goddamned President.

Since Jason was tight with his sister, he had started going up there with her. He seemed to think he was really something now that he was hanging around with the Dead. Ever since then he'd started to think his shit didn't stink.

Crystal rolled her eyes. She knew this was going to end up being nothing but trouble somehow, but hell if he'd listen to her. Up until now, Jason hadn't taken Crystal with him when he went, which was fine with her. She was smart enough to know better than to think those guys were anything to mess with. *Hell no. Count me out.* But even as she thought the words, she had to confess that a part of her deep down was just a little bit curious.

Crystal wondered if Jason hadn't brought her around there because he knew she was just enough of a smartass to say something to get them into trouble. If that was the case, he was wrong. Crystal knew when to keep her mouth shut. If either of them were likely to do the wrong thing, she knew it was Jason. But the club seemed to not mind having him around, since he'd been going up there for a few weeks already.

"I'm going with you?" she asked to clarify.

"I just said so, didn't I?"

***

An hour later, they pulled into the lot. The Evil Dead's San Jose Chapter clubhouse was buried back in an old industrial park on the seedy side of town. It was the last place on the dead-end street, its parking lot backing up to a set of railroad tracks, ensuring total privacy. Crystal couldn't image anyone coming down here unless they had a reason.

As Jason parked, Crystal took in the place. It was an old two-story red brick building that had once housed some sort of manufacturing company. There were dirty multi-paned windows up high in the walls.

Marnie was supposed to already be here. The place was packed. Bikes, mostly. The lot was covered with them. But there were cars, too, parked off to the side of the building.

Jason parked over near the bikes, like he thought he was something special. Like just the fact that his sister was their President's current pussy was supposed to get him special privileges.

They climbed out of the car, made their way inside, and

fought through the crowd, working their way to the bar.

Crystal stuck close to Jason's back, her eyes taking in the place. They'd walked into a big room with a high ceiling. The place definitely had an industrial feel with brick walls and grimy multi-paned windows set up near the ceiling. There were pool tables off to the left and hard rock music was blaring. Jason led her through a sea of black leather vests, all with the three piece patches on the back proclaiming the wearer as a member of the MC.

She noticed the men's eyes touch on Jason, and then slide past him to land on her. None of them welcomed him or smiled. The most he got was a nod, but several, she noticed, shook their heads after he'd past as if he wasn't worth their time. But it wasn't so much the looks they gave Jason that worried her as it was the looks they gave her. They were intense, hungry, filled with more than a little interest, and these men didn't have any problem letting her see it.

They made it to the bar on the right and sidled up to Marnie who had a place of honor on one of the few barstools.

Marnie turned when she saw them and Jason leaned down, his head dipping to hear her as she grabbed a handful of his shirt and pulled him close. Whatever she yelled to Jason, Crystal couldn't hear it over the blasting music. She let her eyes move to the man sitting next to Marnie with his hand on her thigh and his other holding a beer. Crystal figured he was maybe in his forties, which put him quite a bit older than Marnie, who Crystal knew was only a couple years older than herself at twenty-two.

She studied him. His dark hair was graying at the

temples, but he was still a very attractive man. Power radiated off him, something Crystal knew Marnie was drawn to. Yes, she could see his appeal. But at the same time, Crystal recognized the fact that he could be a dangerous man.

Mack was his name. Crystal had heard Marnie talk about him often enough over the last few weeks. Mack *this* and Mack *that*. That's all she talked about.

Crystal watched him raise his beer bottle, and then pause for a moment with it halfway to his mouth as his eyes connected with hers. She felt a chill run over her skin as she looked into those eyes. Yes, he was definitely not someone to mess with. Breaking eye contact with her, he waved two fingers at the guy behind the bar and then nodded toward her and Jason. A moment later, two bottles of beer were being set before them.

Crystal's eyes connected with his again, and she mouthed the words, "Thank you."

He winked at her, and then turned and began speaking to the guy next to him.

A couple of hours later, the party was getting wild, Marnie was getting drunk and loud, and Crystal was starting to get a headache. She made her way through the crowd to a filthy bathroom down the hall. She splashed some water on her face and looked in the small cracked mirror above the grimy sink. She was long past ready to go, but she knew Jason wasn't anywhere near ready to leave yet.

She'd seen a side of him tonight she'd never seen before, and she didn't like it. She'd also seen the looks the members gave him. She could see in their expressions that they put up with him because Mack was with his sister, and that was the *only* reason they didn't run his ass off the property. She was amazed Jason didn't see it. Or maybe he did. More likely he was so caught up in thinking he was really something, hanging with the big dogs. She imagined somewhere in his mind he may even be entertaining thoughts of actually becoming a member one day. If he did, those thoughts were delusional. This bunch would never really let him in. They'd tolerate him as a hang-around, but he'd never be prospect material. Even she could see that.

Yes, she could read all of that on this very first night she'd come up here.

They'd partied and had a good time tonight, but Crystal had a feeling it would be the last time she'd ever attend one of these parties. Jason had been acting like a know it all ass since they walked in. For the first time, she was embarrassed to be with him.

Slinging her leather shoulder bag on the edge of the sink, she began rummaging through it until she dug out a small bottle of aspirin. She shook out a couple of tablets and popped them in her mouth. Then she cupped her hand under the faucet and brought it to her lips to chase the pills down.

Twisting the cap back on the bottle, she jammed it back in her bag and took out lip gloss. When she was through, she checked her look in the mirror, fiddled with her hair a bit, and turned toward the door. As she headed down the hall and back into the big room, she immediately knew something was different. Half the guys were shoving out of the front door. Glancing over to the end of the bar where they'd been standing, she noticed the stools were now empty and there was broken glass all over the floor.

What the hell had happened?

Crystal made her way out the front door as well. She pushed through the crowd and out to the parking lot where she found Jason, Marnie, Mack and half the club.

Marnie was shouting at Mack.

"You're being an ass."

Mack was ordering her brother off the property. And according to him, Marnie was welcome to "take her bitchy ass with him".

The next thing Crystal knew, Jason was driving off the lot with Marnie in the rebuilt '78 black corvette that he and Crystal had arrived in.

As she stood there, staring after the car, she'd wondered how the hell she was going to get home. The asshole had just left her there. And in a way, she was glad.

Turning, she walked back into the clubhouse and returned to the spot they'd been occupying at the end of the bar. She needed to get her jacket, which she'd left there. As she gathered it up, she looked down at the broken glass, where the tussle had obviously started. Grabbing a waste basket from behind the bar, she bent and began picking up the broken pieces, completely embarrassed that she was even connected with those two.

A few moments later, a pair of boots appeared in her peripheral vision. She turned her head, her eyes following up the legs to look up at the man who stood over her. She took in the leather cut and then his face. Good God, he was gorgeous. He had dark hair and a beard and the sexiest brown eyes she'd ever seen. He was intimidating as hell with the stern look on his face as he stared down at her a long moment. Then as Crystal knelt there, stupidly mute, the stern look faded and his warm brown eyes crinkled at the corner as he smiled, revealing gorgeous white teeth.

"You don't have to do that, darlin'. That's what we've got prospects for." His eyes cut over her head to the man behind the bar, who turned his palms up and shrugged as if he didn't have a clue why she was down on her knees.

Before she could respond, Mack appeared at the man's side, also staring down at her.

She looked up at him and apologized, even though *she* hadn't done anything wrong. "I'm so sorry. We were guests here. That shouldn't have happened."

She wasn't even sure what she was apologizing for, since she wasn't even sure what actually *had* happened. She supposed she was just apologizing for Jason being a jerk.

Mack put it more bluntly.

"Your man's a dick."

She nodded. After tonight, she couldn't help but agree with him. "I'm beginning to see that."

"Why the hell are you with him?" the other man asked.

"I'm starting to wonder that myself," she murmured. "It's becoming apparent he's just a braggart and a jerk."

"You're the only one out of the three that gave a shit enough to apologize. And you didn't even do anything," Mack noted.

"I'm so embarrassed they acted like that."

Mack nodded. "Thanks for caring enough to do that"—he lifted his chin to the waste basket in her hand—"but that's not your responsibility."

Crystal looked down at the glass remaining on the floor. "Still. I feel bad. Let me at least pick up the glass."

Mack studied her with a frown, as if he didn't understand her logic at all. Then he'd shocked her by caring enough to say, "Since your ride left, Wolf will take you home."

Then he'd turned and walked off.

She looked up at the man he'd called Wolf. He nodded to Mack, and then his eyes dropped to her. He offered her his hand. "Come on, darlin'."

She put her hand in his, and he helped her up, their eyes holding. Then he turned and led her out to his bike.

"What's your name?" he asked as he handed her his helmet to put on. Up until that point, Crystal had never even been on a bike before. She took the helmet and strapped it on. "Crystal."

He nodded. "You live with Jason?"

"*I did*. Probably not after tonight."

"You got a place you can stay? A girlfriend or family?"

She nodded. "A girlfriend."

He ended up taking her to Jason's place so she could pack a quick bag. Luckily Jason wasn't there, so she didn't run into him. When she came back out, Wolf glanced around. "You got a car?"

"Yes. Jason's driving it."

He whistled and asked in an impressed voice, "That

'vette's yours?"

She smiled. "He rebuilt it for me for a birthday present. Jason's kind of a gearhead."

Wolf nodded. "He give you the title?"

And Crystal's stomach had sunk. Actually, he hadn't. "No."

He nodded, and then let the subject drop. "Climb on, cupcake."

He took her to her friend's apartment.

When he dropped her off, she thought she'd never see him again. But the next morning he pulled up driving her 'vette. One of his club brothers pulled up behind him in an old pickup truck. When she came outside, Wolf climbed out of the driver's side.

"That's a sweet ride, girl."

She looked at him in amazement. He grinned, lifted her hand, and dropped the keys and title into them. She looked down at them, dumbfounded. "How did you...?"

He grinned and shrugged. "Green and I can be real persuasive when we need to be."

She looked down at the title. "He signed it over to me?"

"Yup. There's a bill of sale in the glove box. It says you paid him a hundred bucks for it. Just take it down to the DMV and get the car put in your name."

She looked up at him in awe. "Thank you."

He winked at her.

That's when Green leaned out the driver's window of the truck. "Your boyfriend's a douche, darlin'."

Wolf looked over the hood at him. "I don't think he's

her boyfriend anymore, Green."

"Then hell, come on back to the clubhouse next weekend." Green grinned and waggled his eyebrows.

The next thing she knew, Wolf was backing her against the side of the car, boxing her in. "He's right. Mack told me to tell you you're still welcome anytime, darlin'."

"Oh, did he?" She said breathlessly, more than a little affected by him.

"Tonight's Fight Night. I'll pick you up."

"You're picking me up?"

He put his hands on the roof of the 'vette on either side of her. "You got a problem with that?"

Staring up into his eyes, she shook her head. "Nope."

He grinned and winked. Then his hands slid from the roof, he stepped away, turned, and walked back to the truck. Green put it in gear and they pulled out.

And she stood there, staring after it, until the truck disappeared around a corner.

***

Crystal shook the memory away, punched in some songs on the jukebox, and moved to the closet to get the mop and bucket on wheels. She poured some soap in and filled it with hot water, then rolled it out and began mopping. Mack and Red Dog began upturning barstools.

When they were finished, Mack called over to her, "I'll be in my office. Dog and Cole are waiting out front. Hurry up, babe. I want to be out of here by one."

"I've just got the bar area left."

He nodded and walked off.

She continued mopping and when she was through, she rolled the mop bucket out back where she could dump the water. She took it down the hall and into the big back room to the utility sink in the corner. She dumped out the water, watching the last of it swirl down the drain. When she was finished, she looked around the big back room.

The Evil Dead clubhouse was in an old two story brick manufacturing building. The front contained an open area the club used as their main room. There was an old conference room they used for their meetings and one office that Mack used. On the second floor were the old offices, the doors of each still had the frosted glass on the top half with the black lettering on them proclaiming what each was. Accounting, Engineering, Purchasing, President, Vice President, etc.

Mack, Cole, and some of the other members used those rooms for personal use at the club.

But out in back on the first floor was a huge open area that had originally housed the manufacturing machinery. It was all long gone, but the club had a special use for the cavernous space. They held their monthly fight nights here. They had a steel cage and everything. Ultimate fighting. Two guys would climb in the cage and beat the shit out of each other, and the boys would bet on the outcome. It was a popular night and always packed the house.

Crystal shoved the mop bucket in a corner and wandered over to the cage, leaning her forehead against it. Her mind drifted back to the first time she'd seen Wolf fight. It was the first time she'd seen him with his shirt off and good God, the man was gorgeous—all muscle and beautiful, tattooed skin.

He'd beat the crap out of some guy from another
Chapter that night. She remembered the way he'd looked out
from behind the cage, his eyes connecting with hers. There
was a heat in those brown irises, some confusing message
that was just for her. It had unsettled and confused her
because she felt something respond inside of her.

Then later, he'd cornered her in the hall, backing her
against the wall and asking if she'd enjoyed the fight. She'd
nodded, her eyes skating over him and made some smart-ass
comment about what wasn't to love about two half-naked
men beating the shit out of each other.

He'd grinned. Then he'd lifted his hand, his finger
grazing her cheek. "Does the winner get a kiss?"

It had been the first move he'd made on her. He'd stared
down, waiting, not about to take what she wasn't willing to
give.

She'd gone up on her toes and brushed his lips with a
soft kiss. When she'd opened her eyes, his were still closed.
Then he'd opened them slowly, looked down at her, and gave
her a slow, soft smile. That's all it had taken for her heart to
fall completely over the edge for him.

That's all it had been that first time. Just a single, soft
kiss. She'd slipped from between him and the wall, and that
time—that first time—she'd thought he'd let her go.

But he'd caught her hand and reeled her back in,
corralling her against the wall again. She'd looked up at him,
her breathing coming quicker at the heat flaring in his eyes.
Then he'd kissed her again, and this time there was nothing
soft about it. He'd been all dominant alpha male, taking what

he wanted. And he'd wanted her. She'd given back as good as she got, and he'd growled his approval.

That first night the fiery chemistry between them had ignited into full blown heat.

Soon they hadn't been able to keep their hands off each other, stealing any moment they could to be together.

"Crystal," Mack hollered from the hallway door, breaking into her thoughts and shaking her memories away. "You back here?"

She hustled toward the door and out of the shadows. "I was just dumping out the dirty water."

"Let's go, babe."

She followed him to the main room. The lights were all out, and she trailed Mack out the front door.

Dog and Cole stood just outside the entrance, smoking cigarettes.

"Let's go home," Mack said to them.

They mounted up, but waited while she climbed in her car and fired it up. Then they followed her out of the parking lot and down the street. When they got to the four lane highway, she turned right and they turned left, roaring off on their Harleys.

***

Twenty minutes later, Crystal stood staring up at Wolf. She was pressed against her bedroom wall in nothing but her bra and panties. Classic Wolf. First thing he always seemed to do was back her up against the nearest immovable surface. Wall, door, car... it didn't matter as long as it was something solid he could pin her against.

"Wolf." She looked up into his face. His teeth flashed in the dim light as he grinned.

"In the flesh."

"What are you doing here? You scared the crap out of me."

"Got your blood pumping though, didn't I? I can see your pulse pounding in your throat." She watched his eyes drop to it as his hand came up, his warm palm covering the pulsing vein, and she swallowed. His nearness did things to her, things she couldn't deny. He knew. He always knew the effect he had on her. The effect they had on each other. Still, she had to fight it. She couldn't just give in. She licked her lips.

"You're not supposed to be here. Cole said so."

His grin faded a bit. "I know what he said. I don't need you to tell me."

"Then why are you still here?"

"Because I can't fucking stay away from you, Crystal. And you know it."

"We can't." She tried weakly to push against his chest.

"You feel it, too. Don't try to deny it." His palm came up to cup her cheek, and he moved in closer, crowding her against the wall. Against her will, she found her head turning into his palm, her eyes sliding closed, and she heard him whisper, "There's my baby."

God, she had to be strong. One of them had to be. "Wolf. Please, just go."

His thumb brushed over her lower lip, and her eyes opened up into his. As she watched, his gaze dropped to her mouth, and he pushed down on her lip, sliding his thumb in. She closed around it and watched his eyes flare.

"Love your mouth. Always have."

And then his mouth came down on hers, and he replaced his thumb with his tongue.

Crystal felt her body melting, her knees going weak as they always did when he kissed her. Yes, Wolf was *that* good at kissing. As if he knew, as if he felt her grow weak, his strong arms were there wrapping around her waist, pulling her tight against him, holding her up as his mouth ravished hers. Her moans were muffled by his tongue.

With a growl, he pressed her back against the wall, pinning her there and freeing his hands to roam over her curves.

She found her own hands drifting up over the smooth leather of his cut, her arms encircling his neck. Her touch fired a response in him, like it always had. His hands grabbed her ass and pulled her flush against him as he growled into her mouth.

She broke off, pushing him back. "They told you to stay away."

"I can't, babe. You know I can't." He slammed her back against the wall.

Crystal wanted a man who took what he wanted, a man who wasn't easily deterred or put off. And that described Wolf to a T. But at the same time, she knew Wolf well enough to know the kind of man he was, and because she did, she felt safe in letting him be aggressive with her, and she felt safe in showing that side of herself to him—the side that wanted him to be forceful and aggressive, because in her heart she was sure of one thing. And that was knowing he'd never take more than she wanted to give.

"Face the wall, Miss Devereux."

Crystal smiled. He wanted to roll play. She could always count on Wolf to mix it up. She turned around.

"Hands up."

She placed her hands high, flat on the wall. He tapped her bare foot with his boot. "Spread your legs, Miss."

"Are we playing good cop/bad cop?" she asked over her shoulder as she obeyed his command.

"What do you think?" He stepped closer, crowding her against the wall.

"I think there aren't any good cops."

"I guess that makes me a bad cop. But I get the feeling you like bad boys, Miss Devereux. In fact I think you hang out with a bunch of bad boys. One in particular, and I aim to find out his name."

She gave him a smug look over her shoulder. "I'll never tell you anything, Officer Friendly."

"Oh, we're about to get real friendly. I'll need to search you for concealed weapons, ma'am."

She glanced down at her skimpy bra and panties. Right.

His hands slid over her skin and around to the front of her bra. Cupping her breasts, he squeezed until she came up on her toes with a moan.

"What do we have here? Feels like you're packing some big guns. A pair of double Ds, Miss Devereux?"

Her hand came down off the wall, and she reached

behind her, stroking over the front of his jeans.

"And how big a weapon do *you* have, Officer?"

His hand came down and covered hers, squeezing it and thrusting into her hand. "Maybe if you're a really good girl and cooperate fully, I'll let you find out."

"I am cooperating."

He took her hand and put it firmly back on the wall, holding it there as he leaned in to admonish in her ear, "Then maybe you should keep your hands where I told you."

"Yes, sir."

He released his grip on her wrist, and his hands slid down over her ribs, down past the curve of her waist to her ass. "Let's see what other deadly weapons you've got on you. He squeezed her cheeks. "Hmm. Could be deadly. Could be used against a man." She pushed back into his hands and rubbed up against his crotch.

His hand came down with a firm smack on her cheek. "Behave or I'll have to get nasty." He drew a gun from the small of his back and held it to her cheek, stroking her skin with the side of the barrel. "Understand?"

She had to smile. He was really getting into this. She'd felt how hard he was. "Yes, sir."

"Good answer." He set the gun on the nearby highboy dresser. Then his hand slid around to her front and dipped into her panties, his finger hooking right into her, bringing her up on her toes with another moan. "Now this, Miss Devereux, this could definitely kill a man." He pumped into her several times. "At the very least bring a man to his knees."

She dropped her head, pressing her forehead against the wall, totally caught up in what his wicked hand was doing to her. His other arm came up under her armpit, his hand pressing against the wall as he moved in on her, his mouth at her ear.

"Hmm. Very cooperative, now, aren't you?"

"Are you...?" Her voice broke as his thumb tortured her clit with gentle caresses. "Oh, God."

"You had a question for me?"

"Are you...ATF?"

"ATF are pussies. I'm DEA, lady. And I fully intend to get all the information out of you that I came for."

"W-what information?" God, what he was doing with his hand felt so good, she could barely concentrate on the game.

"The man you're involved with, the one that pays you all those late night visits."

"How do you know about that?"

"I've been watching you."

"You have?"

"Um hmm. What's his name, Miss Devereux?" He ramped up his relentless stroking.

She panted. "I'll never tell you."

"Oh, I think you will." He withdrew his hand and stepped away. "On the bed," he ordered.

She turned and looked at him. They may be playing, but his expression was totally serious. She stepped over to the bed and eased down on it. He stepped closer, standing over her. She tilted her head to look at him. He shrugged off his cut and tossed it on the dresser. Next came his t-shirt. He tore it off and dropped it on the floor. Then he reached to the small of his back, and a pair of silver handcuffs flashed in the dim light pouring from the closet. Her eyes fell to it, and she swallowed.

She bolted off the bed, making a dash toward the door, but he grabbed her arm and reeled her back in. "Going somewhere?"

She struggled.

"Go ahead. Fight me, Miss Deveraux." Then he lifted her and tossed her roughly onto the bed, manhandling her with ease. She scurried across the mattress, but he clamped his hands around her ankles and yanked her backward. He flipped her onto her back and straddled her, easily overpowering her. Grabbing both wrists, he pinned them to the bed above her head.

"Get off me." She tried to buck him off, but he was like an immovable rock. His full weight settled on her, but she still struggled, giving him exactly what he wanted. He grinned down at her as she continued to fight him.

"I'm not going anywhere, so fight all you want, lady." When she finally tired, her breath heaving in and out, he trailed his nose along hers, lulling her in with promises. "Cooperate, and I'll go easy on you."

She nodded, relenting. "All right. I give."

He studied her warily as he released his hold and moved to stand by the side of the bed.

She came up on her elbows and stared back at him, just as wary.

"Lie back," he ordered with a lift of his chin toward the

headboard.

She crawled backward, reclining against the pillows to stare up at him.

He again lifted his chin. "Arms above your head."

She did as he asked, and he snapped the cuffs on her. And then she watched wide-eyed as he pulled his belt loose. Her eyes followed it as the smooth leather slithered free of his belt loops. She sucked in a breath as he loomed over her to wrap the belt around the handcuffs and then around the post of the headboard, yanking it tight.

"What are you going to do?" she whispered, her insides tightening with her desire. God, this man could take alpha to a whole new level.

He planted his fists in the bed, one on each side of her as he loomed over her. "I'm going to get what I came for. I'm going to get all the information out of you I want. I'm going to have you twisting with need until you tell me every single thing you know."

"I'll never tell you a damn thing," she panted, kicking out at him, her whole body twisting and bucking.

He barely managed to deflect her blow from hitting him smack in the family jewels.

"Assaulting a police officer will get you three-to-five, Miss Devereux," he ground out coming down on top of her.

"Three-to-five years? I highly doubt it."

"Three-to-five hours, Miss Devereux. In this bed. At my mercy." He gave her a wicked smile. "But go ahead and fight me. I like it that way. I bet you do, too." He dipped his head to whisper in her ear, his breath caressing her skin. "I'll let you in on a little secret. I'm all about the struggle, so keep going, you're just making me harder."

That just drove the need in her to refuse to submit. She renewed her fight again, thrashing and twisting, but with her hands restrained above her head, there was nothing she could really do but prolong the inevitable. Even so, she wasn't going to make this easy for him. But with every kick she tried to land, his body locked her down further, until she was practically immobile.

When she finally lay motionless, panting from her exertions, he brought his mouth to her ear again to whisper, "Tell me about him. Tell me about this man that visits you at night."

"He knows what a woman likes, he knows how to get inside my head and make me forget everything but him."

"Really. Is that so? What else?"

"He's an amazing kisser. When he kisses me, I forget everything. I forget where I am. I feel like I'm the only person in the world he cares about."

His mouth came down on hers, his tongue delving inside. He kept at it, relentlessly plundering, barely giving either of them a chance to breathe.

Finally, he broke away. "Say his name."

"Never," she panted.

"Oh, I think you will." He rose up, straddling her hips to look down at her.

Her eyes fell to the hand at his hip as it drew the knife from the sheath. He brought it to her chest and she held her breath as he gently lifted each strap of her bra and cut through them. Then he moved to the center of her bra and sliced through it as well.

"Was that really necessary?"

"You bet it was, baby doll."

Her chest heaved up and down as he returned the knife to its sheath and then pulled the bra free, tossing it aside. He sat back, his eyes coasting over her body, his warm palms landing on her stomach and then moving slowing up to cup her breasts. He squeezed, kneading them as his eyes flicked up to watch her reaction, to see the desire flare to life again.

"I can play nice. Or not. It's all up to you."

He squeezed again, and her head fell back, her eyes closing as a moan escaped her lips.

"Say his name," he whispered, brushing his thumbs over her nipples, bringing them to sensitive peaks.

She shook her head, rolling it from side-to-side on the pillow. His hands released her, and a moment later he pinched both nipples. Hard. She arched her back as the sharp jolt zinged through her, and she bit her lip against crying out. *Oh God*, it felt so good.

"Tell me." His voice was sharp with demand as he applied more pressure.

She shook her head. "Never."

He slid down her body, licking and nuzzling and nipping her skin. Her eyes followed his every movement. Then he settled between her legs, his broad chest holding her thighs wide and tucked under his arm pits. She couldn't move. He had her held totally immobile and open and at his mercy. He tore the lace of her panties, yanking them off with one strong tug, and she yelped.

His eyes, dark and hungry, lifted to hers just before he settled his mouth down over her. The flat of his tongue stroked with long slow swipes. She bit her lip, her head falling back. She felt his mouth leave her a moment before she felt a sharp nip on her thigh.

Her head came up as he ordered, "Keep your eyes on me."

She looked down her body at him.

"Do you understand?" he pressed.

She nodded and watched as his mouth settled over her again. His laving tongue stroked over her again and again until he had her worked into a frenzy, twisting with need for more. Her body began to undulate, revealing the need she fought so hard to control. He lifted his head, shifting and a moment later she felt him slide two fingers inside her, gliding up and rubbing until he found her G-spot. Her head fell back again when he found it, and she couldn't stop the moan that escaped as her control unraveled.

"Bingo," she heard him whisper as he began stroking it, first slow, and then fast, and then slow again. She writhed, and then his thumb stretched up to massage her clit. Her hips lifted in a dance as old as time, straining to meet his every stroke. A thin sheen of sweat broke out across her body as she struggled with the need he was driving higher and higher with every touch.

When he had her balancing on the edge of orgasm, he backed off and she twisted, lifting her hips, straining to get back his touch. "No, please."

He tormented her with his tongue. Soft swipes that only brought her gently back down, and then he began with his fingers again, bringing her right back up to the edge. This time he pressed his palm down on her lower belly, increasing the pressure of his fingers as they massaged the G-spot deep inside her.

"Tell me his name," he demanded as he continued his assault.

She thrashed. "I can't. I can't."

He backed off again, and she thrashed all the more.

"Please," she begged.

"You can stop it all with a name, sweetheart. Give him up, and all the torment stops."

Her head thrashed back and forth on the pillow. "I can't. You know I can't."

"Can't or won't?"

"Can't. Won't."

"You can and you will, Miss Devereux."

He began again. This time when she would have rocked against him, he held her immobile, completely vulnerable to whatever he chose to do to her. Keeping steady strokes on her clit with his thumb, he ramped up the torment until her body trembled, and her breath came in desperate little pants. Oh God, she didn't know how much longer she could take it without breaking.

This time when he backed off, she could tell their play was getting to him just as much as it was her. But she also knew he liked to drag this out as long as she could bear it.

"How far do I have to take this? Hmm? How much more

can you take, pretty lady? I can keep at it all night."

They stared at one another, neither budging.

"Tell me his name," he ordered.

"Shane," she taunted him with a name she knew would piss him off.

His teeth came down on her inner thigh again, and she yelped as she heard him growl, "Not funny, Crystal."

She must have really gotten to him if he broke the game to use her first name.

"Tell me his name," he growled again in a sharp tone.

"Never. I'll never tell you a thing."

"Don't make promises you can't keep, Miss Devereux."

He slid from between her legs to stand at the foot of the bed. Her eyes watched every move he made as he kicked off his boots and jeans. He wanted her all right. His cock was rock hard. He grabbed it, giving it a long slow stroke.

"You want this?"

She stared at him, refusing to answer, refusing to tell him she was craving it.

"Maybe I'll fuck his name out of you."

He knelt between her legs again, his fingers delving into the slick wetness between her legs, stroking it up and over her. "Baby, you are definitely in need, aren't you?"

Then he moved over her.

With one hand planted in the bed next to her upstretched arms, his other wrapped around his cock, he hovered above her, dominating and controlling every moment, every touch. She heard him suck in his own breath as he guided his cock to poise at her entrance. He teased her, rubbing the head to her clit and back again. She writhed, pleading with her body, offering herself in silent invitation. *Take me. Please take me.*

She gasped as he settled down over her, his movements stilling as he brushed the hair back from her face and nuzzled her neck.

"Tell me," he whispered in her ear.

"Please," she begged.

"Tell me, and I'll be gentle." His voice cajoling and coaxing.

Wolf knew how to sweet-talk his way into her pussy as well as her heart. But she also knew he didn't want her to give in. Not really. So she did the only thing she could. She shook her head.

He lifted his head to stare down at her a long moment, and she could see the look in his eyes, he practically willed her to obey. When she kept her mouth firmly shut, he grinned and lifted back, settling on his knees between her legs.

"Rough it is, then."

Grabbing her behind her knees he pushed her legs up, pinning them up to the bed, and she caught her breath. He stared down at her, his cock lined up with her entrance.

"Last chance, kitten."

She could see the heat glittering in his eyes, the feral savage need to take.

When she stayed quiet, he paused one last moment before he plowed into her in one savage thrust. She gasped as he planted himself to the hilt and held himself there, rock hard. They stared at each other as he pulled out and slammed back into her, his hips bruising her thighs. He began his pounding assault, slow at first, and then faster with more power. She watched as sweat formed on his skin as his muscles flexed with every driving roll of his hips as he thrust into her again and again. He was like a fierce sleek animal dominating her into submission.

She felt her traitorous body relenting, welcoming him with a new flood of lubrication. She couldn't stop herself as her inner muscles clenched down in its own pulsing cadence. She could see he felt it too, and for a moment she thought he'd break, but then she watched him clench his teeth struggling to regain his unyielding control.

Mastering it, he changed his pace, sliding deep in a slow torturous drive she was sure was designed to send her spiraling past any limit she tried to hold on to.

Her hands itched to feel his skin, to stroke his muscles, to touch the light sheen of sweat she could see at his temple. The handcuffs rattled as she tugged involuntarily at her restraints, and her inner muscles clamped down on him, touching him the only way she could, the only way she had left.

"Nuh-uh, sweetheart. Don't think you can control this, control me."

"I'm not, I—" She broke off, overwhelmed with surging need. "*Please.*"

Leaning over her, he gripped a handful of her hair, his mouth coming down on hers while he continued his brutal relentless onslaught until the need for oxygen took precedence. He broke free and dipped his head, his eyes going to where they were joined.

Oh God, could there be anything better?

She loved everything about the way he was with her, the way he let that animal inside him out when they were together, turning all dominant; an alpha taking its mate. His name was so appropriate. He *was* a wolf. And tonight, he was *her* wolf.

It didn't matter that he wasn't supposed to be here. It didn't matter what anyone else thought of their crazy relationship. All that mattered was having each other, and the connection they had that no one else understood. No one else could ever understand this.

Soon she could see the need building in him. He needed that release as badly as she did, but he'd wait. He'd wait until she said those words. He'd wait if it killed them both. If Wolf had one thing, it was steely control over his release.

"Tell me," he ground out, between clenched teeth, his jaw tight. "Tell me, and this torment stops for both of us."

She knew the game was over. He'd reached his breaking point, and he needed her to give in now. She also knew the way his mind worked. She had to be the one to give in, because he never would.

"Wolf," she panted. "His name is Wolf."

With a groan, one hand left her leg and his thumb began stroking over her. He knew exactly how she liked to be touched, and he gave it to her, until she was thrashing with need. She soared higher and higher as he kept at her.

"Give it to me, baby," he rasped as he continued to thrust into her, changing his angle so that every stroke drove over her G-spot again and again.

She let go and soared over the edge, her l
him with the contractions that shuttered throug
She could tell he felt them as his thrusts becam
then he went solid above her as his climax rocke
him as well.

They were both breathing hard as his body came down
on her. She relished the weight of him and tugged on her
wrists, longing to wrap her arms around him. The metal of
the cuffs clinked together and he stirred, his eyes lifting to
them. Reaching up, he undid the leather belt, freeing her
from the bedpost. Bringing her arms down, he unlocked the
cuffs and gently rubbed her wrists.

"You okay, kitten?" He brushed his mouth over her
inner wrists, kissing them softly.

She nodded.

"You're being quiet." He stared down at her, studying
her as his hand cupped her face, his thumb stroking tenderly
over her cheek. "Was it too much?"

She shook her head. "I would have stopped you if it was.
It was amazing."

He grinned and pressed a kiss to her mouth, his lips
barely touching her. Then he shifted and wrapped his arms
around her. He cuddled her close, spooning her from behind,
his arm locked tight around her, and she felt his mouth at her
ear.

"You gave my name up way too easy, kitten."

She grinned and wiggled her ass into his crotch. "As if."

He tightened his arms around her, and she felt his dick
hardening. She shifted and locked it between her legs,

earning a groan from him.

"You ready for round two already?" he growled in her ear.

She giggled and protested in a whine, "I need *sleep*."

"Mmm. Me, too."

His hands encircled both her wrists, and he crossed her arms over her chest, holding her back pressed against him, locking her down tight and close.

"Wolf, you're squishing me."

"Shh, go to sleep, baby doll."

His body was like a furnace, and the heat of it soon relaxed her. She listened to him breathe. Four or five breaths in, his breathing changed and his muscles began to relax, his body settling deeply into the mattress. She felt his hold on her loosen as he drifted off.

Wiggling and twisting, she managed to turn in his arms and snuggled down into his chest, her face pressed into the curve of his neck. His arms tightened around her for a moment, and then he relaxed back into slumber. She could feel the steady beat of his heart, and she soon drifted off as well, secure in the warmth of his embrace, exactly where she wanted to be. Where she would *always* want to be.

CHAPTER TWO

Wolf stood staring down at Crystal as she slept. God she was beautiful, the early morning light casting her in soft shadows. His eyes moved over her body, exposed where she'd kicked off the sheet. He noticed the small bruises from the little nips he'd given her inner thigh. Perhaps he'd been too rough with her, but Crystal never complained. She seemed to enjoy, even crave, their rough play as much as he did.

He was tempted to wake her, but he didn't. He thought about leaving her a note, telling her how beautiful she was, telling her he'd gotten called out. Club business. But he figured she'd know. She'd been around the club long enough to know that when the club called, the brothers answered. Always.

So he didn't wake her, and he didn't leave a note. It was a decision he'd come to regret. Because if he'd known the events that would transpire, he would never have walked out that door.

But he hadn't known, so he bent and brushed a soft kiss on her forehead and whispered, "Love you, babe."

A kiss she never felt. A note she never saw. A sentiment she never heard.

***

Crystal felt the warmth of the sun on her bare back as it poured in through the white sheers that covered her bedroom window. It felt delicious. For a moment she imagined herself lying on a beach in the sun. She shifted in the bed and immediately felt the ache in her thighs, and memories of last night came flooding back.

Wolf.

Her eyes popped open, and she turned her head on the pillow, her arm reaching out, her hand finding only empty bed and cold sheets.

"Wolf?" she called.

Only silence replied.

She lifted up, her eyes glancing around the room. Any trace of him was gone, as if he'd never been there at all. She could have convinced herself it was all a dream if not for the aching soreness between her legs.

Once again she felt the emptiness return, like it always did, that feeling of being used. Used and cast aside until the next time he needed to scratch his itch.

She flung the sheet back and swung her legs out of bed. Picking up her cell from the nightstand, she checked it for any texts or missed calls. Nothing. Rising, she jerked on a short robe, jammed her phone in the pocket, and headed toward the kitchen. After starting the coffee, she stood at the sink, staring out the window, her fingers drumming on the counter. It was times like this, when the agitation and pent up anger boiled through her, that she wished she still smoked.

Yanking open the cabinet, she pulled down a mug. Coffee would have to do. Coffee and maybe a shot of Baileys. She lifted the carafe and filled her cup. As she returned it to the burner, her phone rang. She dug it out of her pocket and looked at the screen. Angel.

Pressing receive, she put it to her ear. "Hi."

"Morning, doll. What are you up to?"

"Just got up. Working my way through my first cup of coffee," Crystal replied, tucking the phone between her ear and shoulder as she reached for the Baileys and unscrewed the cap to pour a hefty shot into her mug. "What's up?"

"We're all over at Crash and Shannon's. Since the boys left at the crack of dawn this morning, the girls decided to get together for some Bloody Marys. And they beat coffee any day, so get your butt over here."

"You and Shannon?"

"Mary is here, too. Natalie's watching the kids."

"I've got a bathroom to scour." Crystal threw out the excuse.

"Who *are* you? June Cleaver? It's Saturday. Get your butt over here, now. You know with three kids I rarely get out," Angel whined.

Crystal heard Shannon in the background. "Is she coming over?"

Angel's voice replied, "She says she has a bathroom to

scour."

Shannon yelled loud enough for Crystal to hear. "I've got a bathroom she can scour!"

"Did you hear that? Get over here," Angel ordered into the phone.

Crystal grinned and rolled her eyes. "Okay. Okay. I'll be over soon."

***

Twenty minutes later, Crystal was pulling her car into the garage of Crash and Shannon's warehouse style loft. Crash had converted an old two story brick warehouse in Oakland to a beautiful living space. On the outside it looked like an abandoned building, but on the inside the loft was the shit.

Crystal got on the freight elevator and rode it up to the second floor loft. When she threw back the gated elevator door, she was greeted by Angel who stood there with a big grin and held out a Bloody Mary, complete with celery stalk.

"Good Morning, Sunshine," Angel greeted her.

Crystal took the drink, chugged back a slug, and replied, "What's so good about it?"

"Did someone wake up all cranky this morning?"

Crystal followed Angel past the pool table on the left to the open floor plan kitchen with its granite island. She took a seat on one of the stools at the bar. Shannon and Mary were mixing up more drinks.

Crystal's eyes slid over Shannon. She was a tall slender blonde that looked totally put together, even with her hair up in a twist and yoga pants on. "I hate you," Crystal growled as she bit into her celery.

"Hate me? Why?" Shannon's beautiful smile faded.

"Because you look like a movie star at ten in the morning."

Shannon's smile returned. "Yeah, you're a real dog with your thick, glossy dark hair and those big gorgeous eyes. I really feel for you, girl."

"Come on, let's go up on the rooftop with these drinks," Angel suggested.

They made their way through the loft and up the metal stairs that led to the roof. As Crystal looked around, it was obvious that Shannon had definitely had an influence on the place already since moving in with Crash. Previously there had only been a couple of Adirondack chairs and some wooden crates. Now the crates were gone, there were cushions on the chairs, as well as two loungers, and a nice table.

"Wow. Nice upgrade," Crystal commented as they all sat down.

"Thanks. I love what Crash did with his loft, but the roof...it needed a little help."

"You ain't lyin'."

"So, how are you doing, Crystal? I haven't seen you in a while," Shannon asked.

"I'm okay."

"You look tired," Angel noted.

"I didn't get much sleep last night."

"Oh, really? What's his name?" Mary asked.

"Right away it's a guy?"

"I'm just saying…" Mary lilted.

Angel gave Crystal a knowing look. "Shane?"

Crystal huffed out a laugh. "No. Actually Cole told me to steer clear of him. At least until he gets his patch."

"And once he gets his patch?" Shannon prodded.

Crystal gave a sly smile. "Let me see. How did he put it? I believe his words were 'I could have at him'."

They all giggled.

"So, if it wasn't Shane, what or *who* kept you up all night?" Mary prompted.

Angel stared at her, urging her when she didn't reply. "Crystal?"

"It was Wolf, wasn't it?" Shannon asked.

When she didn't reply, they all knew.

"Crystal!" Angel's mouth fell open. "You and Wolf?"

"Maybe." Crystal shrugged like it was no big deal. But she knew this was all news to Angel. Shannon knew. And Mary had most likely heard from Red Dog, but Crystal had never spoken of her affair with Wolf to Angel. She'd have kept it a secret from all of them if she could, but Shannon had witnessed the fight Wolf had with Shane, and had dragged her off and wormed the whole story out of her. A story she'd kept from her best friend, Angel. And now Angel knew.

"Spill. What happened?" Angel demanded.

"Oh, all right. He was at my place when I got home."

Mary frowned. "You mean waiting out front for you?"

"No. I mean he was waiting inside for me."

Mary's brows shot up. "*Inside?*"

Crystal nodded. "Sitting in the dark in my bedroom."

"Whoa. Wait. Is that creepy or sexy?" Shannon asked.

Angel gave her a look. "Have you lost your mind? Of course it was sexy. This is Wolf we're talking about."

"Just sayin'. It would kind of freak me out." Shannon shrugged and took a sip of her drink.

"So, what happened?" Angel pressed Crystal for details.

Crystal lifted one shoulder. "What usually happens."

"You are *so* bad," Mary teased leaning back on her chaise lounge. She lifted her sunglasses off her eyes and looked over at Crystal. "Was he good?"

Crystal couldn't hide the smile pulling at her mouth. "Wolf is *always* good."

"So, then why are you so in the dumps this morning?" Angel frowned, studying her.

"That's not the problem."

"Then what is?" Shannon asked.

Crystal gave her a look. "You should know."

"Oh. That."

"Oh, what?" Angel asked, frowning, looking from one to the other.

"Cole ordered Wolf to stay away from Crystal."

"Why did he do that? And why am I just now finding out about all of this?"

Mary polished off the last of her drink. "Well, this has been fun, ladies, but I can't stay. I have a nail appointment."

"You can't go. I baked a breakfast casserole!" Shannon turned to give her a stern look, ruining it with her smile.

Crystal sniffed the air. "Speaking of casseroles, do you smell something?"

Shannon's smile faded, and her eyes got big. Then she jumped out of her chair and darted for the door. "Oh crap."

Crystal, Angel, and Mary looked at each other, and then burst out laughing.

"Hey, every bride burns a meal or two," Angel defended.

"Yeah, but eating the burnt remains is supposed to be the groom's job," Crystal replied.

Mary giggled and waggled her fingers in the air as she headed to the door. "Ta-ta, ladies. Enjoy your meal."

"Chicken-shit!" Crystal called after her.

Mary stopped in the doorway and turned back, flicking her waist length hair over her shoulder. "Mama Wu didn't raise a stupid daughter, honey."

"Mama Wu raised a chicken-shit!" Crystal called after her in good-natured fun.

"I'll tell her you said that."

"Mama Wu loves me. She knows I'm right."

The door closed on Mary's laughter.

Angel turned to Crystal. "Well, come on. Let's go see if it's salvageable. But you're not off the hook. I still want the full story on you and Wolf."

"Okay, okay."

They both got up and began collecting glasses to carry inside.

***

Crystal took a small bite, put it in her mouth, and then spoke sarcastically around the mouthful. "Umm. Yum."

Angel almost snorted out her drink as she began to laugh.

Shannon took a bite and threw her fork on her plate. "Okay, okay. It's terrible."

They all giggled.

A moment later, Crystal was covering her mouth and jumping off her barstool to run for the bathroom as her stomach cramped. Reaching it just in time, she vomited into the toilet.

When she came back out, Angel asked, "Are you okay?"

"It wasn't that bad, was it?" Shannon asked, frowning.

Crystal shook her head and moved back to her barstool. She reached for her Bloody Mary glass. "I don't know. I just suddenly felt nauseous."

"That's just how I was when I was pregnant with Brayden. Every time I even smelled eggs, I'd..." Her voice faded off as a shocked look formed on her face.

Crystal watched her two best friends look at each other, then Angel looked back at her.

"Crystal...you're not *pregnant*, are you?"

"What? No. *Hell no.* I can't be. I'm on the pill."

Shannon frowned. "Yeah, but you were sick with that bronchial infection last month, and you were on antibiotics."

"So?"

"*So?* They make the pill ineffective. Didn't you read the prescription?" Angel asked.

Crystal stared back with what she was sure was a deer-in-the-headlights look. "Shit."

Angel took the drink out of her hand, walked over and dumped it in the sink. As she did, Crystal thought about the two shots she'd done with Red Dog at the end of the night last night. Before her scrambled brain could get any further than that, Shannon took her by the arm and hustled her back into the bathroom with Angel hot on their heels. Shannon pulled a box down from the shelf and handed it to Crystal.

She looked down at the box in her hand. It was a pregnancy test. Her brow rose. "You keep these in stock?"

Shannon shrugged and admitted a little shyly, "Crash and I have been trying."

"You have?" Angel squealed, excitedly.

"No luck yet."

After Crystal peed on the stick, they all stood around staring at it for three minutes watching the little plus sign form, until it couldn't be denied. It was positive. Crystal felt the room spin.

"I think I need to sit down." They guided her over to the couch. Shannon got her a bottle of water, and she sipped on it, again thinking about the shots she did last night.

"So who's the father?" Angel asked softly.

Shannon sat down next to her and took her hand. "Is it Wolf?" When she didn't answer Shannon pressed, "Shane?"

She'd had her period since the one time she'd been with Shane. But Wolf had been with her one night last month. No wait, twice.

Oh God.

"I haven't been with Shane."

Shannon frowned. "You haven't? I thought…"

She shook her head. "A couple of months ago. Once. But not since then. It can't be his. There's just been…"

"Wolf?" Angel's face was soft with sympathy as she

prodded.

"Yes."

Shannon and Angel exchanged a look.

Crystal felt the blood drain from her face. "What am I going to do?"

"You should tell him," Shannon advised.

Crystal shook her head. "No. I can't. He'll be so pissed."

"No, he won't," Angel insisted, frowning. "Why do you say that?"

"He doesn't want a kid."

Shannon cocked her head. "How do you know that? Have you asked him?"

"No, but…"

"Men don't know what they want until you give it to them," Angel advised.

"Oh, really? Is that how it goes?" Crystal asked with a smirk.

Angel smiled. "Kind of."

"Are you afraid Wolf won't step up?" Shannon asked hesitantly.

"I don't want him if it's that way," Crystal replied with conviction. The last thing she wanted was a man who resented her, or who was with her because he felt trapped. She finished the water and set it down. "Promise me this is between us. You can't tell Cole or Crash. Promise me." She searched both their faces.

Shannon nodded. "All right. I promise."

Angel squeezed her hand, looking meaningfully into her eyes. "Take some time to get used to the idea yourself. You don't have to share the news with him right away, or decide anything yet, but no matter what you decide, he needs to know."

Crystal just stared at her. If anyone knew about that, it was Angel.

"Crystal, you know how things went down with Cole and me. He was so upset that I'd kept it from him. And now look at how happy we are."

Crystal nodded. "But that's you and Cole. Wolf…he's…"

"He's what?"

"He's always been so adamant, right from the start, that he wasn't looking for an ol' lady."

"You think Cole didn't say the same thing to me?"

Shannon smiled. "I think Crash may have said about the same thing to me, too."

"See?" Angel insisted.

Crystal managed a tremulous smile. Her friends meant well. And in their cases, things had worked out. She was glad for them. But she and Wolf were a different story. They had such a complicated relationship as it was, if you could even call what they had *a relationship*. And now to add this to it? She couldn't even imagine what Wolf's reaction would be. He was such a hard man to figure out. He took the term complicated to a whole other level.

On one hand, he didn't want to be tied down. No strings. That had been his requirement from the very start. Yet, at the same time, he was so territorial and possessive of her. Hell, when they first met, he'd made sure the rest of his brothers knew to back off her.

She nodded, more to reassure her friends than anyone else.

CHAPTER THREE

Crystal was behind the clubhouse bar, slinging drinks for the club's weekly Friday night party. The place was packed with members, hang-a-rounds, friends, and sweet-butts.

Crystal was partially distracted by her thoughts. A week had passed since she'd discovered she was pregnant, but she still hadn't come to terms with her situation or worked up the courage to say anything to Wolf. God, what a coward she was turning out to be.

Red Dog reached across the bar and tugged on a lock of her hair. "You doin' okay, doll?"

She blinked, putting a smile on. "Sure, Dog. You want a beer?"

"Does a bear piss in the woods?"

She popped the top on a bottle and slid it in front of him. "I'll take that as a yes."

Red Dog grinned and took a long pull of beer. Her eyes drifted over his shoulder, and her smile faded. Wolf strolled in with his arm around Misty.

She watched as he greeted several of his brothers with back slaps, and then his eyes lifted and connected with hers. He had the gall to wink.

Red Dog noticed her gaze aimed at the door and twisted to look over his shoulder. He let out a loud, "Don't even concern yourself, Crystal. She's ain't worth it. He's just trying to make a point."

"And what is that point, Dog?"

"That he can't be caught. Can't be tied down."

"Yeah. I think I've had my nose rubbed in that 'point' before."

"Then fucking do something about it."

Crystal looked at Dog, and then smiled. "You're right, Dog. I should do something about it."

She saw the curious look in Dog's eyes as he watched her plunge her hand in the tub of ice, pull out a bottle of beer, then throw the hinged end of the bar top up. She saw Dog out of the corner of her eye as he twisted with a frown, following her with his eyes. He was probably going to be real surprised when he saw what she was about to do, because she had a feeling it wasn't what he'd meant *at all*. And she also knew there'd be hell to pay, but right now she was an emotional, hormonal wreck, and she didn't give a fuck.

She made her way through the crowd. Wolf was now off by the pool table talking to Cajun while Misty was standing off by the jukebox, looking bored and self-righteous.

Crystal walked right up to her, taking in her trashy outfit, a short halter mini dress in bubblegum pink with a plunging neckline that went all the way to her navel. The little tramp.

Misty noticed Crystal coming toward her, and Crystal sure as hell didn't like the way she looked her up and down like she wasn't worth her time. *Think again, bitch.*

"Would you like a beer?" Crystal asked, holding out the bottle.

"I don't drink beer," Misty said with distain.

"Aw, that's too bad because I've got a cold one right here *just for you.*" Then she twisted the cap off the beer, shook it and sprayed it all over Misty, who shrieked her lungs out. Crystal had a moment's satisfaction watching Misty's big hair dripping with beer, and her makeup running down her face.

"You little *bitch!*" Misty shrieked, holding her arms in front of her trying to fend off the worst.

Crystal continued to spray her, until suddenly two strong arms locked around her waist and dragged her back. Cole's voice growled in her ear.

"That's enough, Crystal. Goddamn it."

Crash grabbed the bottle out of her hand. "Damn, girl."

"You bitch!" Misty shrieked again, and Green got in front of her as she tried to rush Crystal, claws ready to scratch her eyes out.

"Whoa there, babe. Back off," Green barked, his hand against her chest, pushing her back.

Cole squeezed Crystal, giving her a little shake. "Don't suppose I even have to ask, but *what the fuck*, babe? You know better than this. This shit does not fly. Not in our Goddamn clubhouse. You hear me?"

She nodded.

"I mean it, Crystal. You want to take her out, have at her. But it won't be goin' down on Dead fucking property. We clear?"

"Yes, Cole. We're clear," Crystal replied tightly.

***

Wolf was at the pool table talking with Cajun when all the shit went down. One minute everything was chill, the next all hell broke loose. Looking over, he was shocked to see Crystal smack dab in the middle of it—Crystal hosing down Misty with a bottle of beer. *Jesus H. Christ.*

Before he could shove his way through the wall of leather clad brothers to get to them, Cole had Crystal in a chest lock from behind and, by the look on his face as he bent his head to her ear, he was reading her the riot act.

Shit.

As Wolf shouldered his way through the crowd, his eyes focused on the hold Cole had on Crystal, and a shot of pure adrenaline zapped through him. Suddenly he was filled with the overwhelming feeling of wanting to tear his VP apart for putting his hands on her like that.

He glanced to the left and saw Green restraining Misty—Misty, who was now drenched in beer and stinking like a brewery. If the situation wasn't so fucked up, he'd have a hard time holding back his laughter, something his brothers weren't even trying to do as they were all now laughing their asses off. Every one of them except Cole and Crash, who knew just how fucked up this situation truly was.

When Wolf stepped between the women, it was Crystal

who had all his attention. He glared at her, his temper flaring. Then his eyes lifted over her head to Cole. Cole looked ready to tear him a new one because he knew exactly who was really to blame for this shit.

"You and I need to have a talk," Cole said through his teeth.

Wolf nodded once and bit out, "Let her go."

Cole stared him down. "You want to say that again?"

Wolf swallowed his anger. "Let me talk to her a minute, VP."

Cole released her, and Wolf clamped a hand around her forearm and dragged her through the crowd to the back hall.

***

Crystal was fuming as she stumbled behind Wolf as he pulled her into the hall. Then he did what he always did—he backed her into the nearest wall. She stared up at him. He was pissed at her, yet again. It took her right back to that fight night last fall, and how he'd pinned her against the wall in this very hall, telling her how he was going to wipe the floor with Shane that night.

"A cat fight, Crystal? *Really*? What the hell's gotten into you?"

"Leave me alone. Let me go." She slapped him.

Struggling between them was almost foreplay, but he didn't respond like he usually did. Instead he glared down at her coldly.

"Don't do that again."

"Then let me go." She pulled but his hands were clamped tightly around her wrists now.

"We're not done. So just settle down."

She wouldn't look at him, but she did stop struggling.

Wolf took a deep breath and slowly blew it out, and she knew he was trying to calm himself down. "Congratulations on your ability to create drama out of absolutely nothing."

Her eyes flashed to him then. "Nothing?"

"You've seen me with women before, and you've never gone off like this. I told you they don't mean anything to me. What's so different about Misty? Why is *she* any different?"

She refused to answer.

"Crystal…" He shook her. "Tell me."

"You've never gone back for more before. You're usually done with them by now."

"I told you, they don't mean anything to me."

"And do *I* mean anything to you?"

"You're reading too much into this. I've got to throw the guys off track, don't I? I can't let them know about you and me."

"Answer the question. Do I?"

"You *know* you do."

"No, I *don't* know."

"Yes, you do. You fucking do." He took her head in his hands. "Baby, you know I care about you."

She stared up into his eyes. It would be so easy to just believe him. But Dog was right, if Wolf being with Misty bothered her, she needed to do something about it. So she did. She asked him for something she'd never asked of him before. "Then prove it."

His chin pulled back an inch, and he frowned down at

her. "I shouldn't have to prove it."

If a future with her was ever going to mean anything to Wolf, she had to know. Especially now. So, she did something else she'd never done before. She pushed. "Prove it or I'm gone."

As he searched her eyes, almost as if he couldn't believe her words, she teetered on the verge of telling him about the pregnancy. But his next words stopped her cold.

"You know men like me don't do ultimatums."

That was all it took. She felt her heart breaking, falling to the floor and shattering into a million pieces. The one time, the *only* time she'd ever actually wanted something from him, had the courage to ask for more, he let her down.

"Yes, *that,* I do know." She shoved out of his hold and stalked away, knowing if she stood there a moment longer she would end up a bawling mess. Crystal didn't do the whole crying thing. Not over *him.* And if she did, it sure wouldn't be in front of him.

She dashed down the hall out into the main room and up the open metal stairs to the second floor. She darted down the hall, checking doorknobs looking for an open one. She needed a place to hide and lick her wounds until she could go down and face everyone.

Damn it, they were all locked. She got to the end of the hall and tried the last one on the right. Cole's. The knob turned. *Thank God.*

She stepped inside, closed the door, and collapsed on the bed. Her head in her hands, she burst into tears, letting the hormonal emotions wash over her. She was usually so thick-skinned. They all thought of her as a tough bitch that would never in a million years burst into tears. Not Crystal. No way.

But there she was... an emotional wreck. It had to be the hormones, which only brought her thoughts spinning back around to the pregnancy. She was pregnant. With Wolf's baby. God, it still hadn't sunk in. It still didn't seem real.

But it was. And clearly, he wasn't looking for that kind of relationship with her. If he found out, he'd think she'd done this on purpose. If he flipped his lid over the idea of being given an ultimatum, how would he take *this?*

She wiped the tears away. She had to pull herself together. She had to be strong.

***

Wolf let Crystal go, staring after her. She'd said Misty was different because he'd never gone back for more before, that he was usually done with them by now. Only one thought had gone through his head. *Maybe because she's the only one who had ever gotten this reaction out of you?* But he couldn't say those words to her. Hell, he could barely admit them to himself.

Wolf liked to believe he understood women. But this whole situation with Crystal was spinning out of control. There was something more to this, something she wasn't telling him. And he'd be damned if she was going to walk away without settling it. He yanked open the hallway door and moved into the main room, intent on going after her.

He didn't get three steps into the room before Green waylaid him.

"Bro, do something with Misty. She's one drenched,

pissed off *bitch*."

"Can you get her out of here for me? Take her home?" Wolf asked him.

"Fuck no."

"Please."

"God, you're pathetic when you beg." Green rolled his eyes. "You're gonna owe me for this one."

"Anything, man. Do you know where Crystal went?" Wolf glanced to the bar, but she wasn't there.

"I think she went to the john," Green supplied, nodding toward the bathroom in the corner.

"Thanks, Brother." Wolf moved past Green and was again waylaid. This time with a firm hand in his chest and an immovable wall of leather cut and pissed-off brother.

Cole got right in his face and growled, "We need to talk. *Now*."

Wolf took a deep breath. *Shit*. Last thing he needed right now was a lecture from his VP, but fuck if he saw anyway around it. He followed Cole up the stairs to the second level.

***

Footsteps sounded coming down the hall, getting nearer, and Crystal froze.

Cole's angry voice carried through the door. "This shit's got to stop."

Oh, God. He was headed for his room.

She glanced around, looking for a place to hide, and her eyes fell on the closet. She dashed inside, closing the louvered doors. As she attempted to slow her breathing and make no sound, she realized she could see a tiny bit through the slats. A moment later, the hall door flew open, practically bouncing against the wall and rattling the frosted glass upper half. In strode two sets of boots, and she heard Cole's voice.

"Swear to Christ, Wolf. I'm done with this shit."

"Sorry."

"Sorry? That all you've got to say?"

"Cole, what the hell do you want me to say?"

"I want you to fucking grow a pair and handle this. I told you to cut her loose. But you didn't, did you?"

"Cole—"

"What?"

"It's not that easy."

"Yeah. I know. So I'm gonna make it real easy for you."

"What are you talking about?"

"You know how she feels about you, and yet you keep rubbing her nose in shit like this. Apparently, Misty's a major trigger for her in a way other girls you've been with have never been. Not sure why the hell she's any different."

"Okay, I won't bring Misty around anymore."

"It's gone too far for that, Brother."

"What do you mean?"

"I saw this coming. Shit, I didn't want to see it go this far. But one of you has to go."

"What?"

"And we all know it's not gonna be you."

"What the fuck are you saying?"

"Mack's done. He's gonna hate to let her go, but he's gonna find someone else to run the bar."

"No. I can't be the reason for that."

"Mack loves Crystal. Hell, we all do. She runs that bar like a pro. Place has never been cleaner. But we can find another bar manager."

"Cole, don't do this. Please."

"It ain't up to me. You want to try to talk Mack out of it, good luck, Brother. I just spent ten minutes trying, and I can't get him to budge."

Crystal heard the door open and slam shut as Wolf stormed out.

Then she heard Cole mutter, "Christ."

The door opened and closed again—this time quietly— and she heard Cole's boots retreating down the hall.

Crystal slid down the wall of the closet and let the tears flow. Well, she wasn't about to wait for them to ask her to leave. If she wasn't wanted here anymore, she was done. Her car was parked out back. She just needed to get her purse and walk out.

But then they'd all know. Hell, she'd be damned if she'd slink out of here with her tail between her legs. Fuck that.

Standing, she wiped her face and stepped out of the closet. Then she exited Cole's room, quietly closing the door behind her, and headed down the hall. She took several deep breaths and let anger stiffen her spine. She just had to get through tonight.

* * *

Wolf sat in the club's meeting room at the long conference table. Mack sat at the head, lighting a cigar. He puffed on it, and then shook out the match. Pulling the cigar from his mouth he glared at Wolf through the smoke.

Wolf had just finished laying out his case, hoping to talk Mack out of this shit. But one thing he knew about Mack— Mack was gonna do what Mack was gonna do. Hell, hadn't Cole tried to tell him that not five minutes ago?

But Wolf had one thing going for him—Mack loved Crystal. When it came down to it, he really didn't want to run her off. But he'd do it, if push came to shove. Wolf had no delusions about that. When it came to hard choices, Mack never had any problem making them.

"So prove it."

Wolf didn't miss the irony of the fact that those words had been said to him twice tonight.

"You promise you can stay away from her, then prove it." Mack paused to point the hand that held the cigar at him. "Don't go running over there tonight like I know you want to."

When Wolf glared at him, Mack continued.

"Yeah, I know you. You think I don't?"

Wolf ground his teeth and let his eyes drop to the table. If he had to grovel to his President to make sure Crystal stayed, he'd fucking do it.

"You do," he confessed.

"Damn right, I do." Mack shifted in his seat, relaxing a bit. "You stay away from her, and maybe I'll let her stay."

Wolf nodded. "Done."

Mack nodded toward the door. "Get the fuck out. I'm gonna have a chat with Crystal."

Wolf's eyes slid closed for a moment. *Shit*. Then they opened, he stood up, and walked out.

***

Crystal stood behind the bar, pulling a beer for Cajun who was teasing her about the whole show she'd put on, when her eyes were drawn to the conference room, and she saw Wolf walk out. He looked at her, and then turned away as if he was done with her. She felt her heart break all over again.

Mack followed him out a moment later and approached the bar. He took a seat right in front, his eyes drilling into her.

"As entertaining as all that was, we're not going to have any more little displays like that, are we?"

"No, sir."

"Good."

She felt her eyes getting glassy with tears.

"Why don't you take the night off? In fact, take the rest of the week off. Get your head on straight. Okay, darlin'?"

Crystal swallowed and nodded. "Sure."

Then she moved to the opposite end of the bar to grab her purse. Her eyes connected with Red Dog sitting at the end. Grabbing her purse up, she noticed him frown. She lifted her hand to him, waggled her fingers, and gave him a wink. He relaxed back onto his bar stool, apparently convinced she was okay.

Then she moved through the crowd and headed out the door, desperate to get to her car before she broke down.

***

Mack looked over at Cole at the end of the bar. "Send Wolf somewhere for a few days."

Cole nodded, taking a hit off his cigarette. When he blew the smoke out, he offered, "He can do that Temecula run we were talking about. Seventy miles from the Mexican border far enough for you?"

Mack nodded at Cole's attempt at a joke and looked meaningfully at his VP. "This is the last time I'm dealing with this shit."

"Understood." Cole tamped out his cigarette and moved off his barstool to find Wolf again.

CHAPTER FOUR

Wolf rolled up at the meeting place where he was to meet two of his brothers from the club's Chapter in Temecula, California. The place looked inconspicuous enough for a drop. Not much traffic, out in the middle of nowhere… A lone roadhouse with two bikes parked out front.

But still, he had a bad feeling. The hairs on the back of his neck prickled upward. It was a feeling that Wolf had learned a long time ago not to ignore. He glanced up and down the road. A single tractor-trailer lumbered past, kicking up a trail of dust in its wake. As the sound of its motor faded into the distance, Wolf dropped his kick stand and shut his bike off.

He strode inside. It took a moment for his eyes to adjust to the dim bar. When they did, he took the place in. A long bar stood at the back wall, a busty blonde bartender leaning against it, smoking a cigarette and flipping through a magazine. She looked up when he entered. His head swiveled. There was a pool table on either side of the door. His eyes located his brothers at the table on the right. Not another soul in the place.

They greeted him with smiles and back slaps—Digger, a stocky bald man with a Fu-Manchu mustache, and Weed, an old hippie with a long gray braid down his back and a gold tooth.

They were there to meet the club's Mexican drug connection—a meet that had taken days to arrange.

He wasn't there long before a car pulled up outside. They watched through the window, past the neon beer signs as four Mexicans got out.

As they entered, Weed moved to the bar. He distracted the bartender, while the men made the exchange. It all happened very quickly. A pound of black tar heroin wrapped in a folded newspaper landed on the green felt. Digger quickly tested it for purity. At his nod, an envelope of money slid out of Wolf's vest. The newspaper wrapped around the bundle and disappeared into Digger's inside shirt placket. Wolf handed over the envelope and watched as the man thumbed through the stack before nodding and tucking it into his jacket.

A moment later, the men disappeared as quickly as they'd come.

Wolf and Digger moved to the bar, stopping where Weed stood flirting with the blonde.

"You ready?" Digger asked.

Weed turned to look at him. "I just got this beer. Give

me a minute."

Digger turned back to Wolf, rolling his eyes. "Guess we're gonna hang out here 'for a minute'."

Wolf chuckled. "Guess I'll head on back."

"Already? You in a hurry?"

Wolf shrugged, not really interested in hanging around now that the deal was done, especially when he still had that tingling sensation warning him. About what, he didn't know, but something was off.

"Must be some hot pussy back in San Jose waitin' on him," Weed snickered.

If he only knew the truth, Wolf thought.

"All right, Brother," Digger pulled him in for a hug, slapping his back. "Good seeing you."

Wolf walked out, pausing by his bike, his eyes searching up and down the road as he strapped on his helmet. Nothing. Throwing his leg over the bike, he fired it up.

***

The man stood in the shadows of the building watching the lone bike pull away. He waited until it disappeared over the rise. Then his eyes fell to the other two parked bikes, and he grinned.

He moved around to the back of the building, entering through the back door. Moving quietly through the hallway that contained doors for the men's and women's restrooms, he paused at the corner, peering around the edge until he could see the two MC members sitting at the bar.

His fingers tensed on the two Glocks in his hands. Then, smiling, he moved around the corner. The dumb motherfuckers never saw him coming.

Bam. Bam. They were down on the floor, a pool of blood already forming around their head wounds.

The bartender screamed. He stalked around the bar, backing her up against the wall on the far end. She had nowhere to go. He saw the look of horror as she took in his face, a face he saw reflected in the mirror behind the bar. He smiled, only half of his face lifting, the other half frozen in a paralyzed droop.

His eyes dropped to her tits. They swelled over the top of her slutty tank. He wished he had time to waste. She'd be fun to play with. But he couldn't risk it. Not with two dead bodies already bleeding all over the linoleum.

He grinned. "Sorry, sweetheart."

Then he raised one gun and shot her point blank in the forehead. Her body flew back against the wall, a large blood stain trailing down the cheap wood paneling as she slid to the floor.

He moved around the bar and searched the bodies, coming up with the newsprint wrapped prize.

"Bingo."

He stared down at the two bikers on the floor. He'd love to take their Evil Dead cuts from their dead bodies. What a prize *that* would be. Almost better than the drugs. But if he tried, he'd end up covered in blood. And that wouldn't do, now would it? His eyes fell on the silver Evil Dead rings they each wore, and he smiled. *Well, now, those would have to do.* They would be a sweet consolation prize, and he could easily slip them off without getting too messy. He knelt and pulled them off. Then he stood and unloaded the rest of his clip into their bodies, chuckling as they jerked and twitched with each shot.

When he was empty, he strolled out the back, whistling all the while.

***

Wolf pulled up to the clubhouse, dropped his kickstand, and shut off his bike. It had been a long week. He knew they'd sent him on this damn run just to get him out of town and away from Crystal. He'd kept his word to Mack. While he'd been gone, he hadn't called or texted her. But now, hell he had to admit he couldn't wait to at least lay eyes on her. Even if it was just to see her behind the bar in the clubhouse, pulling a beer for him.

He headed inside, but didn't get ten feet before Red Dog walked up and shocked the shit out of him by punching him right in the face. Wolf fell back against one of the pool tables. Wiping his bleeding mouth with the back of his hand, he snarled, "What the *fuck*, man?"

Red Dog stood over him, two-hundred and fifty pounds of pissed-off biker. "She's gone. Because of *you!*" Dog jabbed a fist in Wolf's chest. "It wasn't enough you treated her like shit, but you had to drive her away, too?"

"What the hell are you talking about?" Wolf asked getting to his feet. "And get the fuck out of my face, motherfucker." He shoved Red Dog back. Not an easy task when the man was a six-foot-four wall of muscle.

"Don't play fucking dumb with me, asshole. *Crystal*! That's what I'm talking about. Like you don't fucking know."

"Crystal? What do you mean she left?" His eyes moved frantically around the room, searching, positive Dog must be fucking with him.

"She ain't here is she? She's gone. Because of *you!* So, tell me, Wolf, is this the part where you're gonna stand there and pretend you don't give a shit?"

Wolf shoved past him and headed toward Mack's office. He didn't bother knocking. The door banged against the wall as he burst through.

Mack was behind his desk, on his cell. He glared up at Wolf, and then bit off into his phone, "Let me get back to you."

Wolf stood in front of the desk, his fists clenching and unclenching at his sides. He'd never felt so close to tearing apart his own President.

Mack tossed his cell on the desk and lunged to his feet, roaring, "Who the fuck do you think you are coming in here like that?"

Wolf roared back just as forcefully, "You ran her off? After you gave me your fucking word if I left her alone, you'd let it ride, you'd let her *stay.*"

"Sit the fuck down!" Mack ordered. Then he walked over to the door and slammed it shut.

Wolf collapsed into a chair, not because he wanted to, but because if he stayed standing, he knew he'd be tempted to take a swing at Mack.

Mack retreated behind his desk, probably for the same reason. Wolf had seen him tear apart more than one brother.

He knew Mack was fully capable of laying him out with one punch if he thought twice about it.

"I see you've heard."

Wolf stared him down. "Did you run her off or not?"

"No, I didn't fucking run her off. I made you a Goddamned deal, didn't I? You keep *your* end of it?"

"Yes, I fucking kept it. You sent me out of town to make sure of that, didn't you?"

Mack ran a hand over his face. "Did you ever think of the possibility that she left on her own?"

Wolf shook his head, emphatically. "No way. She wouldn't do that. She loves this club. She's happy here."

"You sure about that?"

Wolf's eyes narrowed.

Mack huffed out a sigh and leaned back in his chair, the leather creaking. "You put her in a bad spot, Wolf. You know women better than any of my guys, yet how are you so blind when it comes to Crystal? How are you the last to see it when it comes to her?"

Wolf dropped his eyes. Every fucking word was true, and it shredded him to be confronted with it.

Mack continued his flaying words. "You drag a woman through the dirt long enough, she's going to eventually wise up and realize your ass isn't worth it, no matter how much she loves you."

At that, Wolf's eyes shot up. *Love?* Christ, did everybody see it? Was it that obvious? He thought they'd played it so cool all these years. Fuck, he was an idiot. "Did she talk to you? Did she tell you she was leaving?"

Mack shook his head.

Wolf was on his feet in an instant, hope soaring in him. "Then how do you know she left? Maybe—"

"Sit down." Mack cut him off.

He obeyed reluctantly, fearing what he was about to hear.

Mack leaned forward, resting his arms on his desk and gave it to him straight. "I heard it from Cole. Crystal told Angel she was leaving. Stopped over there to say goodbye on her way out of town."

Wolf felt his stomach drop. It couldn't be true. She couldn't have left town. *Left him.* And without even saying goodbye? No way. He couldn't accept that. He surged to his feet again.

"I've got to go." He paused, looking at Mack, giving him at least that shred of respect, waiting for the old man's nod of approval.

He got it and was out the door in a flash.

***

Mack stared at the door of his office, wondering if one of his best guys was going to be useless to him for a while. He'd known more than one brother to have his head messed up by a damn broad. Messed up so bad in fact, that they couldn't fucking concentrate on the job at hand. That kind of distraction could get a man killed. It could also get a brother killed whose back he was supposed to be watching.

Shit.

He picked up his cell, his thumb moving over the screen, and put it to his ear. When his VP came on the line, he gave him a head's up.

"Wolf's on his way, and he's not in a good place."

"Right," came Cole's reply. "I'll deal with it."

Disconnecting, Mack tossed the phone on the desk. Women. They caused him more trouble than every other rival they had put together.

Fucking hell.

***

Red Dog blocked Wolf's way to the door, and Wolf could see the intent in his eyes—he wasn't done with him.

"You want a piece of me, let's go outside," Wolf growled at him.

Dog's eyes flared with warning. "We take this outside and one of us ain't comin' back."

Wolf glanced over and saw Shane standing by the bar, watching. "What about you? You got something to say?" Wolf growled at him.

Shane tightened his hold on his beer bottle, but he just shook his head. "You made your own hell. I ain't got to add to it."

Wolf nodded understanding. Shane wasn't going to do anything to screw up getting his patch. Not when he was so close. So Wolf made it easy for him. "You get your patch, you come find me."

"Count on it."

Wolf shoved past Red Dog, half expecting another blind punch, but Dog let him pass. Wolf walked out of the clubhouse, slamming the door and stopped in the parking lot. His eyes skated over the line of bikes sitting in the sun, but he didn't really see any of them.

She was gone. Good and truly gone, and he felt like a part of him had just died. Just fucking died. He felt a tightness squeezing his chest, and it felt like he couldn't breathe.

Fuck. What had he done?

***

Wolf tore up the gravel driveway of his VP's house. The place was set out in the country, east of San Jose. He shut his bike off and went around back. Cole met him on the deck, obviously having heard his bike roar up the drive. Wolf's eyes slid past him to where Angel stood in the partially opened sliding glass door.

"Where is she?" he asked her.

Cole looked back at his wife, and they both waited for her response.

Her eyes moved between them, and then she told Wolf softly, "I don't know."

Wolf clenched his jaw. He didn't buy it. She knew. She had to know. "Angel, please. I know she was here."

She nodded. "Yes, she was here."

"I know how tight you girls are, there's no way you'd let her leave without knowing shit about her plans. She had to have told you where she was going."

She shook her head. "I'm sorry, she didn't."

"Bullshit." He took a step toward her, but Cole brought him up short. He slammed a hand into Wolf's chest, grabbing a fistful of his shirt and shoving him back.

"Back off, Brother. She told you she doesn't know."

Wolf's jaw tightened as he stared down his VP. Then his eyes moved back to Angel, and he shook his head. "I can't believe you just let her go."

With that, Cole tightened his fist in Wolf's shirt and shook him, growling in his face, "Don't you dare put this on Angel. It's your fucking fault she's gone. *You're* the one who never made her your ol' lady. *You're* the one who strung her along all this fucking time, so don't think you can come here and put the guilt on Angel or anyone else. It's nobody's fault but yours."

"She didn't talk to you before she left?" Angel asked quietly, and there was something in the way she said it that had a bad feeling snaking down his spine. Was there something he was missing? He searched Cole's face. Did his VP know something he wasn't saying? Brothers didn't lie to one another. Not if he straight up asked. "Cole?"

He shook his head. "I got shit to tell you, Wolf."

His eyes moved to Angel for one final appeal. "Please, Angel. She didn't even say goodbye. I can't just let her go like this."

"But you did let her go in every other sense of the word, didn't you?" she asked him, slicing another piece of him.

Fuck, he hated to be confronted with the truth, with his own inadequacies.

Expectations. Fucking expectations. They'd been the bane of his existence. Why? He didn't fucking know, but he was sure it had to do with a father that never thought he was good enough. Instead of continuing to beat his head against the wall in a futile attempt to convince a man who would never be convinced, instead of continuing to try to prove himself, what did he do? He joined an MC and became exactly what his father always expected of him—a big nothing in his father's eyes. The disappointment he'd always told him he was.

No, Wolf didn't do well with living up to other's expectations.

So he supposed he'd never tried with Crystal—ran like hell from anything resembling a commitment. And where had that gotten him?

He met Angel's eyes, seeing the contempt in them, but also a tiny bit of sympathy. He wished he could explain. "You don't understand."

"I think she does," Cole corrected him, then twisted to say over his shoulder, "Go back inside, Angel."

Like any good ol' lady, she didn't hesitate or question. The sliding door slid shut.

"Sit down," Cole ordered, pushing him down into a chair next to a patio table on the deck.

Wolf collapsed into it and leaned forward, his elbows on his knees. His VP sat in the chair next to him and leaned forward as well. Wolf looked over at him. "Tell me the truth. Did Mack run her off?"

Cole shook his head. "No, Wolf, he didn't. I was here when she came by. This was her choice."

Wolf looked at his hands, shaking his head.

"She sold her 'vette two days ago."

Wolf looked up at him startled. "What?"

"Some guy gave her eighteen for it."

"Shit."

"So if you're worried about her, that'll tide her over, help her start a new life."

Wolf cradled his face in his hands wondering what in the hell he'd done. He could feel Cole's eyes on him, watching his reaction.

"You could have made her your ol' lady anytime you wanted, but you didn't. And I get that." Cole glanced back at the house. "Relationships are hard work under the best of circumstances. The life we lead? Takes a special kind of woman to put up with it. Shit, Wolf, the burdens I walk through that door with some nights, I can't even tell you how Angel deals with me. But she does. And I thank God every day she does."

Wolf nodded. "You're a lucky man."

"You're right. And I don't need you to tell me that, because I know it." He bumped his fist on Wolf's knee. "There's a lot to be said for having an ol' lady, Wolf."

When Wolf remained silent, Cole huffed out a sigh. "I told you to either step up or cut her loose. What'd you do? Neither."

"Cole, I—"

"You gonna tell me you weren't still seeing her? You gonna look me in the fucking eye and lie to your brother?"

Wolf met his look. "No. I won't lie to you, Cole. I was. I couldn't stay away."

"And how's that gonna play out now?"

Wolf lifted his hands in a helpless gesture as if he'd given up. "I don't fucking know. I can't believe she's gone."

"Crystal wanted more, Wolf. You can't blame her for that."

Wolf nodded. No, he couldn't blame her for that. She'd wanted more, and maybe that's what had scared the hell out of him.

"You don't want an ol' lady, I get that. If all you want is to get laid, fine. Go find you one of Sonny's girls. But don't think for a minute you'll ever find the caliber of woman it takes to be an ol' lady in that crop, because it's just not gonna fuckin' happen, Wolf."

Wolf stayed quiet.

"You had something with Crystal. Maybe more than you want to admit. You don't want to talk about this, fine. You do, I'm here for you. But, I ain't Dear Abby. You're a grown ass man, make a fucking decision. You either want her or you don't. You either step up or shut up. Got it?

"Got it."

They were quiet for a minute and then Cole asked, "You try calling her?"

"Called her. Texted her. She's not answering."

"Maybe you just need to give her some time and space."

"Yeah." Wolf nodded, but hell it was tearing him up.

"What happened to your face?"

Wolf absently touched his cheek. "Dog."

A grin tugged at Cole's mouth. "He always had a soft spot for Crystal."

Wolf nodded back. "Yeah."

"You may get the same thing from Crash when he sees you."

"Fuck."

Cole chuckled. "Go home, Brother. We're meeting tomorrow. You're gonna give us the lowdown on what's goin' on down at the Temecula Chapter."

Wolf nodded again, but stayed seated.

They sat quietly for a moment.

"Cole?"

"Yeah?"

"I need to ask you something. And I need you to not be a dick about it."

Cole grinned. "Not making any promises on that one, bro."

"Did I fuck up?" he asked in all seriousness and watched the grin fade from his VP's face.

"You tell me."

Wolf didn't answer, he just dropped his eyes to stare unseeing at the deck.

Cole stood. "Go home, Wolf. Drink a bottle of Jack and sleep it off. Either you shake her off or you don't. Only time is gonna tell."

Wolf got to his feet. Cole pulled him close in a bear hug and pounded on his back. "Love you, Brother."

"Love you, too, man."

When they broke apart, Cole smacked him open-handed in the face, right where Dog had decked him.

"Ow. Fuck, man."

Cole grinned. "I'm letting you off easy. That should have been a punch."

CHAPTER FIVE

Wolf sat at the table in the clubhouse's meeting room. Mack had called an emergency meeting just after he'd pulled away from Cole's house.

They all sat there, staring at Mack. Wondering what this was about.

"Just got word. Lost two men from the Temecula Chapter." Then he looked right at Wolf. "Digger and Weed."

There were shocked murmurs throughout the room.

"What?" Wolf barked. "How?"

"They were found shot dead at the drop. Thirty-year-old bartender along with them."

"Jesus Christ," he whispered.

The eyes of every brother in the room swung to him. Wolf's gaze moved from Mack to Cole, who sat at his President's left.

"The heroin was long gone." Mack drew his attention back with that statement. "You want to tell me what happened?"

Wolf frowned. "What happened? I don't know what the fuck happened. They were all alive when I left."

"Humor me. Let's go over it."

Wolf gritted his teeth. He didn't like being questioned, not about his loyalty to this club. Not about two brothers being murdered. But he understood Mack's need as President to get to the bottom of what happened.

"I met them at the bar. Place was empty except for the two of them and the bartender. Santos' men came in, we made the deal. They left. I left a couple minutes later. Weed was hitting on the bartender, wanted to finish a beer he'd just ordered. I walked out, got on my bike, and rode away. End of story."

Mack and Cole studied him.

Finally, Cole nodded and looked at Mack.

"You saw no one else? No one pulling in? No one pass you on the road?" Mack drilled him.

He shook his head. "No one. Didn't pass another soul headed back that way for at least half a mile. Place is out in the sticks."

Cole looked to Mack. "We got a plan? Any suspects?"

Mack shook his head. "Santos got his money. It's possible his men came back to get the drugs, but it would fuck-up a long standing relationship, and for what?" Mack shook his head again. "Doesn't make sense."

"Random hit?"

"Who knew about it?"

Cole shrugged. "Someone could have been following

Santos' men. Decided the two in the bar were a better target than the four in the car."

"Possibly."

"You got any other possible scenarios?"

"No, VP. I don't. Do you?" Mack snapped in an irritated voice.

Cole shook his head. "What'd Temecula have to say?"

"They've got two dead brothers and a couple hundred grand in product missing. They're a little upset," Mack replied in a sarcastic voice.

"They have any ideas?"

He shook his head, his eyes again meeting Wolf's.

"I got nothin' to do with this, Prez. I swear to you."

Mack nodded. "I know you don't. I wasn't questioning you killin' two brothers, just needed to know what you saw." Then his eyes moved around the table. "We got two brothers to bury. Dog, make the arrangements for the trip down there. Notify every Chapter. Everybody in the fucking state attends. Mandatory."

His order broke the five-hundred-mile rule, where only Chapters within five hundred miles were mandatory to attend a funeral, but no one in the room was going to bring that to his attention.

"You got it, boss." Red Dog nodded solemnly.

***

A month after the club buried two of its brothers, they still had no idea who was to blame. Temecula wanted heads on a platter, and they were growing more and more frustrated that they had none.

The police had no more on the murders than they did.

Tensions between the club and the cartel were at an all-time high, and the club was contemplating pulling back from the drug trade all together. Many feared this was the work of a rival cartel, a Mexican drug war that none of the Chapters wanted to get in the middle of.

The money, always a strong draw, was becoming less and less worth the risk. A pile of money wasn't worth shit if you weren't around to spend it. It didn't take a genius to figure that out.

It was becoming a long tense period as winter gave way to spring.

***

The man stood off in the distant desert scrub land, a hundred yards out from The Pony. He had a perfect view of the brothel that stood about fifteen miles east of Reno, just two miles on the other side of the Truckee River from Interstate 80. This late at night it was dark out in that stretch of Nevada desert, except for the lights of The Pony.

A large illuminated sign stood on a pole by the road, marking the entrance into a well-lit gravel parking lot large enough to accommodate a dozen tractor-trailers and four times as many cars. There was a large brick ranch house that looked from the outside like any ordinary house, except for the two large modular add-on wings attached to the back. The front of the lot was well lit for customers. The back was shadowy darkness broken up here and there by dim security lighting, half of which were not in working order, which had made his task that much easier.

Taking a drag off his cigarette, he watched as the flames licked up the walls of the building. Thick black smoke bellowed out of the roof as the insulation, drywall, and cheap modular units quickly succumbed to the fire he'd set with the powerful accelerant.

He looked down the road back toward the Interstate. Off in the distance, over the slight rise, he could make out the sound of fire engine sirens stuck on the other side of the tracks as the midnight freight train came through like it did every Thursday night, like clockwork.

He'd timed the setting of the blaze perfectly. The place would be totally engulfed before they ever pulled up.

A total lost cause.

He chuckled as he dropped his cigarette to the dirt and ground it out with his boot.

***

Crash lay in bed with Shannon cuddled up against him when his cell went off. He reached over and grabbed it off the nightstand, squinting at the time on the readout. *3:00.*

Shit. No good news was ever delivered in the middle of the night. But with life in an MC, they unfortunately weren't all that rare. He put the cell to his ear.

"Yeah."

Cole's voice came on the line. "Just got word. The Pony burned to the ground."

"You're shittin' me. When?"

"Jason said it started around midnight. Place went up quick. By the time the fire trucks pulled up it was fully engulfed."

"Anybody hurt? Are all the girls okay?"

"Yeah, they're fine. Jason and Dolly got everyone out as soon as the smoke detectors went off."

"Thank God." Crash blew out a breath. "Well, guess you made a good decision when you picked Jason to manage that place."

"Yeah, we're damn lucky to have him. Him and Dolly, both."

"So, what's the plan?"

"We're meeting at the clubhouse in the morning. Heading out at first light."

"All right. I'll be there."

"We got a shit-ton of stuff to deal with. Jason said they didn't have time to get the money out of the safe. The girls are all a wreck, and we need to set up something temporary for them."

"Christ. Do they know what started it?"

"Jason said the inspectors will be out in the morning, but he heard rumblings among the firemen tonight that an accelerant was probably used."

"Great. How many enemies do we have *this* week?"

"Too many to count, Brother."

"You think it's somehow connected with the hit in Temecula?"

"Hell, something like this, it might not even be club-related. Could be someone out to shut down legal prostitution in the state of Nevada. Could be a jealous boyfriend of one of the girls, or a customer's wife. Could be a disgruntled ex-employee, or a religious fanatic. The list is endless."

"Shit."

"Yeah. Get a couple hours sleep, we got a long ride in the morning."

"Right." After he disconnected, Crash pulled Shannon's sleeping body close, spooning her from behind.

"Everything okay?" she murmured in a sleepy voice.

He kissed her behind the ear. "Everything's fine, sweetheart. Go back to sleep."

***

Shannon stood in front of the bathroom sink, still dressed in her nightgown, looking down at the pee stick in her hand and its little minus sign. She felt like crying, like dissolving into tears. But then she looked in the mirror and saw Crash come through the doorway, shirtless in a pair of sweatpants hanging low on his hips. His hands closed over her upper arms, and the heat of his body pressed against her back.

His voice murmured in her ear, soft and comforting, "Babe, it'll happen."

She nodded, so overwhelmed with sadness she couldn't speak. Crash took the stick from her hand and tossed it into the wastebasket, then he pulled her around, taking her face in his hands and forcing her to look at him.

"Princess, it hasn't been that long."

Her eyes dropped. "It's been six months, Crash."

A tear rolled down her cheek, and his thumb came up to brush it away. "Baby."

She knew her reaction was breaking his heart, so she tried to smile and brush it off with a shrug, putting on a brave face. Her hands came up and closed over his wrists, pulling his hands from her face. "I'm okay. We'll just keep trying."

Crash smiled down at her. "I'm not complaining about that part, am I?"

She tried to laugh at his teasing, but her heart wasn't in it.

"Aw, sweetheart—"

"I'm fine," she tried to cut him off.

"No, you're not," he whispered, pressing a kiss to her forehead.

"I will be. I'll be fine. You have to leave. The club is probably waiting for you."

"They can wait a couple minutes."

Suddenly, taking her by surprise, he bent, wrapped his arms around her thighs and lifted her. She squealed as he walked her backward out of the bathroom and straight to their big four-poster bed. Dropping her to the mattress, he came down on top of her. His palm came up, and he brushed the hair back from her face as he stared down at her.

"I love you, you know," he murmured.

"I love you, too."

"You gonna miss me while I'm gone?"

"You know I am. When will you be back?"

"Not sure. There's some trouble up at The Pony we have to take care of. It'll probably be a couple of days."

"You're going to Reno?" she asked, remembering the place he was talking about.

"Yeah. Probably shouldn't have told you that, but I don't want you worrying."

She frowned. "Is everything okay?"

"Everything's fine, Princess. Just got some logistics to work out, that's all."

She studied his eyes. She knew he wouldn't tell her even if there was trouble. He'd never want to worry her. She loved him for wanting to protect her like that, but still she wished she could be for him the rock he was for her. "I'm not that fragile, Crash. Not like I used to be."

He brushed soft kisses all around her face. "I know you're not."

"I'll be a good mother."

He lifted his head then, frowning at her sudden change in topic. "Of course you will. I don't have any doubts about that. Did you think I did?"

She looked away, lifting one shoulder in a slight shrug. "I just thought, you know, maybe you were worried about the panic attacks, and maybe you weren't as excited about trying to have a baby."

"You haven't had a panic attack in months. I thought you felt safe now. Don't you?"

"Yes I do. You make me feel safe, Crash, you do. I just wasn't sure if it still worried you." She shrugged again.

"I'm not worried about what kind of mother you'll make. You'll be a beautiful mother, Shannon. And as far as me not being excited about all this baby-making, I guess I have to admit, I do kind of like our time alone, just the two of us."

"Will you miss it?"

A smile pulled at his mouth, and his brows rose. "Hell

yeah, I'm gonna miss it. But you give me a beautiful daughter, and I'll forgive you."

Shannon's brows rose at that one. "Oh, really? And if it's a boy?" .

"Guess we keep tryin'."

"And if we keep having boys?"

"Sucks for you then, 'cause we keep tryin, babe. I want a girl." He kissed the tip of her nose. "One just like her mama."

"I love you," she whispered, filled with emotion for this man who could always tease her out of her melancholy.

Crash got a mischievous look on his face and rolled over, settling Shannon on top to straddle him as he taunted, "Prove it, Princess."

"I thought you had to leave." Her eyes moved to the pack he'd tossed on the bed. He'd been stuffing a change of clothes in it earlier.

He smiled up and smacked her lightly on the ass. "I do, so shut up and let's get busy, woman."

Shannon grinned down at him. "Yes, sir."

***

Later that morning, after Crash had left, Shannon sat at the kitchen island, drinking coffee with Angel who had come over to cheer her up. She stared at the calendar that she had taped to the refrigerator. The one she used to keep track of her cycle. And then she frowned as her eyes focused in on Saturday's date, and she straightened.

"This weekend is Crystal's birthday. Have you talked to her?"

"Not in a while," Angel replied sipping her coffee.

"She's working as a receptionist at a tattoo shop in Grand Junction, Colorado."

"Oh, really? How is she doing?"

Angel shrugged. "After she lost the baby, she was kind of depressed for a while. She always put on a brave front when I talked to her, but I know she's hurting. I should have gone out there and visited her, but Brayden was sick with those ear infections, and well, I just never went."

Shannon nodded. "I can only imagine how she feels."

"She wasn't very far along, but still, it hit her pretty hard."

"I miss her. It's hard when she's so far away."

"We should go see her," Angel suggested.

Shannon thought a moment, and then said with a sly smile, "I've got a better idea."

"What's that?"

"The boys are all out of town this weekend. Crash said they'd be gone at least three days." The wheels started turning.

"Yes. So?" Angel cocked her head at Shannon. "You're getting that look in your eyes. What are you planning?"

"I need to be cheered up. All this trying at baby-making has taken its toll. And since I'm not pregnant, I'm going to drink this weekend. So, I was thinking..."

"Yes?"

"With the boys out of town, maybe this is the perfect opportunity for a girl's weekend. And since its Crystal's birthday..."

"Yeah?"

"I'm thinking Vegas."

"Vegas? I don't know, Shannon. I'm not sure I can swing that. Vegas can get expensive."

"My treat. I'll pay for everyone's rooms. And I bet I can get the company jet. Even with my father gone, my mother is still on the Board of Directors. I'm sure she'd let us use it. You, me, Mary, Crystal, and Natalie if she wants to go."

"You're serious?"

"Absolutely. Who can you get to watch the kids?"

"I don't know. If Natalie comes, I'll need a sitter for TJ, Melissa, and Brayden. And Mary will need someone to watch Billy."

"How about Mary's mother?"

"Mama Wu?" Angel frowned, thinking. "The kids do love her. Maybe she'll do it."

"Good. It's all set."

"Whoa, whoa, whoa. You're forgetting one important roadblock. The guys will kill us."

"They won't be here. They don't ever have to know."

"I can't lie."

"Okay, fine. We just won't tell them until we get there."

"I don't know, Shannon."

"Don't you want to cheer up Crystal for her birthday?"

Angel sighed in defeat. "Okay, fine. But what if she says no?"

Shannon bit her lip, thinking. "She'll probably use work as an excuse. So...we'll just have to circumvent that."

"How?"

"We'll call her boss first and talk him into letting her

have the weekend off."

Angel grinned. "You are so devious."

"Not devious. Just good at removing roadblocks."

"Um hmm. What about that big two-hundred-pound roadblock you call a husband? What are you going to do when he flips his freaking lid over this?"

"You know what they say. Better to apologize later than to ask permission first."

"Oh, is that what they say?" Angel grinned, but still looked unconvinced.

Shannon pouted. "Come on. You know they'll never let us go. We have to just do it and beg for mercy later. Where's your sense of adventure?"

"It's overshadowed by my sense of self-preservation. And by the way, *mercy* isn't going to be high on those boys' lists when they get a hold of us."

"Come on. Those boys *live* for adventure. We deserve a little ourselves. And hey, it might shake things up a bit. Nothing like really good make-up sex. Am I right?"

"Make-up sex *is* pretty good." Angel bit her lip, considering. "Of course we might get our asses spanked first."

"Win-win." Shannon gave her a look that said it was a no-brainer.

Angel rolled her eyes. "Okay, I'm in."

Shannon held her hand up for a high-five, and Angel smacked her hand, then she reached for her phone. "What's the name of the tattoo place?"

Angel thought a moment, biting her lip again. "Umm."

Shannon's shoulders dropped. "Please tell me you remember."

"I'm thinking. I know he's some big-shot famous guy."

"Famous?"

"Famous in the tattoo world. He's like a super star or something. Crystal told me he was contacted by some network producers trying to work a deal for a show about him. That channel that does the biographies of interesting up-and-coming people did a piece on him. He's supposed to be really good. He's even got a coffee table book out with photographs of some of his best work. And I think there's a line of prints you can buy, too."

"Hmm. Sounds cool. Now if we only *knew his name*." Shannon gave Angel a look.

"I'm thinking. I'm thinking."

"Think faster."

"He's Irish, I remember that." Angel snapped her fingers. "Oh…what's the name of that famous Irish Whiskey?"

Shannon frowned. "Jameson?"

"That's it! Jameson. Jameson O'*something*."

Shannon huffed out a breath, her hands landing on her hips. "O'*something*?"

"Arg. I can't think of it. But, it's him and his three brothers. I remember Crystal telling me that much. Wait. That's it."

"What's it?"

"Him and his brothers…that's the name of the place, *Brothers Ink*."

Shannon rolled her eyes and looked the number up on her phone.

CHAPTER SIX

Crystal stood at the reception counter in the tattoo shop she worked at. She'd been there three months, and the place was starting to feel like home. Maybe not in the same way that the clubhouse had, but she had to put that behind her and stop thinking about it.

The shop was a two story brick building on Main Street in Grand Junction. The building itself dated from the turn of the century, but it had been gutted down to the gleaming wood floors and exposed brick walls and totally remodeled, but still leaving that old character that fit so well in the Colorado town. A huge chrome sculpture of a buffalo sat in the entrance.

The shop belonged to a man named Jameson O'Rourke and his three brothers, Max, Liam, and Rory, hence the name, *Brothers Ink*. They were all extremely talented, but Jameson was the star. He was a very gifted, brilliant artist. A real star at what he did. This shop was where he'd gotten his start, but now there was talk of him moving to L.A. or some other place for bigger and better things.

Crystal had been hired to work the reception desk. She stood staring out the large front window, her fingers drumming on the counter. The three inches of beaded bracelets that stacked up her wrists clicking against the Formica, restlessness rumbling inside her. Her birthday was coming this weekend, and she missed her friends. She missed them terribly. Trying to start a new life in a new city where she knew no one was hard. Sometimes she questioned the insanity of the decision. When she'd left San Jose, she'd just driven, just gotten in her car and driven until she'd found herself in this town. She'd liked the rustic look of the place and stayed a few days, trying to decide what to do with her life, how to start over, even questioning her decision to leave at all. There were so many times on the drive that she'd felt like turning around.

Her thoughts took her back to Wolf. She remembered a birthday she'd had when she'd first started working the bar at the clubhouse. She'd been alone one afternoon, setting up for another Friday night, when Wolf had come in and taken a seat at the end of the bar. She'd looked over and smiled.

"Hey, Wolf. Can I get you a beer?"

He'd nodded.

When she'd brought it over to him, he'd had a cupcake sitting in front of him. She'd frowned at him, eyeing it as she'd slid the beer across the bar top. He'd given her a sly grin as he stuck a candle in it, pulled a lighter from his pocket, and flicked it open. His eyes connected with hers as he brought the flame to the candle. Then he'd pushed the cupcake toward her.

"Happy Birthday, Crystal."

She'd sucked her lips in and felt her eyes sting with tears. No one at the club knew it was her birthday. And she'd meant to keep it that way, letting it pass quietly. But then she'd stared down at that cupcake, and she'd realized how nice it was when someone knew, when someone cared enough to do something to let you know you mattered. She'd whispered, "How did you know?"

He'd winked at her. "I have my ways."

She'd frowned at him.

He'd shrugged. "I do security setups. I run backgrounds on every potential prospect... *and* every employee." He'd waggled his brows. "I know everything about you, babe. Down to your bra size."

She'd stared at him, and then a smile had broken out on her face. "Oh, really?"

He'd grinned. "Really, babe. Now you gonna make a wish and blow out your candle?"

The phone rang in the tattoo shop, shaking her from her memories.

She picked up the receiver. "Good morning, *Brothers Ink*. How may I help you?"

"Crystal?"

She frowned. "Shannon?"

"How are you?"

"I'm great. God, it's so good to hear from you. How are you?"

"Good. Angel and I were sitting here having coffee, and we just realized it's your birthday this weekend."

"Oh God, don't bring that up."

"What's the matter? Not wanting to turn thirty?" Shannon teased.

"I'm staying twenty-nine forever."

"Sorry, kid. It doesn't work that way."

"Rats."

"So, anyway, we've decided a girl's weekend is in order."

"You're coming here?"

"No. We were thinking bigger."

"Bigger?"

"Vegas, baby."

"Vegas? Are you insane?"

"Nope. I already made reservations. Don't worry about the cost. It's on us. Your birthday present."

Crystal bit her lip. "I appreciate the thought, but I can't. I have to work this weekend. Pretty much every weekend."

"No excuses. You're coming."

"Really, Shannon, my boss would never let me off." Crystal noticed someone out of the corner of her eye and turned to see the man himself standing with his arms folded looking at her. And he wasn't happy.

Shannon's voice sounded in her ear. "That's why we already asked him. I'm betting he just walked over to your desk, didn't he?"

"Yup."

She heard both Shannon and Angel giggling through the

phone. "Pack your bags, sugar. He said yes. Oh and by the way, he was a little pissed you didn't mention your birthday."

"I hate you."

"You love me."

"I've got to go."

Shannon giggled. "I bet you do. See you tomorrow night. I just emailed you all the info."

Crystal quickly said her goodbyes and hung up the receiver, her eyes on her boss. "Sorry about that. Did you want something?"

"Were you going to tell me?"

"Tell you what?" Crystal played dumb. He looked pissed. At her. Oh God, what had Shannon done, going straight to her boss like that? Crystal wanted to crawl under the desk in embarrassment. Not only had Shannon called him, but then he comes out and catches her on a personal call. *Shit*. But it had been the only one since she'd been here. He couldn't possibly be upset about that, could he? Although, she had to admit, he had a temper—a true Irish temper. She'd seen it on occasion, but in all the months she'd worked here, he'd never turned it on *her*. In fact, he'd never been anything but nice to her.

His brows rose. "Were you going to tell me that it's your birthday Saturday?"

She swallowed. "They shouldn't have called you. I'm so sorry."

"Your girl, Shannon, told me you were turning thirty, and they want to treat you to a girl's weekend. She seemed sure that you'd make excuses for not being able to go. Work, specifically."

"We work every weekend. It's when you're the busiest. I couldn't possibly go. And she shouldn't have called you. I'm sorry about that." Crystal frowned. "Was she that last call I put through to you? She used a Texas accent. That little fraud."

"Don't change the subject." He glared at her.

She huffed out a breath. "No. I wasn't going to tell you. Why would I? It's not exactly something I'm looking forward to. Thirty. Woohoo. I'm so excited." She twirled her finger in the air.

A slow grin formed on his face. "What's wrong with turning thirty? Things just get better, Ace." He winked. "I'm thirty-eight. You sayin' I've lost my sex appeal?"

Her eyes skated down him as he stood with his muscular arms folded, leaned back against the L-shaped end of the counter, his legs crossed at his booted ankles. He certainly hadn't lost it. He was tall and built with a long dark blond ponytail and pretty blue eyes. From the expensive boots he wore to the watch on his wrist, he was head-to-toe GQ. Ralph Lauren had nothing on him. Except maybe the tattoos that ran up his forearms revealed by the expensive denim shirt he wore rolled up at the sleeves. No, Jameson O'Rourke had *not* lost his sex appeal.

But he wasn't really Crystal's type. Maybe he was just a little too polished, which was strange for the profession he chose. But since he viewed what he did as an art form, she guessed it made sense. The shop was lined with framed art. All of it his.

"No, of course not. You haven't lost your sex appeal."

He grinned. "Maybe this isn't an appropriate conversation to have with your boss."

"Pretty sure not." Crystal rolled her eyes.

He nodded toward the phone. "They must be pretty good friends to go to all this trouble."

"They are, but I can't leave the shop. Not for a whole weekend."

He lifted his chin toward her work area. "Wrap up whatever you were doing and get out of here."

She frowned. "What?"

"Go. Get. You've got a bag to pack. And if I know women, you've got shopping to do before your trip."

"I *can't go*."

"The hell you can't."

"Jameson…"

He turned and ambled off, saying over his shoulder. "You're still here in an hour, you're fired."

"*Fired?*" Crystal whined at his retreating back.

He kept walking. "Happy Birthday, Ace."

CHAPTER SEVEN

Cole stood by his bike in the gravel parking lot of what once was The Pony, one of Nevada's most successful brothels—a brothel the Evil Dead MC owned. Not outright on paper; their ownership was buried in dummy corporations a mile deep.

"Let me bum a smoke," he asked Red Dog who dug a pack out of his vest and shook one out. So much for trying to quit. At this rate, he was going to have an ulcer as well. Pulling his silver Zippo from his pocket, Cole lit the cigarette up, drawing hard. He flipped the lighter closed and shoved it in his pocket, letting the smoke expand in his lungs and the nicotine flood his system like sweet nirvana. Blowing out the smoke, he said, "Thanks, Dog."

They both watched as Crash approached them from the rubble of the gutted building. Beyond him, Cole could see Mack still talking with the Fire Marshall.

Crash reached them with the update. "He says it's

definitely arson. And the way he's questioning Mack, I'm betting he thinks it's an inside job."

Cole exhaled and squinted through the smoke. "So, they think we burned our own Goddamn business down? A business bringing in a ton of money? For what? Insurance money?"

Crash shrugged. "Hey, don't shoot the messenger. I'm just telling you what he's thinking."

"Does he know where it started?"

"Says it was at the back of the rear wing, where the lighting was probably the worst."

Jason walked up and Cole turned on him. "I thought we had security cameras?"

"We do. But we also have a ton of customers coming and going at that time of night. We don't have someone staring at the monitor non-stop. Dolly and I are busy with customers and payments and keeping the johns in order."

"I thought we had dogs. What happened to the two Dobermans you kept out back?" Cole prodded.

"They found their bodies behind the building. They were shot."

"And you didn't hear that shit?" Cole snapped.

Jason held his hands out. "Look, everything happened so fast. One of the girls reported hearing something, but then the smoke detectors started going off, and then the building filled up with smoke. People were panicking, and we were just trying to get everyone out."

Cole ran his hand through his hair in frustration. "You do a good job, man. I'm not trying to blame you. I'm just fucking pissed."

"What's the next step? You planning to rebuild?"

"Not sure. Mack's gotta work that out with the state licensing board; I'm not sure how it all works. Maybe they'll let us set up something temporary and keep the girls working. Maybe not."

Jason nodded.

"They all doing okay?" Red Dog asked.

Jason shrugged. "They're all pretty shook up. Dolly's with them. The Red Cross is putting some of them temporarily up at the Kingman Motel."

Cole lifted his chin toward Jason. "Give us a minute."

Jason nodded at the look Cole gave him that meant he needed to discuss club business, and that wouldn't be happening in front of him.

When Jason walked off, Cole's eyes swung to Crash. "They recover the safe?"

"It's buried. They're pulling it out now." He nodded toward a couple of firemen working through the debris.

Cole nodded. His mind went over every enemy they had. Burning the place to the ground was a little drastic for a pissed off client or jealous boyfriend, but not outside the realm of possibilities. Cole couldn't help thinking this had to be directed at the club. If someone wanted to hit them where it'd hurt, this was definitely a way to do it. Financially, it was going to be a major hit.

"You think this is connected to Temecula?" Crash asked in a low voice.

Cole's eyes swung to him. "If somebody wants to fuck

with us, they're doing a damn fine job of it."

"If there is a connection, it pretty much rules out another cartel in the Temecula hit. There's no way a cartel would bother with this." Crash nodded toward the rubble.

"So who does that leave?"

"Another club, I'm guessing."

"But which one? DKs? Death Heads?"

Just then Green came hopping on one foot across the parking lot toward them.

"Oh look. Here comes Peter Cottontail," Red Dog bit out with a grin.

"I stepped on a motherfucking nail!" Green shouted.

Dog shook his head with a smirk. "You dumbass."

***

"We have to text the guys. We can't wait any longer," Angel insisted as they rode the elevator.

"Speak for yourself." Mary turned to her with a not-on-your-life expression "I'm not telling Dog a thing. How stupid do I look?"

"Come on, Mary. We agreed," Shannon insisted. "We have to tell them all at once, otherwise they'll hear it from each other, and it'll just be that much worse when we get home."

"You're joking, right?" Mary arched an eyebrow.

"Just get your phone out. If we're going down for this, at least we'll go down together."

"Why can't we just tell them when we get home?" Natalie asked, biting her lip.

"Are you worried about Mack?" Angel asked with a

book

fiction

1st ed.

WOLF

WOLF

WOLF

book

fiction

1st ed.

WOLF

WOLF

WOLF

book

fiction

1st ed.

WOLF

WOLF

WOLF

teasing look.

"Of course not! It's… well… we just arrived and I was hoping we'd get at least one day in before we were all ordered home."

"They can order all they want. We're here, and they're there. What can they do about it?" Shannon insisted.

"I wouldn't underestimate them. The only thing we've got going for us is that they don't know where we are," Natalie murmured.

"Exactly, so why are we texting them?" Mary whined.

"I can't lie to Cole," Angel insisted. "I have to tell him."

Mary let out a heavy sigh. "Oh, all right. But don't say I didn't warn you if this all blows up in our faces."

They all pulled their phones out and typed off a text. Then they looked at each other.

"Ready? Set? Send."

"Five bucks says our phones all go off before the elevator doors open," Mary insisted, watching the numbers illuminate as they climbed to the eighteenth floor.

"I've got an idea. Why don't we all turn them off and get drunk?" Crystal suggested.

"Excellent plan!" Shannon concurred, shutting her phone down and tossing it in her bag.

***

After hours standing in the hot Nevada sun and smelling the burnt remains of The Pony, the boys had finally finished getting shit in order, loaded up, and pulled out.

Twenty minutes later, the six bikes rolled into a gas station to fill up before heading back up to San Jose. They all dismounted.

Wolf pulled the nozzle from the pump, unscrewed his gas cap, and shoved the end in the tank, squeezing the handle. His eyes slid to Green one pump over who was rambling on some random topic, like he often had a tendency to do. Leave it to Green to start yammering on about something no one gave a shit about. Like his favorite brand of waffles, or why dogs drool.

"Do you believe in auras?" Green asked.

Wolf gave him a look, which didn't shut him up, not that it ever had.

"I watched this show about it the other day, and it said the color of someone's aura reveals what they're really feeling."

Before Wolf could respond, Green's attention was distracted as a car pulled up, and a hot blonde got out. The girl began pumping gas and Green, abandoning his conversation, wandered over to flirt with the woman.

Shaking his head at Green's totally *un*surprising behavior, Wolf turned to Cole. "So, Jason's gonna call you with an update tomorrow?"

Cole glanced over. "After he meets with the County Sheriff and the District Attorney, yeah."

Wolf nodded. Then a commotion drew his attention. Glancing back, he saw the woman Green had been flirting with duck into her car and come out with a handgun which she aimed over the roof of the car toward Green.

"Get away from me or I'll shoot your junk off!" she yelled. Then she jumped in her car and sped away.

Green shouted after her, "We're soul mates! The sooner you figure that out the less creepy I'll seem."

Wolf held back his laughter long enough to call out, "Hey, Green!"

"What?" Green replied, still staring after the disappearing car.

"I think her aura was a bright shade of '*fuck off and leave me alone*.'"

The guys all burst out laughing.

"I think she liked me," Green said, still staring.

"I'm no expert, but when a woman threatens to shoot your dick off, I'm pretty sure it's time to back the fuck off." Cole chuckled.

"Wolf, think I can track her down by her plate number?"

Wolf rolled his eyes. "Let it go, bro."

Red Dog shook his head as Green walked past him back to his bike. "Your behavior is completely embarrassing, but highly entertaining at the same time. So keep it up."

Cole snickered. "Why can't Green find a girl? The mystery continues."

Green slammed the cap back on his gas tank. "Screw this, I'm goin' inside and getting me some snacks."

"Get me a pack of smokes and a water, will you?" Cole shouted after him.

Red Dog chuckled. "Better give him a list or he'll end up in the booze aisle."

Green's response was to keep walking but lift his arm up, flashing them all the finger over his shoulder.

Crash chuckled at that as his cell went off. He pulled it

from his pocket, looking at the screen. Incoming text from Shannon. He smiled as he swiped his thumb over the screen to open it. His smile faded as he read it.

"Jesus Christ."

Cole frowned over at him as he screwed the cap on his gas tank and hung up the nozzle. "Problems?"

"It's Shannon. She's in Vegas."

"Vegas? You know about that?"

"Hell, no."

"What's she doing there?"

"Apparently a *girl's* weekend."

"Girl's weekend?" Cole straightened. "Fuck, Angel better not be with her." Cole's cell went off, and he yanked his phone out, looking at the text he'd just received. "Goddamn it."

Red Dog looked over. "What's goin' on?" A moment later he was pulling his own ringing cell out of his pocket. He looked at the screen and roared. "Mary's in *Vegas*! What the fuck!"

Mack chuckled as he leaned back against his bike, shoving his sunglasses up on his head. "That's what you boys get for goin' soft on your ol' ladies. They think they can get away with pulling shit like this. Those three loose in Vegas; that ought to be good."

Cole glared at him. "Shut the fuck up."

Wolf looked over at Red Dog, frowning at the look on his face. "You okay, Brother?"

Dog turned away, growling, "Shit like this makes my eye twitch! Leave me alone."

Mack continued to laugh until his cell chimed an incoming text, and the shit-eating grin on his face faded. He whipped his phone out, read the text, and growled, "Goddamn it!"

"What was that you were saying, Mack? Something about not being able to control an ol' lady?" Wolf taunted with a grin.

"Shut up, Wolf. Thank your lucky stars you don't have one." Mack ran his hand down his face and growled. "I can't believe this. Natalie told me she was painting the hallway this weekend."

"You sure she didn't say painting the *town* this weekend?" Wolf continued to torment.

Crash looked at Cole. "Women are such better liars than us."

Cole growled back. "They don't lie better, they just lie so much bigger."

Red Dog added, "Yeah. A man's lie is like 'I was at Joe's house'. A woman's lie is like 'It's your baby'."

Wolf chuckled.

Crash grinned over at him. "I wouldn't be so quick to laugh, Wolf. Crystal's with them."

Wolf's smile disappeared.

Mack threw his leg over his bike and lifted it off the kickstand, growling, "All the shit we got going down right now and they pull this stunt? Wait till I get my hands on that woman. Let's go."

"Where? Back to San Jose?" Green asked as he walked out with an armful of assorted snacks.

"No, dumbass. Vegas."

"Vegas? We're really going to Vegas? *Ooow, slots!* I'm in!" Green tossed the snacks to the ground and jumped on his bike.

"How far is it?" Mack growled at his VP.

Cole was already pulling it up on his phone. "From here, close to three hundred miles." He slid his phone in his pocket. "We can be there in about four hours."

They all mounted up, firing their bikes up and a moment later, they roared out onto the street, one hoard of angry, pissed off bikers.

CHAPTER EIGHT

Shannon reclined on the chaise by the pool at a swank hotel in Vegas. She flipped from her back to her stomach adjusting her sunglasses and looking over at the other girls. Crystal was to her left, Angel to her right, Natalie the next chaise over, and Mary's chaise was empty. She lifted her head to scan the pool and saw the petite Asian beauty in the water, standing waist deep in the shallow end. Her hand pulled her waist-length silky dark hair to the side as she flicked her gaze over her shoulder, to a man who was admiring her full back tattoo. It really was beautiful artwork—a stunning peacock surrounded by flowers, its long tail curving down her hip. The gorgeous hunk in the pool lifted his hand to trail a finger down her spine, smiling at her. Red Dog would flip his shit if he saw, but Shannon knew Mary was just flirting. She only had eyes for her big redheaded Viking.

"Your drinks, ladies."

Shannon looked up to see a bare-chested waiter with a tray of refreshment standing behind their chaises. Her eyes, hidden behind her shades, skated over his muscular body as he began taking the drinks from the tray and setting them down on the small table between them. She smiled. The perks of staying at a five star hotel, they certainly thought of everything, even gorgeous eye-candy staff.

Just as she was reaching for her Appletini, Shannon heard booted feet and saw the waiter's eyes widen as he looked at something just over her head.

"Beat it," she heard in a deep growly voice.

The poor boy lifted his empty tray in front of his chest, as if that would be any protection, and stepped hastily back.

Shannon saw Angel's eyes widen as she pulled her own sunglasses off and looked beyond Shannon, murmuring under her breath, "Crap."

Before Shannon could twist to look behind her, she felt a sharp slap on her bare cheek, revealed beneath the skimpy bikini she had on. And then a weight against her hip as someone sat on the edge of the chaise with her.

She twisted to see Crash's big body, his hand now slowly rubbing over the skin he'd just smacked with his palm, and a grin pulling at the corner of his mouth.

"Hello, Princess."

She swallowed, looking beyond him to the line of leather-clad bikers standing with arms folded, booted feet spread, looking intimidating as hell. Cole stood at the foot of Angel's chaise, Mack at the foot of Natalie's, and Wolf at the foot of Crystal's. Green stood off to the side, his eyes scanning the many other bikini-clad hotel patrons lying around the pool. Red Dog stood off to the side, his eyes scanning the pool, obviously looking for Mary.

Her eyes returned to Crash.

"W-What are you doing here?"

"You didn't really think this little trip of yours was going to fly did you?"

"Come on," Mack snapped at Natalie.

"Let's go," Cole growled down at Angel.

"Go where?" Shannon whispered, looking back at Crash.

"To the rooms you've paid for," he replied, and she couldn't tell if he was pissed about her paying for all this.

He pulled her to her feet, and she grabbed up her bag. Angel rose from her chaise, as did Natalie.

As Crash pulled Shannon behind him back toward the hotel, she saw Red Dog walk over to the edge of the pool and snarl, "Mary, get your ass over here."

Mary swam to the edge near his booted feet and looked up at him, biting her lower lip.

"Hey, baby."

Red Dog didn't hesitate in reaching down, grasping her around each wrist and hauling her dripping wet body straight up and out of the pool. Then he bent and hefted her over his shoulder. She squealed as his hand came down in a loud smack on her wet ass cheek. Then he walked over to her chaise, grabbed up her bag, and followed behind them.

Shannon saw Crystal still on her chaise.

"What about Crystal?" she asked.

"Don't worry about Crystal. Wolf can take care of her.

It's you that you need to be worried about right now."

"Crap," she whispered.

"Exactly, sweetheart. And you're in a pile of it."

***

Red Dog carried Mary to the bank of elevators. When the doors for two different elevators slid open, he took the second so they could have it to themselves. Stepping inside, with her still slung over his shoulder, he twisted so her head was hanging near the row of buttons.

"Push the button for your floor, Mary."

"No," she refused.

His palm came down in a smack on her cheek with the sharp crack echoing in the confined space.

"Ooww," she howled.

He jabbed the button for the top floor.

"That's not my floor," Mary informed him.

"Don't matter. It'll give us a nice long ride." He dropped her to her feet then, his eyes skating over her bikini clad body. "Had half the guys down there drooling over you. You're such a little exhibitionist."

Her hands landed on her hips. "Since you met me in a strip club, I guess you already knew that."

"Even back then, when you were dancing, I don't think you ever realized how stunning you are."

Her chin lifted at the compliment. Damn, it was hard to stay angry at him when he said sweet things like that. She was glad he hadn't shown up five minutes earlier or she'd be bailing him out of jail for assault on the guy at the pool. "You are such a party pooper."

"Don't give me any of your sass. You're in a shitload of trouble, China doll."

"I knew we shouldn't have texted you boys."

Dog shook his head. "Even if you hadn't, it wouldn't have mattered. Two minutes after you texted I got a second one."

She narrowed her eyes. "From who?"

He grinned. "Mama Wu ratted you out, babe."

"My mother? That didn't take her long."

"She likes me better than you."

"She does not. She's terrified of you."

"She loves me. Every Tuesday I bring her Crab Rangoon from Jimmy Wong's."

"She sold me out for a fried dumpling?"

"Well, they're pretty good wontons." He reached over and hit the emergency stop button.

"What are you doing?"

"Just rode 400 miles for you, Mary. Now you're gonna make it worth the trip." His hands went to her ass and with a toss, he had her up and pinned to the wall.

She grinned at him, happily wrapping her legs around her man and pulling his head down to hers.

***

"Whose idea was this?" Crash asked Shannon as he followed her into her hotel suite.

"Mine."

"Thought so. You footing the tab?"

"Maybe."

"I'm gonna cut you some slack here, seeing as how I

know how upset you were before I left."

"We just wanted to do something nice for Crystal's birthday."

"I've got no problem with that. But you and the girls loose in Vegas? I've got a big problem with *that*." He studied her. "I know we haven't been together long—not like Cole and Angel, not like Dog and Mary, so let me be clear. You don't ever pull a stunt like this, Princess."

She stared up at him.

"I mean it. Do not pull this shit again. If I'd come home and found you gone…" He shook his head. "You think I need a flashback to the day you gave yourself over to that piece-of-shit Brit? You think I need a reminder of that?"

Crap. She hadn't thought of what would run through his mind when he found her gone. "I'm sorry, baby."

He grabbed her up and tossed her on the bed, coming down on top of her.

"Yeah, and you're about to spend an hour on your back showing me just how sorry you are, sweetheart."

She grinned up at him, cupping his face in her hands. "Maybe I should get in trouble more often."

"Baby, I'm beginning to realize troublemaker is your middle name."

"*Crash!*"

***

Natalie opened the door and walked into her suite. Mack stalked in behind her, booting the door shut.

She stormed into the bathroom, slamming the door.

He gritted his teeth. She may have the hot Irish temper

of a true redhead, but he wasn't about to let her win this match.

He threw the door to the bathroom open, and it bounced against the wall. He had to fling out his arm to keep it from bouncing back in his face. The bathroom was huge, and she stood four feet from him, her arm moving up and down as she violently yanked a brush through her hair again and again.

His eyes swept down over her body. She was wearing a one piece bathing suit, but she still had a great body with a nice firm rack and killer legs.

"You tryin' to give me heart failure?"

Natalie tossed the brush to the vanity with a clatter. "No, I'm not trying to give you heart failure. Honestly, you are so dramatic."

"Oh, I'm dramatic? Is that right?"

She flung her arms out. "Looks that way to me."

"You know how much shit I'm dealing with in the club right now? You think I've got time to drop everything and chase you across Nevada?"

He advanced on her, and she took a step back, her tone suddenly changing. "Okay, I can see you're angry."

"Angry? Woman, angry doesn't begin to cover it. Try livid."

"I don't see why this is a big deal."

"Think we had this fight once already."

"What fight?" Natalie frowned.

"This. You. A girl's weekend in Vegas. Thought I was pretty clear," he bit out tightly.

"And I thought *I* was, too," she bit right back.

"I see there's only one way to deal with you."

Her hands landed on her hips. "Oh, really? *Deal with me*? Is that what just came out of your mouth?"

Without answering, he grabbed her by the arm, pulled her out of the bathroom and over to the bed. Then his hands were at her waist and she was flying through the air to land on her back.

She looked up at him in shock. "Did you just manhandle me?"

He grinned down at her, tearing off his cut. "Yeah, woman, I did. And you know what?"

"What?"

"You liked it." With that he moved over her, his mouth coming down on hers, silencing any protest she was about to make. A moment later, her arms slid around his neck as she moaned into his kiss.

And a moment after that, she broke off long enough to say in a panting voice, "It took you long enough to get here."

"Smartass," he growled with a grin before his mouth came down on hers again.

***

Cole backed Angel up, advancing on her across the hotel suite, the look on his face thunderous.

"Do I gotta remind you who you belong to, Angel?"

"Cole—"

"Not playin' with you, babe."

"I know who I belong to."

"You want a trip to Vegas, all you had to do was ask. I

can swing it; it's yours. What you do not do, babe, is sneak off behind my back."

"Cole, it was just a girl's weekend."

"Then I put some guys on you."

"Prospects?"

"Prospects. Brothers. Whoever I have to keep you safe."

"We were perfectly fine, Cole."

"You forget how easily a drink can be dosed? Huh, Mama? Only takes your back to be turned for a second for something to be slipped into your glass. They get you alone, cut you off from the group, you're fucked. You forget that happened to you? You forget where I found you?"

"No, Cole. I'll never forget." She looked at her feet. He lifted her chin with a finger.

"I'm not makin' this point to bring up bad memories. I'm makin' this point to make you understand. None of that would happen if you got my boys covering you. Watching you."

"Cole, I'm sorry."

"Babe, I know you're sorry, but I'm still pissed. You're lucky you texted me. If I'd have gotten back to San Jose and found you gone…"

Angel's eyes filled with tears.

"Cryin' ain't gonna save you this time, Mama."

She closed the space between them, pressing against him, her mouth brushing his softly, hesitantly, almost as if she was asking for permission, persuading him to open for her. And he did. His body remained stiff, unyielding, but she kept on until suddenly she felt her back hit the wall as he trapped her against it.

"I'm still pissed, Angel."

"I know." She pulled his head back down to hers and replied between kisses, "Let me make it up to you."

"Oh, you will definitely be making it up to me. You may be making this up to me until Christmas, sweetheart."

***

Crystal watched the little trail of men heading into the hotel with their ol' ladies, and then her eyes swung back to Wolf. He glanced over to see Green was occupied before his eyes returned to her.

"How are you, Wolf?" He didn't respond, and she watched him move to stand at the foot of her chaise, his hands in the hip pockets of his low slung jeans, nothing under his cut but a short-sleeved black *S&S Carburetor* tee that revealed his muscular tanned biceps. He had on a pair of dark sunglasses, but she could still tell when his eyes slid over her body, and she never felt so exposed, lying there in her little black string bikini. Finally, his eyes returned to her face.

"Let's go to your room."

"I'm not going anywhere with you."

"We need to talk. Don't think you want me sayin' what I've got to say to you, here." He lifted his chin, indicating the pool area and all the sunbathers who right now had nothing more entertaining to do than watch the show the out-of-place bikers were putting on. Since Cole, Crash, and Red Dog were gone, their attention had turned to Wolf and Green.

She swallowed. "We have nothing to talk about."

He pushed his sunglasses up on his head. "Seriously?"

She lifted her chin and rested her head back on her chaise, attempting to ignore him. "You're blocking my sun."

"Babe, you do not want to test me right now or you'll end up just like Mary—slung over my shoulder with your ass in the air."

She lifted her head, her eyes taking in the dead serious look in his eyes. Yep. He'd do it, too. She wouldn't put anything past him. Huffing out a breath, she swung her legs over the side and surged to her feet to bite out, "Fine!"

"Fine," he bit back without a second's pause.

She flung on her cover-up, snatched up her belongings, and marched toward the hotel, Wolf trailing behind and every eye in the place following their exit. When she reached the bank of elevators, she jabbed the call button and stared straight ahead. She could feel Wolf's presence at her side, feel his closeness. Hell, the very air crackled with his nearness, just like it always had when he came around her.

The doors opened, and they stepped inside. She punched the button for the eighteenth floor as the doors slid closed.

"You got a room to yourself?" he asked.

"Yes," she replied, not looking at him, keeping her eyes on the flashing numbers above the door as the elevator ascended.

"You gonna look at me?"

"I'm trying not to," she replied tersely.

"This how it's gonna be?"

"Apparently." She heard him give out an aggravated sigh. Too bad. Let him be aggravated. She owed him nothing. But even as she tried to keep up the cold exterior, she could feel her insides turning to jelly. She fiddled nervously with the big silver cuffs she wore on both wrists. He affected her still. Hell, he probably always would. She wasn't sure what his intention was or what he wanted to talk about, she just prayed she had the strength to get through it. Maybe if they had a discussion, he'd leave her alone. Perhaps he just needed closure. Perhaps, if she was being honest, they both did.

The elevator dinged as the doors opened. She stepped out, and he followed her down the hall to her room. She slid her keycard in the slot and opened the door. Tossing her things on the bed, she turned to face him as the door clicked shut.

His eyes scanned the wall of floor-to-ceiling windows that provided an excellent view of the sun setting over the Spring Mountains in the west. He moved to stand in front of them.

"Nice view."

"Thank you. So what did you want to talk about?"

With his hands shoved in his pockets, he turned back to look at her. "Why'd you leave? Why didn't you say goodbye? Why wouldn't you pick up my Goddamn phone calls? Take your pick, Crystal. Where do you want to start?"

She moved to the small bar and cracked open a bottle of water. "Do we really need to do this? What's done is done."

"Yeah, babe, we really need to do this."

"Fine. I left because I overheard Cole say Mack wanted me gone. I left because there obviously was nothing there for me anymore."

"Without saying goodbye?"

She let out a breath. "What would be the point?"

His brows shot up. "What would be the point? You're seriously standin' there askin' me that?"

"Wolf—"

"Don't you think maybe I should have been included in this decision of yours? You think maybe we should have talked about it before you just up and left?"

"What would that have changed?" she snapped at him. "Huh, Wolf? Tell me that!"

"You wouldn't have been leaving town, that's for sure. *That's* what would have changed!"

"Did you ever think that maybe I needed to leave? That I couldn't take it anymore? Did you really expect me to stay and continue as we were?"

He yanked his shades off his head, tossed them on the bed, and ran a frustrated hand through his hair. "Look, I didn't come up here to argue."

"Fine. Leave."

"Crystal, stop. Can't we just talk?"

"We are talking. This is you and me talking. So say what you need to say. If I had come and told you goodbye, what would you have said to me?"

He advanced on her. "I never would have let you go. *That's* what I would have told you!"

"That would have been pretty selfish of you, wouldn't it?"

Stopping in front of her, he towered over her. "Yeah, babe. I'm a selfish guy. You're right. But that doesn't mean leaving was the right thing either."

"I had to, Wolf. Why can't you understand that?" she said in a deflated voice.

"I'll never understand that, Crystal. Never."

She turned away. "It's done. We can't go back. Too much has happened."

"It's not done. Not for me." He pulled her around to face him as he stared down into her eyes. "Not for me, Crystal. It won't ever be done."

"Wolf." She stared up at him and felt her heart breaking all over again. "Don't do this. Please. I can't take it."

His hands lifted to cup her cheeks. "One thing I know about you, babe. Your kisses don't lie. They never have."

With that his mouth came down on hers. Not rough and demanding like she expected, but gentle, testing, seeking entry, coaxing her to open for him. It was her undoing. And so she did. Because she couldn't lie—he was right. She couldn't deny the way he made her feel. The way he always made her feel.

When her mouth opened and his tongue delved inside, his hold tightened as he pulled her flush against his body. Her hands landed on his waist, and then slid up under his t-shirt to find the heat of his bare skin. She heard him groan at her touch, one arm dropping to the small of her back to pull her tighter against him.

The long months they'd been apart, the miles she'd put between them, none of it mattered, none of it could dim the feelings they had for each other. It was as if they hadn't been separated. The rightness of being in his arms engulfed her just like it always did when he held her.

A moment later, she found herself flat on her back on the bed, with Wolf on top of her, kissing her like he'd never stop.

The weight of his muscular body pinned her to the bed, his heat surrounding her. His fingers threaded through her hair, tilting her head back, holding her just where he wanted her while his mouth plundered deep. When he finally came up for air and let her breathe, he murmured, "God, how I missed you, baby."

She sucked in several gulping breaths, the feelings she had for him engulfing her.

His mouth pressed soft kisses around her jaw, moving to her ear to whisper, "Tell me you missed me, too."

She swallowed as he continued to nuzzle.

When she didn't reply, he nipped at her earlobe. "Say it."

Her arms strayed around his torso, her palms sliding under his t-shirt to the bare muscles of his back. He groaned at her touch, but then pulled back, hovering above her to stare down into her face.

"Say it, Crystal."

She looked up at the intensity of his expression, the raw need in his eyes, and she couldn't lie.

"I missed you, Wolf. So much."

At her response, his mouth came down on hers again as his body slid up, his knee forcing her thighs apart. When she moved to accommodate his body, he groaned his approval, the sound captured by her mouth.

He lifted again to stare down at her, one hand moving to

tenderly brush her hair back again and again as his eyes moved over her face. Then they locked with hers. "I've missed this."

"This?"

"You under me. You're arms and legs wrapped around me, holding me close, making me feel the way only you do. I've missed *us*."

"Shut up and kiss me, Wolf." She didn't want to think about what his words might mean. If they changed anything, or if they changed nothing at all. She didn't want to know that answer right now. She just wanted to feel, to remember what it was like between them. How she'd never felt with anyone what she felt with this man.

She pulled his head down to hers, lifting to meet his mouth halfway. He didn't stop her. It seemed less talk and more action suited him fine, too.

He rolled them until he was on bottom, and she was astride him. His hands ran up her thighs as they snuggled tight against his ribs. She watched as his hungry eyes skated up her body, taking in the sheer cover up she wore that was open and gaping in the front revealing the black string bikini underneath.

One hand slid up over her hip to the curve of her waist and then behind her, his fingers going straight for the ties. One pull and they came free. Then that hand was reaching up to the strings at the nape of her neck. Another tug and her breasts were bared to him. He wasted no time pushing the cover-up off her shoulders to pool at her elbows. Then his hand at her back was coaxing her down, bringing her breasts down to meet his hungry mouth. He lifted his head, closing the last few inches to latch onto one nipple with a strong tugging pull that had her arching to bring him closer. She moaned at the exquisite jolt that zinged through her.

He let go of her nipple with a popping sound and stared up at her. "My baby likes that."

She moaned her agreement as he moved to the other breast, treating it to the same torment until she was writhing on top of him. She felt his hands stray to her hips to yank the strings of her bikini bottom free. And then they were moving all over her ass as he moaned, the sound vibrating through her nipple. She lowered down on top of him, the soft bare skin of her naked body brushing up against the cool leather of his cut and the cold metal of his belt buckle. She writhed, brushing against the roughness of his jeans and felt the sensation between her thighs.

She rubbed against him seductively as his hands roamed over her. He let loose of her nipple and dragged her mouth down to his, kissing her with a hunger that took her by surprise. There was an intensity to him tonight. She pushed back, straddling his hips and began to pull his t-shirt free.

"I want you naked, too."

***

I want you naked, too.

As Crystal's words stole through him, Wolf sat up, more than willing to obey. Her hands slid over his shoulders, helping to rid him of his cut and shirt. Once he'd tossed those aside, he rolled again, putting her back under him. Then he lifted off her, bearing his weight with one hand in the bed while the other fumbled with his pants, barely getting them down far enough before he plunged inside her, not willing to wait another second before feeling her tight around him.

Her head went back in the pillow as he drove into her, and his mouth latched onto her exposed neck as one of his forearms hooked under her knee and pressed her leg up, spreading her wide for him. He began moving, slowly at first. *In and out. In and out.* He lifted his head, his eyes never leaving her face as he moved. He watched every emotion as they stole across her face. Awe. Hunger. Want. Need.

They flashed in her eyes one after another as he moved in deep, long strokes, making her feel every inch, every rubbing thrusting sensation as a thousand nerve endings skated across each other, flaring to life.

"Do you feel me, Crystal? Do you feel *us?*"

She could barely do more than nod as she stared up into his eyes as if hypnotized by them.

"Say it," he demanded, not about to settle for a nod.

"Yes," she panted as her body undulated beneath him.

He changed angles and her head went back again, her eyes sliding closed at the new sensation took her higher and higher.

His mouth came down on hers as his body picked up the pace, his thrusts gaining momentum. He wanted to make it last, but it'd been so long since they'd been together, and he knew his control was hanging on by a thread. This first time was going to be hard and fast, but he swore to himself he'd make it up to her. He'd spend the rest of the night making it up to her.

"Baby," he growled through gritted teeth.

As if she understood, as if she knew what he was feeling, she nodded, clutching at him.

"Yes," she panted.

Hell, he supposed he shouldn't be surprised she understood his need. She'd always understood his needs. They were always so in sync with each other, so attuned with one another. That and she probably could feel the tremors in his arms as he fought back the urge to finish so soon.

"Oh Wolf," she panted as he reached around her leg, his hand searching out her clit, stroking over her as he continued to drive into her.

"I need you to get there, baby."

Then he watched as her head went back, and she moaned out a long wailing sound as she slid over the edge, her inner walls contracting around him, milking him for a response.

He groaned, dipping his head as his release exploded. His arms locked around her, his body went solid, and every muscle flexed as the aftershocks shuddered through him. And then, as if every drop of energy had been drained out of him, he sank down on top of her soft, welcoming body.

He felt her hands stroking over his back, one hand lifting to thread her fingers through the hair at the base of his neck. Her lips pressing soft kisses along his throat. He made a move to slide off of her, but her arms tightened.

"Stay," she whispered, and he could feel the fear in her. Was she afraid he was leaving her? Like there was a chance in hell of that happening.

"I'm not going anywhere. I just don't want to crush

you."

He moved off her then, and this time she let him go. But he pulled her close, tucking her against his side. He only meant to rest for a minute to regain some strength, but he soon felt the miles catching up with him, his body heavy with exhaustion. He pressed a kiss to her forehead.

"Just give me a minute to rest." His hand hooked behind her knee, pulling her thigh across his lower abdomen, needing her body plastered to him. He moaned into the top of her head as she snuggled into his warmth, and that was the last thing he remembered as he slipped into oblivion.

CHAPTER NINE

Wolf heard a banging at the door. He blinked the sleep from his eyes and squinted around the hotel room. Crystal was nowhere in sight. The pounding on the door continued.

Shit.

Tossing the sheets back, he stood and pulled his jeans on, calling out, "Who is it?" as he strode toward the door.

He heard a muffled response. "Narcotics officer."

He pulled the door open to find a grinning Red Dog.

"You're hilarious."

Dog strode in. "*I* thought so."

Wolf watched him glance around the room.

"You get your note?"

"My note?" Wolf frowned, scratching his chest. He didn't have a clue what the fuck Dog was talking about.

"We all got one. Girls got dressed up and snuck out while we were sleeping."

Wolf glanced around. There was no note. Dog stepped

into the bathroom doorway, flipping on the light, and Wolf could hear him chuckle.

"Leave it to Crystal to make a statement."

"What are you talking about?" Wolf stepped beside him. There scrawled across the mirror in red lipstick was his note.

Hey, Sleeping Beauty—
Come find me in the club downstairs when you awaken!
—Crystal

"They're *all* down there?" Wolf asked Dog.

"Yeah. Get dressed. We're going to find 'em. The guys are waiting by the elevator."

***

"Mack had to take a call about The Pony. He'll be down in a minute. He was pretty pissed the girls snuck out on us." Cole mused as they made their way through the crowded club.

"Oh, and you're not?" Wolf asked with a grin.

"Where the hell are they? You see 'em anywhere?" Crash asked, his eyes scanning the crowd.

"Fuck, this place is packed," Cole replied with a shake of his head.

Wolf's eyes surveyed the crowd. The place was filled with a young party crowd. The women were all dressed to the nines in short dresses and towering heels. There was a light show going on like nothing he'd ever seen before. Strobe lights and colored spotlights flashed in perfect time with the music.

"Let's get a drink," Cole shouted, nodding toward one of the bars.

They pushed their way to the front, or more aptly the crowd parted like the Red Sea when people turned to see their cuts. The bouncer had made a noise about wearing them inside, but a hundred dollar bill from Cole and a look of death from Red Dog, and he'd waved them in.

A few minutes later, drinks in hand, the men turned to survey the crowd again.

Dog looked around like he'd never seen anything like this place. He turned to Wolf and yelled in his ear over the driving dance beat. "None of this is real, right?" When Wolf shook his head, he continued, "Okay, good. Just checking."

Wolf grinned over at him. "I thought you were going to deck that bouncer."

"Hey, we're in. Don't worry about that guy," Cole told him.

"Do I look worried? I just hate when you have to be nice to someone you really want to throw through a window."

***

Crystal leaned toward the mirror in the club's swanky ladies' room and retouched her lipstick. Her eyes swept over her reflection. She'd straightened her long dark hair, letting it hang in a glossy sheet. She'd put a rhinestone headband in and teased her hair up in a subtle lift behind the jewels, a la sixties style. She wore a strapless, black lace mini dress that showed a lot of skin. Shannon had loaned her some sparkly lotion that gave her bare shoulders and cleavage a subtle sheen. She'd finished off the look with long, dangling, jet beaded earrings and matching cuff bracelets on both wrists. Her heels were sky-high, accentuating her legs.

Her eyes moved down the mirrored wall, taking in all her dear friends that had made this evening possible. Shannon was dressed in an ice blue sheath that really made her blue eyes pop. Mary was in red satin that looked hot with her long black hair. Angel was in a stunning gold cocktail dress that matched her hair perfectly. And Natalie was in a sexy white and silver sequined dress, her red hair pulled up in a sleek twist.

Finishing off her touch-up, Crystal popped her lipstick back into her tiny beaded clutch, and watched while Shannon touched her own lips up. Their eyes met in the mirror.

"You having a good time, birthday girl?" Shannon smiled at her.

Crystal grinned back. "I'm having a wonderful time."

"Wolf in your bed for the night. That's got to be a little birthday bonus, huh?"

Crystal gave her a sly smile.

"Come on girls, I want to dance!" Angel pleaded, her arm looped through Mary's, pulling her toward the door.

They all headed back out into the crowded club.

***

Cole lifted his chin in the direction over Wolf's shoulder and grinned. "I think somebody's about to rock your world."

Wolf twisted to look over his shoulder, and his breath caught, a fist tightening around his heart. His eyes swept over Crystal, taking in every detail. Jesus Christ, she was beautiful.

He found himself turning slowly toward her. His eyes lifted to connect with hers, and he struggled to make his mouth work.

"Hey."

She smiled at his lame greeting and repeated it back to him. "Hey."

"You look beautiful."

"Thank you."

"Can I get the birthday girl a drink?"

"Okay."

Mack finally shouldered his way through the crowd to join them. His eyes did one long trip down Natalie's outfit, and he turned to his VP. Leaning to his ear, he barked, "Go find us a limo. Now."

Cole frowned at him, not sure he'd heard correctly. "Do what?"

"A limo. One of those stretch jobs that'll hold all of us. Get one. Now!"

Cole gave him a curious look and replied, "Yeah, okay."

He jerked his chin at Green, and the two moved toward the exit.

A half hour later, they all piled out of the hotel and under the portico where a white stretch limo sat waiting, the driver holding the door open. Cole stood next to it.

"Where are we going?" Natalie asked.

"Get in ladies," Mack ordered.

"Mack, you're being all mysterious." She frowned at him.

His brows rose. "Get in the car, Natalie."

"Okay. Okay."

They all slid inside, only to find Green already seated and making himself a drink from the mini-bar.

Mack spoke with the driver, then climbed inside, and the limo pulled out onto the boulevard.

Ten minutes later the limo turned in a driveway and pulled to a stop. The driver got out, came around, and opened the door. Mack slid out, extending his hand in for Natalie. She climbed out, took one look at where they were, and pulled back on his hand.

"Oh, no. No way. Not happening."

The others all piled out and took in the tiny Vegas wedding chapel.

"Mack, you dog. You and Nat tying the knot?" Green asked, still holding his drink.

"Come on." Mack began pulling Natalie toward the entrance. She yanked back, which wasn't easy in her silver heels.

"Mack, stop. We are *not* doing this."

He came to a stop and whirled on her. "Yeah, we are. We *are* doing this. And we're doing this right now."

"Have you lost your mind?" she asked, her free hand going to her hip.

"No. I took one look at you in that sparkly white dress and the idea just came to me. You look like a bride. We're here in Vegas. Let's do this."

"And did my running off to Vegas without your permission have anything to do with this sudden idea of yours?"

Mack lifted his chin and grunted, "Maybe."

Shannon, who'd been busy on her smart phone, looked up and said, "I just Googled this place, Natalie. Cindy Crawford and Richard Gere got married here. So did Angelina Jolie and Billy Bob Thornton."

Natalie whirled on her. "Oh and is that supposed to make me feel better about this? Just look how those marriages turned out."

"Yeah, but they also filmed the wedding scene from *Viva Las Vegas* here. You know, the one with Elvis and Ann Margret? Come on, Natalie, if that's not a sign from God, what is?"

"You can't be serious?"

Mack pulled her around to look at him. "Forget all that. Do you want to marry me, Natalie? Yes or no? I ain't gonna stand here and beg you."

"It would be nice to be *asked!*"

"I just did!"

"The right way!"

"Think she wants you down on one knee, Boss," Crash advised with a grin, one arm pulling Shannon close to his side as everyone stood watching Mack squirm.

Mack glared at him, and then back at her. "Oh, for the love of…"

Natalie raised her brows, waiting. "Well?"

Mack blew out a breath and dropped to one knee.

Angel scrambled to dig her phone out of her purse. "Wait, I've got to get a picture of *this*."

Mack gave her a death glare, but she clicked away

anyhow, grinning like a fool.

"Natalie, will you do me the honor of becoming my wife?"

"Where's the ring?" she asked arching a brow.

"I'll take you to the jeweler tomorrow, and you can pick one out. Anything else, woman?"

"Just one more thing."

"Yeah? What's that? Ask away, because swear to God, this is the last time you'll have me on my knee, baby."

She smiled down at him. "Tell me you love me."

"I love you, Natalie, with all my heart." He stared up at her and, with typical Mack impatience, ruined it by adding, "Now, you gonna marry me or not?"

"Yes, Mack, I'll marry you."

A half hour later, they all emerged, Natalie holding a big bouquet of white roses, with Mack's silver pinky ring around her finger.

CHAPTER TEN

Wolf stood at the hotel suite window with one arm propped high on the glass, looking out over the lights of the Vegas strip below. But his mind wasn't on the view. It was on Crystal.

They'd been doing a dance all evening—flirting, seducing, getting to know each other again. It was almost like they were strangers, hooking up for the very first time. But at the same time, it kind of felt like they were picking right up where they left off.

One thing Wolf realized for sure, he needed to treat her gentle, careful, like a man testing the waters. She needed to be seduced slowly, all night long. And he was up for it. Hell, yeah. He'd give her whatever she wanted. Whatever she *needed*. Right now slow was what he believed she wanted.

Until she walked out and blew that belief all to hell.

Crystal walked out of the bathroom, and he caught her reflection in the glass. Twisting his head, he looked over his shoulder at her and forgot to breathe. She was in a black satin short kimono-style robe, belted at the waist, but with enough gaping open to reveal the matching black satin bra underneath. His hand slid from the glass, his eyes tracking her movements as she padded barefoot across the room to the mini bar. He slid his hands in his pockets, watching as she filled a short tumbler with bourbon. The ice in the glass tinkled as she turned and stalked slowly across the room.

It seemed, for tonight, Crystal wanted to be the seducer. A grin pulled at his mouth. He was fine with that. Oh, yeah. He was definitely fine with that.

Wolf pulled his cut off, tossing it over a chair, his eyes never leaving her.

She stopped at the side table, her hand moving over her smart phone. A moment later a slow sexy saxophone filled the room before she set the phone back down. Wolf's eyes lingered on the phone, a phone he had helped himself to while she was in the bathroom so that he could quickly download an app to track her movements. It was something he wished he'd done six months ago. If he had, then he wouldn't have had any trouble finding out where she'd fled to when she'd left town. He swore to himself he was never going to get caught in that position again. That app was his insurance policy. Insurance that no matter where she tried to run or where she tried to hide, he'd always be able to find her.

Crystal's eyes lifted and met his as she moved toward him. Coming to stand in front of him, she took a sip of the amber liquor, and his eyes slid over her body and down the smooth tan length of her legs. He was distracted from his slow perusal when her free hand cupped the back of his neck, her fingers sliding into the hair at his nape. His eyes met hers and saw the slow burn begin in them.

She handed the glass to him. He took it, taking a slow sip, his eyes never leaving hers even as she twisted, her knee coming up and her inner thigh sliding along the outer side of his jean-clad leg. The sole of her delicate foot stroked along the back of his calf from his knee to his boot top buried beneath the leg of his jeans. She rubbed against him like a cat in heat, seducing him slowly and seductively, enticing him with every tantalizing touch.

Holding the glass in one hand and still not breaking his gaze, his free hand hooked the back of her knee as it brushed against him, and then slid up the outside of her thigh slowly, inch by inch, until his fingertips were skating under the satin robe. Her head lifted, her lips almost brushing his. When he dipped down to connect that last few inches, she pulled back, just out of reach, and a slow smile pulled at the corner of her mouth.

And with that, their crazy dance began. One of teasing and taunting.

She stepped back, her eyes sliding closed as her body began to move to the music, her hips swaying, her body undulating from side to side. Her hands lifted the hair off her neck and then slowly let it fall.

Wolf sipped his drink, watching her every move, taking it all in, enjoying the little show of feminine enticement. Every move she made designed to tempt and seduce. Her eyes opened, her head tilted to the side as she continued to move. He did a slow blink, their eyes connecting.

His baby wanted to play. The fine art of seduction by Crystal. And she was a *master* at it. Every move, every look, every touch was designed to tempt him like Eve tempted Adam in the Garden of Eden.

He sipped his drink and twisted to set the glass down on the dresser. Taking her in his arms, he dipped his head low to bring his face down to hers. She looked up at him, her arms sliding up his chest to his shoulders. His hand lifted to shift through her hair and cup the back of her head, bringing her close. He kissed her slow and soft. That's how she wanted it tonight. A slow, erotic seduction. He was all too happy to give it the way she wanted it. Right now that was exactly how he wanted it, too.

His hand reached for the satin belt tied around her waist. As he pulled, she slowly backed up and the belt slid free, her robe falling open down the front. He followed her, tracking her as she continued her slow retreat across the large hotel suite, the whole time her eyes never breaking contact with his. When she got to the big platform bed, she stopped and he closed in, his hands sliding into the opening of the robe where all of her smooth, flat belly was exposed and her navel peeked out. Her skin was warm and soft under the heat of his large hands. He looked down into her face and saw her mouth part with a soft intake of breath at the touch of his hands. He stroked over her hips to her ass and back. Then he pushed the robe back off her shoulders, its slick satin gliding down her skin to pool on the floor.

She stood before him now in black satin panties and strapless bra. His eyes skated down the length of her and then back to her face, their eyes connecting again. He saw his own hunger reflected in her heavy lidded gaze. She sat on the edge of the bed, looking up at him before crawling back to recline on the pillow. One of her knees lifted, the sole of her foot sliding seductively over the sheet as her body gently writhed in invitation.

He stood there with his weight on one foot, his eyes moving over her, admiring all that silky tanned skin. His head dipped down to look at her from under his brow. He took it all in—her body all laid out for him like a feast for a starving man. And he was *most definitely* a starving man at that moment. Did she know how badly he wanted her? Did she even have a clue?

Dragging out the moment, he watched as her chest rose and fell with her accelerated breathing. Perhaps she *was* as aroused as he. Perhaps she needed him just as badly as he needed her. He hoped so. He prayed so.

At his continued hesitation, she whispered his name, beckoning him softly, pleadingly.

"Wolf."

It broke the spell, and he moved toward her, his knee coming down on the bed between her legs, one palm in the mattress, the other sliding up the calf of her bent leg. His fingertips barely brushed against her skin, and he knew the light sensation was setting sparks along every nerve ending. Determined to string out the anticipation as long as possible, he moved slowly over her, his hand skating up her thigh, over her hip, the indentation of her waist, loving the feel of her silky skin under his palm. He lowered himself on top of her, his weight coming slowly down, his hips settling into the cradle of her thighs. She looked up at him, her eyes wide, filled with desire and want, her mouth parting, her lips soft, inviting.

That look. That look in her wide eyes said it all. It was one of wonder. He'd never been this gentle, never held back like this, never moved so slowly, and he could tell it had her off balance.

Good. He liked when Crystal was off balance. It meant she was unguarded. It meant maybe she'd let him back in.

He had her full attention. Her full awareness. And he loved watching her increased responsiveness to his soft touch.

She had started all this, attempting to seduce him, but perhaps he was turning the tables on her and seducing his way back into her heart.

***

Crystal gasped as the cold metal of Wolf's belt buckle came in contact with the warm bare skin of her belly as his weight settled down on her.

His mouth muffled her moan as his hands slowly stroked over her body. His mouth was gentle, probing, asking, not demanding.

This was all about giving, not taking. Every touch, every movement, every soft word whispered in her ear designed to please her. Tonight it was all about her—giving her pleasure.

This was a side of Wolf she hadn't seen in a long time.

Maybe ever. And it threw her. She wasn't sure what to make of it. Maybe her mind was a little clouded by alcohol, because she didn't want to risk examining it too closely. To be honest, she was terrified she'd pin too much meaning to it, and in the end, it wouldn't mean what she hoped it did.

But Wolf wasn't letting up. He wasn't teasing, he wasn't playing. He was unwavering, resolute enticement, determined to tear down every wall she tried to keep up, every barrier she'd crafted to protect her bruised heart. She'd meant for this to be just a fling, just a taste of what they'd once had. She'd never meant to rekindle a flame she knew was likely to burn her again.

But she couldn't help falling under the spell he was weaving over her.

For the first time, it wasn't all about him. He wasn't thinking about what he wanted, because if he did, this would be completely different. It would be rough, demanding, playful and teasing maybe, but never this tender show of emotion, never this gentle expression of things he obviously couldn't say.

Her hands moved to his belt, and one of his came down to help her, yanking it free, his mouth never leaving hers.

When he finally broke free to breathe, she whispered in a voice frantic with need, "I want you naked."

He rose up to look down at her before moving back off the end of the bed just long enough to shuck his clothes. Then his hot hard body was coming back down on top of hers. His hand moved up, his palm closing over her satin covered breast, gently squeezing.

"Need you naked, too."

Her back lifted off the mattress to help him as he moved a hand beneath her, his fingers snapping the hook open. He pulled her bra free and tossed it aside. His mouth pressed kisses along her jaw, down her neck and across her collarbone to climb to her nipple. His tongue lapped gently until she was threading her fingers into his hair to pull him against her, needing more. So much more.

He latched on, giving a deep tugging pull that had her back arching, her neck sinking into the pillow. But he wasn't letting her lead, he wasn't letting her set the pace, no matter how badly she wanted him to move faster. He spent what seemed like hours lavishing her breasts with attention until she couldn't take it anymore and had to plead with him.

"Wolf, please, I need you."

That didn't hurry him any, either; he just trailed his mouth down her belly, transferring his attention to another area. She felt his hands move to her panties until they were down her legs and gone. He settled lower, between her legs to take up his torment again, only this time with even more determination to drive her crazy. His wicked mouth moved over her again and again and again, tongue delving, probing, tormenting, torturing, teasing... until her head was thrashing on the pillow as she climbed toward orgasm.

"*Wolf*," she gasped.

"Come for me, Crystal. Let me see all that beauty."

His growled words, edged now with raw need worked to push her over the edge with a ragged moan. A moment later he was over her, brushing her hair back, his eyes moving over her face as her eyes opened to barely a slit.

She looked up at the tender look on his face, a look filled with love.

"Baby," he murmured, pressing kisses over her face as her rapid breathing slowed. "Let me in."

As he said the words, his leg moved between hers, his thigh coming up to press against her, his intention clear.

"Yes," she moaned, opening to him as he settled between her thighs.

His mouth came down on hers as she felt his body lift, and then he was at her entrance, gently probing.

"Let me in," he repeated.

She wrapped first her arms and then her legs around him in response, and then pulled him deep in one sweet motion. She felt and heard him groan as he settled.

"Oh God, baby. I've missed this. I've missed you."

Her arms clutched at him as her throat closed, afraid to reply, afraid this fairy tale was going to burst like a soap bubble and she'd awaken alone in her bed.

He began to move inside her with achingly loving care— gentle, slow, unhurried, every stroke drawn out, lingering over every sensation. The deep rumbling groan he emitted gave away the toll this took on his need. But he maintained a tight control on his urge to change the tempo, she could tell by the tremor in his arms and the tick in his clenched jaw. He was determined that this be all about her.

His body worshiped hers with such devotion in every touch. He seemed completely consumed by her, with such attentiveness and awareness of her in every move he made, every groan, every growl, every whispered word of love, praise, and devotion.

His mouth settled over hers, his tongue delving inside as his strokes began to build.

"Harder," she begged.

"Not gonna do you hard, babe. Not tonight."

He kept moving in long gentle pumping thrusts as his hand moved between them caressing, stroking. Intent on building her to another orgasm.

His mouth at her ear, he whispered words of love.

This wasn't heated, rough, passionate sex. This was an excruciatingly tender expression of how he felt about her, how they felt about each other. This wasn't sex, this was making love.

"What are we doing, Wolf?"

"I'm showing you how I feel about you, Crystal."

With that, her head went back, and she crashed over the edge into all-consuming bliss. And a moment later, his body went rock solid above her as he followed her over.

CHAPTER ELEVEN

Wolf's eyes came slowly open. Light poured in the floor to ceiling windows of the luxury hotel suite. The front range of the mountains was visible in the distance. He took in a deep relaxing breath, feeling totally sated from last night's bout of endless sex. He turned his head on the pillow, expecting to find Crystal, her dark hair splayed across the bright white of the pillowcase, his arm already moving across the sheets toward her. All he encountered was cool emptiness. His head lifted, his eyes moving around the room. He turned toward the bathroom door.

"Crystal?"

It was open, the light off. He twisted, reaching for his cell on the nightstand and checking the time.

He threw the covers back, swung his legs over the bed, and pulled his jeans on. Then he moved through the hotel suite. She was gone. Along with every trace of her—her purse, her bag, her makeup in the bathroom, all gone. No note. He checked his cell. No text or missed call.

Son of a bitch.

She'd run out on him again. The little minx.

And after everything they'd done last night. He thought he'd made it clear with every touch, with every whispered endearment, with every expression of love just how much he felt for her, how much he cared about her, how much he Goddamn loved her. Did it mean nothing to her? Or was she just running scared again?

His eyes fell on the satin belt from her robe where it pooled on the floor still, exactly where he'd let it fall last night. It teased him, laying there like Cinderella's forgotten glass slipper, reminding him of all he'd had last night. He bent to pick it up, his thumb rubbing over the satin fabric. Goddamn it. When he caught up with her, he was going to tie her to the bed with this belt. He shoved it in his hip pocket, a tight grimace forming on his face.

Crystal wanted to play this game, then he was all too willing to take up the gauntlet. After all, no one loved the chase more than he did. This was one chase he was going to love, especially when he finally caught up with her.

Payback is gonna be a bitch, sweetheart.

***

Wolf found the rest of the group downstairs in the hotel restaurant having breakfast. Well, all except for the newlyweds. They probably wouldn't emerge for hours.

He stood at their table.

Angel was grinning down at her phone. "This shot is getting blown up, poster size." She turned to Cole. "I think you should put it up in the clubhouse. Maybe have it framed."

"Let me see." Shannon leaned over to look at the picture, a picture Wolf could see clearly from his position standing above her. It was the shot Angel had snapped of Mack down on his knee outside the wedding chapel.

Angel turned the phone toward her. "Isn't it great?"

Shannon frowned, confused. "Wait? That really happened?"

"A little fuzzy, are we?" Crash asked her with a laugh.

She turned to him. "I don't even remember coming back to the hotel last night."

The waitress returned with a carafe of coffee and began filling mugs.

Crash looked over at Shannon and winked. "Coffee. My other favorite morning thing."

Shannon grinned big and turned red, muttering softly, "Crash."

Cole looked up at where Wolf stood. "You gonna join us, Brother?"

He shook his head.

"Where's Crystal?"

"Gone."

"Gone? What do you mean, gone?"

"I mean she's gone. Her. All her stuff. Woke up and the room was empty."

"What?" Angel asked, stunned.

Wolf's eyes met hers. "She say anything? Tell you she was leaving?"

"No, Wolf. I swear."

His gaze swung to Shannon. "You?"

"Not a word. She seemed so happy last night. I thought everything was fine, and I know she doesn't have to be back at work until tomorrow." Shannon was already moving to dig her phone out of her bag to call her.

"Don't bother," Wolf told her.

"Why not?" she replied softly, pausing.

"I'm going after her. I'd appreciate it if you didn't give her a heads-up on that."

"Okay."

"Did you two have a fight?" Angel asked.

He shook his head.

Cole raised his mugs to his lips, pausing to ask, "You want to talk about it?"

"No."

"Good," he muttered, and took a sip of coffee.

Dog bit out a laugh at Cole's response, then leaned back in his chair and glanced up at Wolf. "How much of a head start she got on you?"

"No clue."

"She fly in or drive?" Dog asked, swinging his gaze to Mary.

Shannon answered for her. "She drove."

"What's she in?" Wolf asked.

"I know," Angel cut in, then added with a cocky smile, "but if you want me to tell you, it's gonna cost you."

CHAPTER TWELVE

Wolf caught up with Crystal eighty-three miles outside of Las Vegas, just this side of the Arizona state line.

All he'd had to do was follow the tracking app he'd installed on her phone. It showed her moving northeast out of Las Vegas on Interstate 15. He'd gunned his bike, weaving in and out of traffic until he caught up with the little red Honda that Angel had told him she was driving these days.

That bit of information had cost him.

She'd made him confess his feelings. Standing right there at that table, she'd made him say the words. And he had. He'd told everyone there that he loved Crystal, had *always* loved her, and always will love her.

Surprisingly, not a single one of his brothers had cracked a joke.

He pulled alongside Crystal, motioning her to the side of the road. Dismounting, he approached her car as her driver's window powered down.

"What the hell are you doing?" she snapped.

Like she had any right to be pissed off. He braced his palms on the frame and leaned in. "Going somewhere, sweetheart?"

At that, she aimed her designer sunglasses toward the windshield, huffing, "I have to get back."

"Bullshit. You're runnin' again."

"Wolf, I have a job to get back to."

"Don't lie to me, Crystal. Don't you dare sit there and lie to me. Shannon told me you don't have to be back until tomorrow."

She stayed stubbornly silent as he called her bluff.

Wolf took in their surroundings as a big tractor-trailer barreled past, the blast of wind rocking her vehicle. There wasn't much around except for endless desert scrubland. But a sign indicated there was an exit coming up, and a billboard in the distance advertised the Desert Palms Motel.

Bingo.

"You're going to follow me to this exit." He lifted his chin to the green highway sign proclaiming the exit number approaching. "We're gonna have this shit out once and for all."

"I'm not going anywhere with you, Wolf."

He leaned down in her face and they locked shades. "We're getting a room and working through this shit, or would you rather do it on the side of the fucking highway, Crystal?"

She huffed out a breath. "Fine."

"Do *not* make me chase you down this road again,

babe."

"I said fine, didn't I?"

She put her car in gear as he headed back to his bike. He followed behind her, making sure she took the exit, before he gunned the throttle, zoomed around, and took the lead. Turning off the ramp, he led her to the motel.

It was a small place, maybe a dozen units in a horseshoe-shaped layout surrounding a blacktop parking lot with a tiny, fenced pool off to one side. A sloped roof overhung the concrete walkway that ran past each unit's door and curtained window.

Parking his bike in front of one of the nearest units, Wolf yanked off his helmet as Crystal pulled into the parking space next to him. He walked back to the tiny office set just off the street, and a few minutes later, he returned with a key.

He slid the key into the lock of unit number one, conveniently right in front of where her car and his bike sat. He pushed the door open and glanced in at the double bed. The air conditioning unit rattled in a poor attempt to cool the place. The room was a far cry from the luxury suite they'd shared in Vegas last night, but it was going to have to do. He walked back to her car, yanked open the back door as she got out the front, and then he grabbed her overnight bag.

"What are you doing?" she asked with a frown.

"Carrying your bag."

"I agreed to talk to you, nothing more."

He continued on past her. "Well, it's gonna be a long talk, sweetheart."

"Wolf!" She followed him inside as he tossed her bag on

the bed. She glared at him as he walked back past her to slam the door shut. She swiveled to him, her hands landing on her hips. "What is your problem?"

He advanced on her then, until she felt the need to take a step back. "My problem? My problem is I woke up alone in an empty hotel suite. My problem is you have a habit of forgetting to say goodbye. My problem is I've got a woman who seems to think any of that is gonna fly with me."

"I'm not your woman, Wolf."

"Keep tellin' yourself that, babe."

She ignored that and moved on. "You're pissed about *me* leaving? Really, Wolf? But it's okay for *me* to wake up alone every time *you* sneak out the door?"

He frowned. "What?"

"*You* do that to *me* all the time, Wolf!"

"Babe, you know how the MC is. I get called out, I have to leave. You know that, Crystal."

"God, you're so infuriating."

He shook his head. Christ, she'd talk him in circles if he let her. But there was one question, by God, she'd answer. "Why'd you run, Crystal?"

"We had a night together. Why are you trying to make it into something it wasn't?"

At that, his chin came back. "Something it wasn't? Just what the fuck are you tellin' me?"

"Wolf, nothing's changed."

"*Everything's* changed. I thought I proved that to you last night."

"We had sex. That proves nothing."

"That wasn't just sex, Crystal, and you know it. You fucking *know it*."

She turned away from him then, apparently not able to meet his eyes. And he knew why, too. It was because she knew every word he said was true. At least she gave him that much. He watched her eyes move around the room. He could almost hear what she was thinking.

"It's not much, but we're the only guests, so no one will hear us."

At that, she turned back to him, her eyes big. "Hear us *what?*"

"Hear us yelling. Or hear you scream when I turn you over my knee and spank your ass, woman."

"Right." She rolled her eyes, and he felt his temper flare.

"Don't tempt me, Crystal. I'm not in the best of moods right now."

"I would have thought after last night that you'd wake up in a great mood this morning." She gave him an arch look.

"Yeah, babe. I did wake up in a really, *really* great mood. It lasted all of about two seconds until I rolled over to reach for you and *you weren't there!*"

"Wolf."

"So let me hear your explanation."

"My explanation for what?"

"I gotta spell it out? Why'd you run out on me this morning?"

"Oh honestly, Wolf. You're acting like I deserted you. It's not a big deal. I just needed to get back."

"In case you hadn't noticed, I just chased you down an

interstate halfway across Nevada, so clue in—it's a *big deal* to me."

"Apparently."

"You want to cut the smartass mouth?"

"What do you want from me, Wolf?" She rounded on him. "We've been apart all this time. We run into each other in Vegas, and yeah, we had a night for old time's sake. It's over. Let it go."

"*Old time's sake?* Is that all it was to you? Are you really standing here tellin' me this shit?"

"Wolf." She ran a frustrated hand through her hair.

"You're scared. That's what this is about. You're scared I'm gonna jerk you around again. That's what this is about, isn't it? *Isn't it?*"

"No, Wolf. I'm not scared."

"The hell you're not."

"What's it gonna take with you? You want another go at it?" she asked sarcastically, her hand flung out indicating the bed. "Fine. Let's go. Let's get to it. *Then* will you let me leave?"

"Babe, seriously?"

"Seriously." Her brows rose in a challenging attitude that only confused him more and was beginning to piss him off.

"Can't we have a damn conversation?"

"Is that gonna move this along?" she asked flippantly.

That did it. Something inside him snapped. He'd be damned if he'd stand here and have her taunt him like this. This was all bullshit. And if he had to prove that to her, he would.

"Fine." He started unbuttoning the flannel shirt he wore under his cut. Then he yanked it and his cut off, dropping them to the floor. Next he tugged his undershirt over his head.

He watched as she stood mutely—*for once*—and stared as he continued stripping. Next came his boots. When his hands went to his belt buckle, he lifted his chin at her.

"Take off your clothes. You wanted to get to it, *let's get to it*," he threw her words back at her.

She stared at him.

"But don't expect sweet from me right now, Crystal. That's not what you're gonna get. That's not the way I want it right now." He watched as her eyes fell to where his hands were working his belt buckle. Then she was moving toward him. Then she surprised him again by dropping to her knees. She brushed his hands aside and looked up at him.

"I know what you really want, Wolf."

He could only stare down at her, stunned as she undid his pants and pulled his dick out. All conscious thoughts scattered as she offered herself up for his pleasure. And suddenly all he could think about was her pretty fuckable mouth, and how badly he wanted it wrapped around his dick, how badly he wanted to sink into it. If that was what she wanted, he wasn't about to stop her. He wasn't that big a fool. Instead, he slid one hand to the back of her head, pulling her closer, guiding her mouth to take him.

If she hadn't driven him to the breaking point, this could have gone differently. He would have taken more care. But now, all gentleness had been stamped out by her taunting comments that he knew had been designed to drive him to the edge. In its place was a demanding, unleashed anger and desire to lash out and show her who was boss.

She'd asked for it. He only hoped she was prepared to pay the price.

"Well, baby, let's put that smart mouth of yours to a much better use, then, shall we?"

His hands tangled in her hair, and he drove his cock into her waiting mouth. He used that grip to command her movements, and to set the pace as he pumped into her. He lost whatever shred of control he had as he fucked her mouth.

She didn't resist, didn't try to pull away or stop him. Quite the contrary. The hunger in her eyes as she looked up practically *begged* him to claim more. Her soft moans encouraged him to take whatever he wanted, however he wanted.

It made him question who really had the control here. But hell, fighting it was a lost cause. He was a goner. She did that to him. She always did that to him. She always found a way.

His fists tightened in her hair as he jerked her hard and his cock exploded, his release shooting down her throat. She took it all, swallowing every drop, and then continued to hold him in her mouth even after his hands gentled and released her.

Wolf locked his legs, fighting the overpowering aftermath that threatened to send him to his knees. She'd sucked him dry. Holy hell.

Releasing him, she looked up, their eyes locking. Then

he was reaching down, grabbing her forearms and jerking her to her feet. They glared at each other.

"You get what you wanted?" he asked.

She had the gall to smile, wiping her mouth with the back of her hand. "Yup. How about you? Are you satisfied? Can I go now?"

"Satisfied?" He shook his head. "Not by a long shot, darlin'. And no, you can't go."

"Why not?" He watched the arrogant smile fade from her face.

"We're not finished yet." With a wicked smile, he shoved her toward the bed. "In fact, we're just getting started."

He reached for his belt, and pulled it free, doubling it in his palm.

Her eyes dropped to it, and then she was darting toward the door. He caught her easily enough, one strong forearm locking around her waist as he hauled her back, pinning her tight against his chest.

"Going somewhere? You were all about pleasing me a minute ago. Lose your nerve?"

"Not the belt, Wolf."

It clattered to the floor.

"My hand then." He bent his head to her ear, his soft beard brushing the side of her face. "And I swear to you, you're gonna feel it for a few days."

He walked her over to the dresser, pushing her over it. She had on a short sundress with tiny straps. His hand fisted in the hem and pulled it up over her hip. Then his fingers were hooking in her lacy panty, yanking them free in one quick tug.

She gasped.

He buried a hand in her hair and pulled her head up until her eyes met his in the mirror. He grabbed his cock with his other hand. He was already hard again as he lined up and drove inside her. Her pretty mouth dropped open, and her eyes slid closed. He tightened his hold on her hair.

"Watch," he growled.

Her eyes immediately popped open as she followed his command.

He took her hard and fast, smacking her bottom with every other thrust. He could feel the way she clenched tight inside with every impact, and it drove him higher.

"Show me your tits."

She didn't hesitate. He loved that about her. She'd fight him if she thought that was what he wanted, but she'd always submit when he needed her to.

He watched as she quickly pulled the straps off her shoulders, and the dress fell to her waist, baring her breasts. He watched as they bounced with every thrust, every punishing smack.

"Very pretty," he rumbled. Releasing her hair, he locked both hands on her hips and pulled her ass tight against him as he continued to pound into her.

But he wasn't anywhere near close to finishing. This time he was going to drag it out for both of them. Pulling out, he turned her around, hoisting her up onto the dresser so that her ass just barely hung over the edge. It was the perfect height. He pushed her legs up with his arms, knowing he'd be able to take her deeper that way.

The soft noises she made as he sunk in deep were almost as good as the feeling of being inside her. She fell back on her hands, her back and head pressing against the mirror bolted to the back of the dresser. It banged against the wall with every driving thrust of his punishing onslaught.

He leaned over her briefly, one hand stroking the side of her face, then trailing down to her breast for a slow squeeze that had her moaning.

"I've missed you," he murmured, his face an inch from hers. "It was hell, these last few months. Not being able to see you, touch you." He slid in and out, his pace slowing momentarily as he reveled in the sensation of her breast thrust up into his hand as she arched her back, seeking his touch.

She lifted her head to try to close the distance, her mouth attempting to capture his.

He pulled back. "You think one night was gonna be enough to make up for all those months?"

When she didn't answer, he punctuated with a deep thrust, pinching her nipple between his fingers. She moaned, rocking her hips against his body.

"Did you?" he demanded.

She shook her head, rolling it from side to side on the glass of the mirror. His hips had her pinned like a butterfly.

"I've never been a patient man, Crystal," he growled. "And you've definitely pushed me way past my limits."

"No, Wolf. I knew it wouldn't be enough."

"And still you ran?"

"Yes."

He kept plunging inside her, but his need to drive her as mad as she was driving him was quickly surpassing his need to pull any unwilling answers from her. "Before this is over, you're going to tell me why. But right now, I don't care to hear anymore lies spill from your lips."

He gathered her up and carried her to the bed, taking her to her back as he came down on top of her. He shoved and kicked the jeans that had been around his thighs, then he moved over her, his hand sliding between her legs.

"Your turn, baby. I'm gonna wear you down until you're a puddle of need, until you're just as crazy for it as I am." He loomed over her, his fingers already delivering on his promise. "You gonna fight me on this?"

She shook her head, giving him the answer he'd expected. "No, Wolf. I'm through fighting."

"Good, baby. I'm through fighting this, too."

CHAPTER THIRTEEN

Wolf stood staring out the motel room window, watching the night fade away as the first streaks of dawn broke across the horizon. It was five in the morning, and his time with Crystal was quickly ticking away with so many things left unsaid. Christ, there were so many things he still needed to say.

He looked back at the bed. Crystal lay there sleeping. After she'd passed out from exhaustion a couple of hours ago, he'd made good on his promise, made sure she wouldn't be able to run out on him again while he'd slept. It was gonna be her turn to be pissed when she woke up this morning. A grin pulled at his mouth. He had no problem with that.

***

Crystal woke, her eyes fluttering open. Wolf was standing by the window, staring out. Early morning light glimmered through the cheap curtains. She blinked, her brain still fuzzy with sleep. Awareness seeped in. They were in a motel room on the state line, where Wolf had brought her after chasing her down. It all came flashing back. They'd ended up in bed, where they seemed to do most of their communicating. Wolf had been demanding after she'd taunted him with her flippant comments—comments designed to push him away and shield her bruised heart, only driving him to be even more possessive.

He'd taken it as a challenge. As if he'd prove her wrong if she thought anything about what they had was casual.

It wasn't. She knew that. They both knew that. What was the use in pretending?

But eventually his aggression had turned sweet, his touch had turned tender, filled with feelings and emotions he always seemed to have such a hard time verbalizing. Those feelings existed. They were there. They were all there, expressed with such sweet passion, the way only Wolf could.

All this flashed through her brain in a microsecond.

She tried to stretch, to move, and panic flashed through her just as quickly. Her eyes darted above her head to find her wrists tied together to the cheap wooden headboard. Her eyes fell on the restraint—the sash to her satin kimono robe.

What the hell?

She pulled, but the knots didn't budge. Her eyes darted to Wolf standing at the window. He turned, her movements having caught his attention.

"Wolf, untie me! Right now, Goddamn you! This isn't funny."

He grinned, moving to stand near the bed. "Wasn't meant to be. I wasn't gonna chance you sneaking out on me again."

God, he was infuriating.

"So you *tied me up?*" She practically screeched it at him.

"Yup. Payback's a bitch, huh?"

"I'll scream," she threatened.

"Go ahead. Ain't nobody around to hear."

"Let me up, Wolf. I mean it."

"Don't think so. Not till we get a few things straight, baby girl."

She quietly fumed at the ceiling, thinking she had it straight already. He'd lost his damn mind if he thought she was going to play these kinds of games with him.

"You up for that conversation now? That conversation you didn't want to have last night?" When she didn't respond, he continued right on. "Time to tell me why you really left town."

"I *did* tell you."

He shook his head; she could see the movement in her peripheral vision as her eyes remained locked on the ceiling.

"No, you gave me an answer, but it was a bullshit one. Tell me the real reason, Crystal." When she maintained her silence, he continued, "There was something going on. I know it. I could feel it back then, but you left before we could talk about it."

Yes, there was something going on. She'd been carrying his *baby!* If only she'd made better choices. If only she'd told him. If only she hadn't left. Her whole life had become one long tortuous game of *if only's.*

Crystal felt her eyes sting as they pooled. She turned her

head, determined to hide the tears from him, determined not to let all the hurt that she'd buried so deep swell up and consume her again. It was always right under the surface, and God, she didn't want to return to that deep dark pit again. It would suck her in if she let it. Only this time she may not survive it.

"Please, Wolf. Please, don't." She knew her voice was shaky, but she didn't anticipate his reaction, didn't realize what the sound of her quavering voice would do to him, how much it affected him. He moved to the bed, his hip brushing hers as he sat by her side. With his hands on either side of her, he leaned in, his whole demeanor changing. Gone was the confrontational Wolf set on provoking her; in his place was a man who suddenly only seemed concerned.

"Baby, what is it? Tell me."

She shook her head. "I can't. I can't. Please, Wolf. Don't do this to me."

He stroked the hair back from her face. She blinked and felt the tears slide down her cheek.

"Crystal, why are you crying? What aren't you telling me? Was it Misty? You know she didn't mean shit to me. Hell, I ran her ass off that night. She hasn't been back, I swear."

She shook her head violently. "No, you ass. I'm not crying about her. Let me go, Wolf." She began her struggles again, tearing and pulling at the sash. It was tied tightly over the beaded bracelets she wore on both wrists, and she felt them cutting into her skin, the strands ripping.

"Crystal—" he started, and she could see true worry

gripping him. "Whoa, baby. Calm down, let me untie you." He reached toward the knots, but she continued to pull and jerk making his task more difficult. She couldn't help it, she was beginning to panic. He couldn't find out her secret. She couldn't let him. What would he think of her if he knew?

He leaned over, his weight coming down on her, trying to settle her down.

"Crystal, damn it, hold still. I can't loosen this if you keep fighting me."

She heard him, but she couldn't stop. She could see the look on his face as he stared down at her. He must think she'd lost her damn mind. Maybe she had. Her body racked with sobs, completely breaking down. Her eyes closed tight against the image of his shocked expression.

She felt something cold, like metal or steel, as Wolf sliced through the sash. It snapped free, the bracelets with it, the beads scattering all over. She heard the knife clatter on the nightstand and then he was pulling her up, clutching her tightly to his chest.

"Baby, you're okay. I'm sorry. I didn't mean to upset you." His hands ran up and down her back as he attempted to comfort her. But all she wanted was to get away, to put some distance between them. She shoved him back.

"Let me go. Let me up."

"Crystal—"

She fought his hold, and he grabbed her wrists, trying to settle her down. That's when he felt them. His eyes flashed down, his thumbs sliding over the ugly rigged scar tissue that marred the inside of both wrists, exposed to him now that her bracelets weren't there to hide them.

The scars were plainly visible—an ugly, horrible reminder of just how deep that dark pit was that had almost completely sucked her in.

She tried to pull away, her actions almost instinctive. Self-preservation and reflex all rolled up in one.

"Don't," she bit out. But he wasn't going to be put off. Not this time. His hold only tightened as he stared down at her wrists. Then his wide, stunned eyes flashed up to meet hers.

"Jesus Christ." His words were barely a whisper, but she heard them. They ripped her heart out.

"Don't pity me. Don't you dare!" she hissed.

"*You* did this?"

She wouldn't look at him.

"Crystal, my God, why?"

"It doesn't matter." She pulled again, and this time he let her slide free. She scrambled off the bed and grabbed the first article of clothing she could find—his flannel shirt. She tugged it on, buttoning a couple buttons to cover her nakedness. She felt exposed enough to him right now. She moved to stand in front of the window, needing space. There wasn't very far she could go, and she knew if she moved toward the door, he'd stop her. He'd allow her space, but only so much. He'd never let her walk out. Not now. Not until he dragged out every wretched detail. Crossing her arms in front of herself, she tried to build up the wall he was determined to tear down.

"The hell it doesn't." He moved to stand behind her. She

could feel him there, and she prayed he wouldn't touch her. She'd break into a million pieces if he did, but at the same time, she felt bereft when he didn't. "Baby, please, talk to me."

She shook her head violently. "It's over. It's done. Please don't make me talk about it."

"I have to make you talk about it. If you can't talk to me, hell baby, who can you talk to?"

"You won't want to hear it," she warned.

"Crystal, I don't run, and I don't scare easily." When she remained quiet, he coaxed, "You're not the only one who has stuff they don't want to talk about. We all have things we hope will never see the light of day."

She felt his hand rest on her shoulder.

"Your secrets are my secrets. Your demons are my demons. Tell me, and you'll never have to fight them alone. I promise you that."

A promise. From Wolf. He'd never once promised her anything.

She whirled on him then, determined to use anger to hold herself together. "Fine. You want to know? I'll tell you. You're right, Wolf, there was something more going on when I left." She watched his jaw clamp shut, and she knew he wasn't sure what she was about to spew at him. Hell, he didn't have a clue what was coming. "I was *pregnant*, Wolf."

She watched him visibly pale, and his voice came out in a whisper. "What?"

"Didn't see that one coming, did you?"

He frowned. "You were pregnant? Why didn't you tell

me?"

She swallowed, regretting for a moment dropping the bomb without any warning.

"Why didn't you fucking tell me, Crystal?" he growled again.

There was the anger. She knew it'd show up sooner or later.

She watched his hand flex at his side. If he'd been another kind of man, she may have expected a backhanded slap. But Wolf would never hurt her, not in that way at least. The hurt he inflicted was always emotional and probably unintentional.

"You couldn't tell me? Couldn't have said something before you walked out the fucking door?"

"What would it have mattered, Wolf? You can't commit to anything longer than a few weeks or months. You wouldn't have wanted any of it. We both know that."

"That would have been my choice to make!" he roared. "Not yours. You took the choice away from me."

She took a step back. She'd seen him pissed before, but never like this. She'd honest-to-God hurt him.

"You went off and had my baby, and never fucking thought to tell me? Where is it? You leave our kid with your mom? Your sister? Huh?"

She shook her head and turned back to the window. He was having none of that. She felt his hand clamp around her upper arm to yank her back around. His face glared down at hers.

"Where's my baby, Crystal?" he roared.

She shook her head again, whispering softly. "There's no baby, Wolf."

"What?" He stared down at her with a frown and a look that told her he was trying to keep up with a storyline that had one too many twists. Then, with an anguished, grief-stricken look, he asked, "You didn't want it? You didn't want my baby?"

"Wolf—"

"Christ, tell me you didn't kill our baby?"

She shook her head, more tears returning.

He ran his hand through his hair, and then moving toward her suddenly, he grabbed her forearms, holding her scarred wrists up in front of her eyes. "You did, didn't you? And then you tried to kill *yourself*."

"No, Wolf."

"You do this?" He shook her scars in her face.

She nodded. She couldn't deny that. She had. "Yes."

He shoved her away as if she were poison.

"Oh, my God." His voice was tormented, like she'd never heard it before.

"Wolf—"

"Oh, my God."

She slapped him then—hauled back and let him have it with a resounding crack that echoed in the small room. Then she screamed at his stunned face. "I didn't kill your baby. I *lost* your baby. I lost *our* baby. I lost *my* baby!" She emphasized the words by jabbing her finger in her chest. "Mine."

He stared at her, frowning for a long moment, and then

whispered, "You wanted it?"

She nodded. "Yes, I wanted it you big, stupid oaf."

He slowly ran his hand over his mouth, studying her. His eyes dropped to her wrists, and then as if the weight of the world was on his shoulders and it was just too much, he collapsed down on the bed, dropping his head into his hands.

She stared at him a long moment until his shoulders shook with a slight tremor. His face was downcast, but she knew he was weeping. For their unborn child? Perhaps for everything they'd lost?

It killed her to see him like this. Wolf, who was so strong, now devastated, broken. She found her feet moving toward him, drawn like a magnet, needing to give him comfort. Dropping to her knees in front of him, she grabbed his wrists, attempting to pull his hands from his face. He fought her on it only for a moment before he let her win. She saw his eyes, glassy with tears, and then she was sliding her arms around his neck.

He latched onto her like a drowning man, pulling her between his knees, her chest flush with his. She felt his face bury into her neck as he shook.

"I'm so sorry, baby. I'm so sorry," he murmured into her ear.

"Shh. Shh." She didn't know what else to say. She knew that no words made this any better or any easier.

"This is my fault. This is all my fault," he muttered.

She shook her head against him. "No. No, baby."

"I wasn't there for you. I should have been there for you. For you both."

"Wolf."

They held each other for a long time, both clutching each other, seeking comfort for something to which there was no comfort, no solace.

Eventually, he took her by the arms and set her away, rising to his feet. Without a word he went into the small bathroom, closing the door. She knew he was a man that didn't let weakness show very often, maybe never. In an MC he couldn't afford to ever reveal or expose any weakness. And she was sure he didn't like her seeing them.

She pulled a pair of jeans out of her bag, slid them and her shoes on, and stepped outside, giving him time. Leaving the door open, she stood on the concrete walkway of the nearly deserted motel. She hugged herself and put her nose to Wolf's soft flannel shirt, breathing in the scent of him. She watched the sunrise, knowing things would never be the same between them after this, but knowing she would no longer be the only one to carry this grief. She'd wanted to spare him from it, but in a way it felt good not to be the only one, not to have to struggle alone with it anymore.

Not that it mattered. It didn't change anything between them. Not really. Wolf was still Wolf. He was still the free-spirited man she'd fallen for all those years ago. Perhaps that's how it should be. She shouldn't want to change him. And if she was being completely honest, she couldn't risk her heart again, because she knew no matter how much he wanted to be what she needed, that wasn't him. He was a lone wolf, and perhaps that was for the best.

***

Wolf stared at his reflection in the tiny mirror over the sink. Goddamn, he was a piece of work. Who the hell was *he* to confront her? Even if she had terminated the pregnancy, how could he condemn her for it? How could he blame her or say shit about it? He'd proven himself unworthy, someone she couldn't depend on when the shit hit the fan. When Mack gave him that ultimatum, he hadn't stepped up; he hadn't chosen her, not really. Oh, sure he'd wanted her to stay, he'd wanted to keep her close, but he was only thinking about himself. Even then he somehow thought he could have his cake and eat it too. He thought he would keep her without really committing. What an idiot he was. What an asshole, he'd become.

What would he have done if she had told him about the baby?

He stared at his reflection, his hands on the sink. He liked to believe he would have stepped up. God, he wanted to believe that with all his soul, but obviously she saw something in him that made her doubt it. Doubt *him.*

The fuck of it was, he couldn't blame her.

He pushed off the sink and strode out of the bathroom. A flash of panic took hold of him when he saw the open door, but his eyes darted to her bag still lying on the floor, and he let out a breath, the tightness in his chest easing.

He stepped outside to find her staring into the sunrise.

He moved to stand behind her.

"Crystal."

She stood there, unmoving.

His eyes moved to the horizon and he swallowed, trying

to find the words, trying to sort through all his feelings and say this right. Hell, there was no right way. No easy way through any of this. In the end he opted for honesty. "I wish I could take away your pain. I wish I could say something to make this all better, but I just don't have the words. I don't know how."

Still, she didn't reply or make a move.

"Let me hold you," he implored softly. "Please. At least let me hold you." At his words he saw her shoulders begin shaking with a new wave of sobs. It broke Wolf's heart to see her like this.

"Baby." He pulled her around and into his arms, holding her tight against his chest. He spoke softly, his mouth at her ear. "This isn't on you. This is on me. You, the baby, those scars you carry? It's all on me, sweetheart. I'm to blame for all of it. Every bad thing that's happened to you, it's my fault."

She tried to shake her head in denial, but he stopped her, his hand coming up to push her head to his chest, stilling her movements. "Shh. It's true. We both know it's true. And I'm so sorry, baby. I'm so sorry. For all of it."

She was quiet in his arms for a few moments. But her next words made him realize she'd only been gathering her armor. She pushed back, putting a few inches between them.

"Let me go, Wolf." She nodded toward her car.

His eyes followed, landing on her vehicle. Ah hell, how was he ever going to do that? He shook his head. "I don't want to let you go. I can't."

"You have to."

"Crystal—I can't. Don't ask that of me."

"Please, Wolf, if you had any feelings for me at all, you'll let me go."

Fuck. That gutted him. His eyes slid closed as the pain of losing her ripped through him. *I need you.* It was on the tip of his tongue. God, he didn't *want* to let go. He *never* wanted to let go again. He opened his eyes and looked down at her. He wanted to keep holding her forever. But something in the way she looked up at him, had him loosening his grasp. He wasn't good for her. He'd done nothing but bring her pain. It was selfish and cruel to think of how hurt he was going to be when she left again. So he had to think about what was best for her.

He let her go, dropping his arms to his sides, and they stared at each other.

"Are you sure this is what you want, Crystal?" he asked one final time.

His insides clenched as she nodded.

She brushed past him, moving back inside the motel room door. He followed, standing unsure in the doorway as she gathered up her things and stuffed them into her overnight bag. She flung her purse over her shoulder and reached to grab her bag off the bed, but he brushed her hand aside and picked it up for her.

Their eyes met.

"Wolf, I can carry it."

"Don't." Wolf stopped her protest with a word. "I've got it."

She turned and headed out the door. He followed her to

the car. She popped the trunk, and he hefted her bag inside, then slammed it shut. She moved to stand uncertainly by the driver's door and Wolf stepped up, taking her face in his hands, and his mouth came down on hers. Softly. Just a brush of lips... and then another. He stared at her a long moment before pressing a kiss to her forehead, holding it a moment before releasing her and stepping back.

"You can always call me. For anything. You know that, right?" he asked, his voice coming out in a deep rumbling rasp as emotion engulfed him. His throat felt tight with it.

Her eyes glazed over and perhaps she suffered the same choking feeling because she could only manage a nod.

He stepped back as she turned, opened her door, and climbed inside. A moment later, he watched her car pull out onto the highway, leaving a trail of dust in its wake.

Wolf stood there forlornly long after the dust settled back down on the road, thinking about everything she'd said.

As the dawn broke over the horizon and the faintest starlight faded away like any hopes he'd had of holding onto her this time, any hopes he'd ever had for the two of them, he turned toward his bike and the long ride back to a life that suddenly didn't mean half as much as it had only hours ago.

CHAPTER FOURTEEN

Wolf sat at the end of the bar at Marty's, a neighborhood joint the guys sometimes frequented. A man sitting halfway down on his left was repeatedly flicking open a silver zippo lighter. *Open, close, open, close*. The sound grated on Wolf's nerves until he was tempted to walk over there and slam the asshole face-first into the bar top.

Marty walked over and leaned his elbows on the bar, saving him from his felony.

"You doing okay, Wolf?"

Wolf's eyes moved from the man to Marty. "Fine."

Marty nodded to Wolf's empty glass. "Can I get you another?"

Wolf nodded, even though he was quickly finding there wasn't enough liquor in the world to fill the emptiness inside him. He'd been back two weeks now. Two weeks. Two long motherfucking weeks since he'd said goodbye to Crystal and watched her drive out of his life for the second Goddamned time.

Two weeks of having his brothers asking him what the fuck was wrong with him. Two weeks of sideways glances from brothers who meant well, but didn't have a fucking clue to the extent of his hell.

Marty returned with his drink, and with one look at Wolf's murderous expression, wisely retreated to service his other customers.

Wolf took a slug of his drink as the jukebox in the corner switched songs. It had a strange mix of current music mixed in with a bunch of oldies. Marty's taste was a little funky, like the man himself.

The mellow sounds of Tommy James and the Shondells' *Crystal Blue Persuasion* drifted out.

Oh, fucking hell.

The song taunted him with memories of Crystal—like he didn't have enough of those. He didn't need another fucking reminder of just how bad he'd fucked up. Now he had to sit here and listen to her name being sung to him in every chorus.

Screw this.

He slammed back the rest of his drink, slapped a twenty on the bar, and headed outside. His bike was parked in the side lot near the front door. He fired it up, but then sat there a moment, considering his options. He could head south toward the clubhouse, but something made him swivel his head north.

Oakland.

There was one thing that had gnawed at his gut since

he'd been back. One thing that he couldn't let go. One thing he had to know.

He popped his bike in gear, twisted the throttle and let out the clutch, rolling out of the lot and gunning it down the street. The roar of his pipes reverberated against the buildings with a deep echoing rumble as he headed north to get his answers.

Twenty minutes later he was stepping off the freight elevator into Crash's industrial loft. His brother stood in front of him, arms folded.

"Brother," he greeted Wolf, his eyes edged with curiosity over the sudden visit.

Shannon was in the kitchen area rinsing out some glasses. She turned, giving him a bright smile. "Hey, Wolf."

"You want a beer?" Crash offered, taking in his demeanor.

"Yeah, sure." Wolf replied and Crash moved to the refrigerator to pull two out.

"You want one, Shannon?" Crash asked his wife.

"No thanks, hon."

Crash gave a jerk of his head toward the stairs to the roof and asked Wolf, "You want to take this outside?"

Wolf's eyes moved from Crash to Shannon and back. "Actually, I was hoping I could talk with Shannon."

Crash's eyes narrowed and he offered, "She's welcome to join us."

Code for *not on your life am I leaving you alone with my ol' lady, Brother*. Wolf understood the message loud and clear. He nodded, his eyes moving to Shannon.

She looked between them. "Okaaay."

They all moved outside. Dusk was falling quickly, turning the sky a deep violet-blue. The lights of the Bay Bridge twinkled in the distance. Wolf took a seat, and Shannon sat one chair over. Crash chose to remain standing, but planted his ass on the low wall, crossing his legs at his booted ankles. He took a slug of his beer, eyes on Wolf.

"You had something you needed to talk about?" Crash eyed him.

Wolf leaned forward in his chair, his elbows on his knees, rolling the beer bottle between his palms. "This stays between the three of us."

"What does?" Crash asked, not quite ready to make any promises without knowing what the fuck this was about. Wolf could understand that.

"It's about Crystal."

Crash's eyes connected with Shannon's then returned to Wolf's as he nodded. "Okay."

Wolf looked at Shannon. "Did you know?"

She frowned at him, her gaze swiveling between Wolf and her husband. "Did I know what?"

"Did you know Crystal was carrying my baby when she left?" Wolf couldn't be more straight-up than that. He watched Shannon swallow, her discomfort plain, and he knew the answer before she ever responded.

"Yes. I knew."

Wolf ground his teeth together and stared out at the horizon. Then his eyes swung to his brother. "Did you know?"

"No, Wolf. I had no clue." Crash shook his head, his eyes unguarded and clear before they moved to his wife who had obviously kept him in the dark.

Wolf nodded. At least his brothers hadn't hung him out to dry.

"I thought she told you. She made us promise not to say anything, but I thought surely she told *you*," Shannon explained in a soft voice.

"Us?"

"Angel and I. We were with her when she took the test."

Wolf shook his head. Unbelievable. "And after she left, you honestly thought I knew? Did I act like a man who was aware of that shit? Did you really think that I would have let her go if I'd known?"

"Wolf," Crash warned in a tone that cut him no slack.

The corner of Wolf's mouth pulled up in a smile that was more sneer than anything else. "And when she lost it, you know about that, too?"

Shannon nodded.

"And the Goddamn suicide attempt, did you know about that as well?" He surged to his feet.

She stared up at him in shock, her voice barely audible. "What?"

He turned on her. "Were you ever gonna tell me? Or was that all part of the secret?"

"Wolf, what the fuck are you talking about?" Crash demanded, straightening from the wall.

Wolf answered him, but his eyes remained boring into Shannon's. "I'm talking about Crystal slitting her Goddamn wrists."

"What?" Shannon paled, her eyes beginning to fill.

"I see she obviously kept that secret from both of us."

"What are you talking about, Wolf?" Crash demanded.

"She tried to kill herself. I saw the fucking scars."

"Scars?"

"Yeah, scars. She has them. She likes to keep them hidden, but they're there. Both wrists."

Shannon covered her face as she burst into tears, and Wolf felt like ten kinds of asshole.

Crash pulled her into his arms, glaring at Wolf over her shoulder for putting this hurt on his woman. "You get what you came for?"

Wolf flung his bottle into the alley below where it shattered. "Yeah. I guess so."

He moved to walk past the two and head out, but Shannon stopped him with a hand on his sleeve. "Wait, Wolf. Don't go."

He froze, his eyes falling to her hand.

"I didn't know. I swear. She never said a word."

Wolf gave a single nod.

Shannon's eyes moved imploringly to Crash's.

"Babe, go inside. Give us a minute."

She nodded and fled.

Wolf stared over at Crash. "I shouldn't have come."

"That was a shit thing to do, Wolf. I know you're hurting, but don't think for a minute that I'm gonna stand here and let you dump on my ol' lady and not say shit about it. Shannon doesn't need to carry the guilt for anything

Crystal did. This shit is all between the two of you." Crash let out a frustrated breath and growled, "Sit down."

Wolf hesitated.

"Sit the fuck down, Wolf."

He sat.

"I take it this is what's been eating at you since we got back from Vegas?"

Wolf nodded.

"And how'd that end?"

Wolf ran a hand through his hair. "Not good."

"What happened?"

"She dropped one bomb after another on me. I didn't handle it well." Wolf shook his head, staring off at the horizon. "Hell, I lost it."

Crash nodded, waiting for Wolf to continue, when he didn't, Crash finally prompted, "Do you want to try to make a go of it with her?"

Wolf shook his head. "Doesn't matter what I want."

"What the hell does that mean?"

"Means I'm trying to do what *she* wants."

"And what's that?"

"She told me if I cared anything for her, I'd let her go."

Crash nodded solemnly. "Is that what you plan to do, then?"

"I have to. I have to think about what's best for her."

"And what about you? You gonna survive this?"

"Gonna have to try."

They sat there a long moment before Crash finally stood up, and Wolf followed. Crash pulled him into an embrace and slapped his back. "Then you'll do what you have to do. And we're all here for you, Brother."

They broke apart. "Yeah."

They moved toward the door, but Wolf stopped him before Crash could open it. "This stays between us, Crash. No one else needs to know. I shouldn't have told you, but hell, I needed someone to talk to."

Crash nodded. "I won't say a word."

"And Shannon?"

Crash's brows rose and a slight grin pulled at his mouth. "Yeah, that might be a bigger problem."

"Crash," Wolf warned.

"I got it, don't worry. She won't say a word."

CHAPTER FIFTEEN

Jameson studied Crystal. Ever since she'd come back from Vegas two weeks ago, she'd been quiet, subdued. She'd reverted back to the Crystal who had walked into his shop that first day, all those months ago, broken and whipped, beaten down by life and barely hanging on.

Jameson would never forget that day. The day she'd walked in looking for a job…

Six months ago—

He was bent over the arm of a client, twisting and leaning to get to a difficult area of shoulder when the bell over the front door tinkled, drawing his eyes up for one brief glance. He saw the back of someone's coat as they turned to close the door. The shop was short a receptionist since his last crazy bitch had walked out, calling him every name in the book. She blamed his tyrannical behavior (he preferred to think of it as artistic drive) and his hot Irish temper on why he couldn't keep a girl in the reception chair longer than a month. That one had only lasted three days. But he'd known from the get-go that she wasn't going to work out. He hadn't even bothered to pull the ad he'd posted.

Now he was stuck going through the whole process of hiring again. Interviewing people was definitely not his thing. But unfortunately, he was stuck doing it. He didn't trust Max with it. His brother and partner would hire the first set of double Ds that walked through the door. Great for eye candy; not so great for accurate receivables.

So, if he wanted a front-end person who could add two plus two, he was stuck with the chore, and he had a couple interviews coming in today.

His eyes strayed to the clock on the wall. If this was his four o'clock—she was early. His eyes again flicked to the entrance. And then he did a double-take.

Holy hotness.

Long dark hair, big eyes, not too much eye makeup, perfect olive skin. She slipped her coat off, uncovering a slender, boyish frame with all the right curves. Low slung jeans hugged her hips and revealed a teasing inch of skin between them and her tight top. Lots of necklaces—all different kinds that somehow worked together in a bohemian style—hung over a nice rack. Beaded bracelets stacked up both wrists.

His eyes returned to the tattoo he was working on as Max moved to the counter to greet the woman.

Jameson kept one eye on the activity at the front counter so he didn't miss Max handing her an application on a clipboard. He also didn't miss the look Max turned and gave him as she moved off to take a seat in their lobby to complete the application. With his back to the lobby, Max had mouthed the word "Wow," giving Jameson big eyes.

Jameson tried to hold back a grin, returning to his work.

In that very first interview, he could see that somewhere buried beneath the shell she'd built around herself was a girl with spunk and spirit. Perhaps it was his curiosity for what had caused her to become so reserved, reticent, and careful that made him want to hire her, or perhaps it was the challenge she posed. He couldn't help the desire that kindled inside him to want to be the one to free her from whatever pain or sorrow that had dimmed that spirit.

She was an enigma, a mystery, and he saw the irony of it. On the outside, she was a perfect paradigm of a receptionist in a tattoo shop. The total rock-chick hard-ass—she had the look down pat. On the inside, somewhere buried under there, was the perfect smart-ass personality to match. He'd bet the shop on it. The only problem was, the way she acted now was more reserved, school-girl type—the ultimate example of who *not* to hire for such an outgoing position, dealing with the types of clientele a typical tattoo shop like his dealt with.

If he'd listened to his better judgment, he'd have sent her packing. But something made him hesitate. Some glimmer shining deep in her eyes. Something that called to him, pleading silently, communicating on some non-verbal level that this might be her last chance; *he* might be her last chance. Some flicker deep in her soul that needed to flame to life again.

***

Jameson shook the memory free. He'd hired her that day, and he'd never been sorry. She kept the place spotless, picked up the bookkeeping he'd taught her in a snap, and was meticulous with running the front desk.

As she relaxed into her position, her spunky personality immerged little by little. When it did, she had a wonderful way in dealing with customers. Her sparkling smile, he was sure, drew in many repeats. He was also sure one or two of his regulars were half in love with her.

Now that girl he'd worked so hard to rebuild—hell, they'd *all* worked so hard to rebuild—was right back in that dark place she'd been in when she first walked in the door. Apparently whatever had happened in Vegas hadn't stayed in Vegas. She'd brought all the baggage back with her. Something big had happened to her. Something powerful and damaging and damning.

Mother fucking hell.

Jameson unfolded his arms, straightened from the wall he was leaning against, and turned to head down the back hall. He strode into the break room. Max was sitting at a table with his other two brothers, Rory and Liam, kicked back in a chair, drinking a beer.

Jameson's eyes flicked to the clock on the wall. Quarter past nine on a Tuesday night. They'd officially closed fifteen minutes ago, although Max had finished up with the last customer a half hour earlier, which was unusual for them. Usually they were finishing up long after closing time. His brothers were obviously intending to take full advantage of the early night and had started in on the beer.

The four of them had worked hard to make a go of it with this shop, working long hours, day after day, and things were finally starting to pay off. Word-of-mouth was getting out about the shop started by four brothers and the primo work they did.

Brothers Ink was finally gaining a reputation.

The four-page spread in *Inked Up Magazine* that had come out last month hadn't hurt either. It was an incredible break for them, one that Jameson fully understood and appreciated.

He moved to the fridge and pulled out a beer. Joining his brothers at the table, he spun a chair around and sat on it backward. He twisted off the cap of his beer and with a snap of his fingers sent it sailing toward Rory's face.

Rory ducked. "Brat."

Jameson grinned and took a long pull off his beer.

"What's the deal with Crystal? I thought going to Vegas was supposed to make a person happy." Max looked over at Jameson for an answer.

Jameson's expression sobered as he leaned forward and rested his crossed arms on the backrest. He shook his head. "I don't know. *Something* happened."

"No shit. She's back to being that same girl who walked in the place months ago." Liam leaned back in his chair and folded his arms.

Jameson nodded. "Yeah."

"She say anything?" Max asked him.

"No, but I'm going to have a word with her. See if she'll open up."

Max nodded once.

Just then Crystal walked in, purse in hand, shrugging into her leather jacket. She looked at Jameson. "I put the month-end paperwork on your desk."

He nodded. "Thanks, sweetheart."

"Stay and have a beer with us, doll." Max grinned at her.

She gave a half-hearted attempt at a smile. "I'm kind of tired. But thanks."

Jameson rose from his chair, the metal legs sliding across the linoleum. "I'll walk you out."

She rolled her eyes. "I'll be fine."

"Don't bother arguing, honey, you know Jamie's rules about someone escorting you to your car at night." Liam winked at her.

She let out a sigh and looked at Jameson. "Right. Let's go, Daddy-O."

***

Crystal walked through the back door that Jameson held for her and into the alley behind the shop. It'd been a long day and she was exhausted. She was parked in one of the spots near the door, so they didn't have to walk far. Stopping next to her car, she slipped her key in the door, but looked up when Jameson's hand slid to the roof.

"Can I talk to you for a minute?"

She frowned, wondering what he wanted to talk about. "Sure."

"Crystal, I'm going to shoot straight with you because

that's the kind of guy I am."

Oh God. Where the hell was this going?

"Okay…"

"You want to tell me what happened in Vegas?"

Crap. Had she really been that obvious?

"Not really."

"Let me rephrase that. *Tell me* what happened in Vegas."

"Is that an order, boss?"

"Does it need to be?"

She looked away, staring down the alley toward the lights of Main Street. She didn't even know what to say. How could she even explain?

"Come on, Ace, talk to me," he teased with his nickname for her.

She sucked her lips in, as if trying to hold in the words, afraid once they started flowing, she wouldn't be able to stop.

"Hey…" His tone had changed, his voice soft, caring. She turned to look at him. His hand came up to brush a strand of hair that the breeze had blown across her face.

She searched his face. "I saw a man I used to know, that's all."

"A man." He nodded as if that explained everything. "Were you in a relationship with him?"

She nodded. "Sort of."

"*Sort of?*"

She lifted one shoulder in a small shrug. "It's complicated."

"How complicated?"

"I…" God, she didn't have the words.

"Did he hurt you?"

She frowned. How could she answer that? "I...like I said, it's complicated. Why are you asking me all these questions, Jameson?"

He took in a deep breath and let it out. His eyes moved down the alley and then back to her. "When you first came here, I could see you were healing. From what, I didn't know. Over the months you've been here, you've healed. You were happy. At least, I thought you were."

"I was," she hurried to assure him, and then corrected, "I am."

He shook his head. "The light has gone out of your eyes again. Just like before."

She looked down. Every word he said was true.

He took her wrist in his hand, his thumb brushing over the stack of beaded bracelets she was never without. Her eyes followed the movement.

"You know, tattoos can cover up some pretty nasty scars. They actually do a damn fine job of it."

She looked at him like a deer caught in the headlights and barely breathed the word, "What?"

He nodded at her bracelets. "Do you wear those to hide something, Crystal?"

She swallowed, not meeting his eyes.

"Talk to me."

"It's not what you think. I'm not crazy."

"I don't think that, sweetheart."

"If you're worried you hired a crazy person, don't. I'm better now." She couldn't have been more shocked that he knew; apparently he'd known all along. "How…how did you know?"

His head tilted to the side, his eyes staring into hers, his words and his touch tender. "I had a girl come into the shop once. It was a couple years back. She wanted her scars covered. She told me she was tired of always trying to cover them with bracelets." He shrugged. "I've wondered… if that was why you always, *always* covered your wrists."

She tried to pull away, ashamed, but his grip tightened.

"Was it because of him?"

"No. It was because of me. Because I was weak." She bit her lip. "You know, it's funny, because up until then I'd always thought of myself as a strong person." She shook her head. "But I'm not. Not when it counts."

Before she realized what he was about, she was pressed to his chest, his arms wrapped around her.

"Babe."

Surrounded by his warmth, his strength, she realized he didn't need to say anything more than that single word. She melted against him and let the feelings of sadness and grief that she'd tried not to feel since she'd driven away from the motel, leaving Wolf standing there staring after her car, engulf her. Now she felt it all. Her eyes filled with tears as her body shook with her sobs.

Jameson's hands rubbed up and down her back as he let her cry it out. He simply held her, and right then, that was all she needed.

***

After she finally settled back down, she let Jameson talk

her into coming back inside the shop.

"So what's going on with Crystal?" She heard Liam ask. As she walked in behind Jameson, she saw Liam's eyes slide past his brother to land on her. He'd obviously thought she'd left.

"Crystal, you okay?" Max asked.

Jameson answered his question. "She's fine. Why don't you guys head on out. She and I are going to be here a while."

Liam, Rory, and Max exchanged a look, but rose from their chairs.

"Yeah, sure. We were just leaving, weren't we, guys?" Max replied.

"You bet," Rory added.

After his three brothers shuffled out, Jameson herded her toward the front and into a chair at his station. Then he grabbed up a binder and slapped it on the padded arm rest.

"Pick something, Ace."

She looked from him to the book, and then smiled and flipped it open. Jameson pulled over a rolling stool and sat. He watched as she turned the pages, studying the designs. She felt his eyes move from the designs to her face, and she lifted her gaze to him.

"You sure you want to do this tonight?" he asked softly. "I didn't mean to push you into doing anything you're not ready for."

She smiled at him, touched by his concern and by the fact that he hadn't pressured her for any details or tried to drag the story out of her. Maybe he could tell she wasn't quite ready to talk. "I'm sure. I have to admit, I've thought about it ever since I walked through those doors."

He grinned. "If you're sure." Then he slid a piece of paper out from the back of the book and laid it on top. He tapped his finger on the design sketched on it. "I like that one."

She looked down at it. It was a beautiful design of intricate flowers with a filigree pattern behind it forming the cuff. It really was stunning. She met his eyes and smiled. "It's perfect."

"I sketched this out last week."

Her eyes took in the gorgeous design. He was an amazing artist. Truly gifted. "It's stunning." Then her eyes lifted to his. "Who did you do this for?"

"For you," he admitted softly.

"Me?" Her eyes returned to the design, glittering with tears. "You *did* know, didn't you?"

He lifted one shoulder in a slight shrug. "I suspected, that's all, Crystal. I didn't know for sure. I still don't know much, do I?"

She met his eyes and gave a slight shake of her head, her throat closing.

"You don't want to talk, that's fine. But if you ever do, I'm here."

"Okay," she replied softly.

A small grin pulled at his mouth as he repeated the word back to her just as softly. "Okay."

That got a grin out of her.

"Let's get to work then." He winked and moved to set up

his equipment.

CHAPTER SIXTEEN

"Wolf finally working his shit out?" Cole asked.

Crash looked over at him and shrugged. "He's doing better. It's just gonna take some time."

Cole nodded. A moment later, his attention was caught by the TV above Marty's bar as they interrupted programing for breaking news. The news anchor was saying, "We go live to our reporter on the scene."

The screen showed a woman standing in front of what looked like a sketchy apartment building.

"I'm reporting live from Parkview Apartments in Sunnyvale, where three women were found dead this morning. The victims shared an apartment in this building behind me, and all seem to have died in similar fashion. Details suggest these deaths were especially gruesome. Police are saying very little, but our sources are reporting the victims were found with their throats slashed. Our sources confirm that all three women were employees of a

local strip club called Sonny's. We'll continue to follow this story as more details emerge. Reporting live, Samantha Edwards, Channel Ten News."

"Christ, man," Crash murmured, his eyes glued to the screen.

A moment later, Cole's cell went off. He pulled it out and looked at Mack's name on the screen. He put it to his ear, growling, "Yeah?"

"You seeing what I'm seeing?" Mack bit out.

"Just saw it."

"Goddamn it. Call a meeting."

Twenty minutes later, they gathered around the table in the clubhouse meeting room.

Mack ran his hand through his hair in frustration before looking over at Cole. "What do we know?"

"I talked with Sonny. He's had no problems. He's got no clue."

Mack stared down at the scarred wooden table. "That's the third hit on a business that has a direct line to our income. I'm not buying that it's a coincidence."

Cole nodded. "I think you're right."

Mack looked over at Cole. "Who the fuck is doing this?"

Cole shook his head. "I don't know, but when we catch them, they're going to wish they were dead."

"Up security on everything. Sonny's, The Pony, all our deliveries... Find out who the fuck is doing this!" Mack roared.

Cole nodded.

***

The man stood in the bushes fifty yards from the clubhouse, just far enough away to be out of sight. He grinned as he watched the men scramble to their bikes. They'd never figure out who was fucking with them. He was just too good. Hell, this was like taking candy from a baby.

He twirled the gold necklace with the tiny locket around his finger—a little memento from last night, one he'd taken from the cute brunette. She'd yelled filthy things at him, calling him a grotesque, hideous monster before he'd finally shut her up. The little cunt.

He'd shown her though, hadn't he? He'd shown her the true meaning of the word *monster*, saving her for last, taking his time, slashing her over and over while she'd screamed behind the duct tape he'd put across her mouth.

She'd been Sonny's headliner. He chuckled. Her head wasn't so pretty anymore, now, was it?

CHAPTER SEVENTEEN

Crystal was on the front steps of the shop, sipping on a cola and enjoying the spring sunshine on her fifteen minute break when Max came roaring up on his Harley. He backed it to the curb, dropped the kickstand, and dismounted. Pulling his helmet off, he twisted, grinning back at Crystal.

Her eyes trailed over his bike. All of the O'Rourke brothers rode, and every time she heard their bikes pull in, every time she looked out the window and saw that line of four bikes—sometimes a lot more than four if they had a bunch of bikers for customers—she'd miss the feel of riding on the back of Wolf's bike.

She'd ridden with Wolf quite often over the years. After a long ride they'd stop somewhere quiet and talk about anything and everything. He'd tell her about growing up with a father who made his life hell and never thought he was good enough. She'd tell him about growing up with a sister who could do no wrong and how in comparison she could do no right. They'd share things with each other, things they'd never shared with anyone else.

Her thoughts went back to one ride in particular. Wolf had ridden her up into the hills to a spot that overlooked the city below. It was a place he'd taken her several times before. In fact, she'd begun to think of it as their special spot.

Dusk had fallen, turning the sky to a gorgeous sapphire blue as the lights of the city sparkled below. They'd sat side-by-side on a big boulder, their booted feet swinging.

"It's so beautiful up here," she'd murmured.

"Um-hmm." He studied the horizon.

"If you hadn't joined the MC, what would you have done?"

"What do you mean?"

She'd shrugged. "I mean, like in high school, what did you want to do with your life?"

He'd grinned at her. "You mean what did I want to be when I grew up?"

Her eyes rolled. "Yes, Wolf. What did you want to be when you grew up?"

"Hell, I don't remember," he'd said with a lift of his shoulder. "I think I had planned to join the Army. Back then I would have signed my life away just to get the hell out of my father's house."

"But you joined the MC instead?"

"Yep. About the time I met Dog." He'd grinned at her, teasing, "It was all downhill from there."

She had given him a sly grin in return. "I'll tell him you said that."

His brows went up. "Like hell you will."

They'd laughed. When they got quiet again, she turned to him. "Do you ever come up here without me?"

He'd turned to look at her, studying her a long moment before shaking his head. "Nope. Just with you."

She had grinned, liking his answer, and then dropped her head to his shoulder. "It's our spot then."

"Yep, kiddo. It is." He had taken her hand, threading their fingers together, then brought their joined hands to his mouth and pressed a kiss to the back of her hand.

"Wolf?" she'd whispered.

"Hmm?" he responded, his eyes back on the horizon.

"Do you ever miss your family?" His jaw pressed against the side of her forehead as he'd dipped his head toward hers.

"All I've got left is my ol' man. And you know how I feel about him. So, I guess the answer is no." He'd hesitated a moment, and then asked, "Why? Do you miss yours?"

She'd shrugged. "Sometimes."

"When's the last time you saw them?"

"Three years ago."

"Maybe it's time you went home for a visit, then." When she hadn't replied, he bumped her with his shoulder. "Hey?"

She'd met his eyes.

"What's the matter?"

"My father has been sick, and I really want to go see him."

"Then you should go." When she'd hesitated, he frowned. "What's the problem, sweetheart?"

She'd shrugged. "You know how I get on with my mom and sister. I just don't know how a visit would go over."

"You need backup, just say the word," he'd told her with a grin.

Her eyes then dropped to his mouth, and she returned his smile. "You offering to be my backup, Wolf?"

"I'll always be your backup, darlin'. Anytime. Anyplace."

She'd grinned up at him, getting lost in his warm brown eyes. He'd meant it. Every word. And she'd loved him for it. In fact, she'd loved him for a long time. She just hadn't known how to tell him.

"I've got the weekend free. Say the word, and you're on the back of my bike, and we're gone."

She'd searched his eyes. "You mean it? You'd really take me?"

"Yes, I'd really take you. If you're ol' man is sick, you need to go see him. Don't let your mom or sister keep you from doing that."

"You're right, Wolf. I should go."

"It's settled then. If your mom or sister gives you any grief, I'll shut that shit down in a heartbeat."

Crystal stared off into space, thinking back on the sweet memory. Wolf had taken her that weekend, just like he'd promised. He'd met her father, the two of them even having a quiet talk. He'd had her back for every barb her mother and sister threw at her. Finally, before the weekend was over, they'd come to have a new appreciation of her, treating her with a new respect they'd never had for her before. It was all because of Wolf. He'd pointed out to them over and over what a good person she was, what a hard worker she was, and how everyone loved her. Finally, having enough, he'd informed them if they couldn't see any of that, they could both go to hell.

Of course, that hadn't gone over well, but she had to admit, they'd changed their tune after that.

"Sometimes people just need to be reminded of shit and put in their place," he'd told her later when she'd thanked him.

Max's voice drew her back from her memories. "Hey, darlin', want to go for a ride?"

She focused in on him as he stood next to his bike, looking up at her. "I'd love one, but it's busy, and you're late. You know how that pisses off Jameson. And no one wants a pissed off Jameson."

He grinned and then his eyes lifted to something over her head and behind her.

"A pissed off Jameson?"

She heard the growled words and winced. Apparently, while she'd been daydreaming, she'd missed the sound of the door opening. "Oh shit."

"Yeah, 'oh shit' is right, Ace."

She twisted to see the man himself standing on the porch behind her, his arms folded over his chest. He may have growled, but his eyes twinkled down at her. Then he lifted them to his brother. "Our hours are eleven to nine in case you forgot."

"I remember."

"Did you remember the paperwork I asked you to bring me?"

"Paperwork?" Max frowned.

Jameson let out a long-suffering sigh. "The shit I left on the kitchen table. The shit I called you about a half hour ago…"

"Oh. Shit. I forgot." Max looked up at him sheepishly.

"Well, go back to the house and get it."

Max grinned. "I was just asking Crystal here, if she wanted a ride."

"That so?" Jameson looked down at her. "You want a ride?"

"Umm. Yeah, sure."

He lifted his chin toward Max. "Go on then. Go with him."

"But the shop," she protested lamely.

"Got it covered, Ace. Go on."

She swiveled to see Max smiling and crooking his finger at her.

She rose to her feet and trotted down the steps to her first ride in a long, long, time.

***

They rode through the backwoods and countryside, Max definitely taking the long way back to the old family farmhouse the four brothers shared outside of town. After they finally pulled down the long drive and he dropped the kickstand, Crystal remembered why she loved riding so much.

Max looked back at her and grinned. "You enjoy that?"

"God, yes. I miss it. Bad."

Max frowned. "Then do it more often."

"Uh, that's kind of up to when I get the chance."

"Why settle for being on the back?"

"What do you mean?"

"You shouldn't need a man to be able to ride. Get your own bike. Then you can ride whenever the hell you want, darlin'."

Crystal smiled, sliding her hands in her back pockets. "That's not as easy as it sounds. I don't know the first thing about riding one of these things."

"I could teach you."

Her eyes widened and her mouth parted. "Are you serious?"

"Hell, yeah. Why not? You're a quick learner."

Crystal was amazed by Max's offer, her eyes skimming over the sleek lines of his beautiful bike. God, it would be awesome to ride one, to be able to ride anytime she wanted, go anywhere she wanted. Shit, how cool would that be? Then she bit her lip. There was just one problem—she couldn't afford a bike.

"What's wrong?" Max asked.

She shrugged. "It's a real sweet offer, Max, but even if I wanted to, I couldn't afford a bike."

"And *do* you want to? Bike aside, I mean."

"Of course, but—"

He turned his back on her and walked toward the garage that was set back from the farmhouse. "Come on, Ace."

She trailed behind him, stopping when he lifted up the

garage door, then followed him inside the huge three-car garage filled with junk. He stopped in front of a tarp-covered shape and pulled the canvas off, revealing an old motorcycle. The front forks were missing the wheel, the handlebars were bent, and the rear fender was damaged.

"It needs a little work, but it's a good bike." Then he shocked the shit out of her by saying, "I'll make you a deal. I'll fix it, but you've got to learn to ride it."

"Are you saying…?"

"I'll give it to you."

"No shit!" A smile burst across her face, and he busted out laughing.

"No shit, Ace."

And so commenced her riding lessons. She spent all her spare time, first watching Max work on the bike, then taking lessons. Not just from him—all the brothers got in on the act, each one of them taking a turn teaching her. She rode every chance she got. As May turned to June, and June to July, and July to August, she was becoming damn good.

Pulling into the shop one day, she strutted inside before opening time to find the four brothers gathered around her reception area. Liam was sprawled in her chair, Rory was sitting on her desk, Max was leaning against the customer side of the counter, and Jameson stood with his feet spread and his arms crossed.

"Good. She's here." Max greeted her, twisting to look over his shoulder.

"What's going on?" she asked, looking suspiciously from one to the next.

"Family meeting," Rory teased.

"Family meeting?" She frowned, her eyes moving to Jameson.

"Employee meeting," he corrected.

"That's what I said," Rory insisted with a grin.

Crystal moved to stand next to Max, setting her purse down on the counter. Max leaned over and bumped her with his shoulder. "How's the bike running?"

She grinned. "Awesome."

"Good," Jameson replied. "Because we're going on a road trip."

"A what?" Her eyes widened.

"Sturgis, Ace."

"Sturgis?"

"Yup. We go every year. Make a mint up there. Customers are lined up out the door," Max confirmed.

"Okay, but why do I have to go?" She frowned, a panic taking hold of her.

"Someone has to do the paperwork and handle the payments, babe. We'll be working non-stop laying ink," Jameson clarified.

"Are you serious?"

"Yeah, Ace, I'm serious. Why?"

"Sturgis? No way." She shook her head.

"It's not up for negotiation."

"I'm not camping out in some campground with a bunch of men. I need a bed and a hot shower," she insisted.

"High maintenance, isn't she, boss?" Max gave her a wink.

"I never met a woman who wasn't," Jameson replied, his eyes on her.

"Hey!"

"You'll have a bed. And hot water," he clarified.

She put her hand on her hip and arched her brow suspiciously. "I'm not sharing. Just so we're clear."

He looked at her, his eyes skating down her body, and he grinned.

"Jameson."

"We're clear, Ace."

"Where exactly are we staying?" Her eyes moved around her desk, landing on each man before stopping on Jameson again. She watched his eyes sharpen.

"You'll have your own room, Crystal."

Liam added, "Yeah. We rent out a storefront on the main drag. There's a small apartment above it that comes with it. Of course, the cable network that's interested in signing Jameson for his own show is going to be providing him with one of those big tour buses."

Rory grinned. "Yeah, we're going to be our own traveling 'road show'."

"Tour bus?" Crystal looked at Jameson, who almost looked embarrassed by it all. He shrugged.

"They're going to do a little filming. See if there's anything worth doing a show with."

"You mean, kind of like a pilot?" she asked.

He shrugged again. "I guess."

"Holy cow!" Her eyes got big.

At her lame response, he grinned. "Yeah, how 'bout

that? *Holy cow.*"

She slugged him in the arm. "Shut *up.*"

CHAPTER EIGHTEEN

"Babe, you seen my long sleeve shirt?" Crash called out from the bedroom when he heard Shannon coming out of the bathroom. He was distractedly stuffing clothes in a duffle bag that sat on the bed. He twisted, looking over his shoulder. Shannon had a funny look on her face—kind of green, kind of anxious.

"You okay?" He frowned, thinking back to all the anxiety and panic attacks she used to have when they first met, attacks he thought were long in the past. But then again, he hadn't left her for an extended period of time, not like this run was going to be, and it crossed his mind for the first time that maybe she was afraid to be alone. He straightened. "Shannon?"

"I'm fine."

"You know I have to go. It's a mandatory run. Sturgis is national. There'll be Chapters from all over the country."

"I know. How long will you be gone?"

"It's fourteen hundred miles, babe. Two days out, maybe six days there, two days back. So, at minimum, ten days."

She suddenly dashed back into the bathroom, her hand over her mouth. This time, he followed and held her hair while she puked. As she bent over the toilet, his eyes skimmed down her back and landed on her ass, to the white telltale stick sticking out of her pocket.

His eyes moved to the wastebasket, and he spied the corner of the recognizable box she'd tried to hide under a wad of tissue. His eyes then moved to her back as her muscles flexed with her heaving. He rubbed her back and couldn't fight the grin forming on his face or the joy singing through him.

She flushed the toilet, and he handed her a washcloth. She moved to the sink, turning on the faucet. Scooping some water into her cupped hand, she slurped it up and spit it out. Wiping her face, she then chugged some mouthwash.

"Sorry."

"Nothing to be sorry for. You okay now, Princess?"

"Yes."

He studied her face. Then he took her by the hand and pulled her into the bedroom. Taking her in his arms, he stared down at her a long moment and then asked, "Were you going to tell me?"

"Tell you what?"

He reached and pulled the stick out of her back pocket. Holding it up, he asked again, "Were you going to tell me before I left, sweetheart?"

Her eyes filled with tears, and she pressed close against

him. He felt her nod against his chest, her face still buried.

"Shannon, look at me."

Finally, she pulled back and met his gaze.

"Aren't you happy?"

She sniffled. "Of course I am."

He eased her onto the bed and knelt in front of her. "Then what's wrong?"

"You're leaving. I'm afraid. I didn't want anything to distract you."

"Baby," he breathed, his eyes searching hers. "You know I want nothing more than to stay with you. Especially now. But you understand I have to go, don't you?"

She nodded. "I'll be fine. I'm being silly. I guess the hormones are already kicking in. I'm just being emotional."

"I love you." He held her eyes for a long moment before dropping them to her stomach. Then he moved in close to kiss her belly and whispered against her skin, "And I love you, too, little Princess."

"Maybe it's a boy."

He shook his head, smiling up at her with a cocky grin. "Nah. It's a girl. My own little princess."

CHAPTER NINETEEN

The San Jose Chapter of the Evil Dead MC rolled down Main Street in Sturgis. They had arrived in town early, before it got too crowded. They could actually find places to park, and there weren't so many bikes rolling down the street that they had to crawl like rush hour traffic. That being said, there was still a line of bikes parked on the street. They found a spot large enough to accommodate all their bikes, and one after another backed into a spot in a move so smooth it could have been choreographed.

Wolf dropped his kickstand. Mack, Cole, Crash, and Red Dog were on his right. Green, Cajun, and their two prospects, Jake and Shane, were on his left. They all dismounted and moved to stand on the curb behind their bikes.

Cole paused to light a smoke.

A woman strolled down the opposite side of the street, her sexy body revealed in a pair of low-cut jeans, a pair of black chaps, and a matching black leather bikini top, complete with fringe. Wolf caught Shane's eyes on her. Not about to miss one of his last chances to torment the prospect before he got patched in tomorrow, Wolf looked over and asked, "You know how a woman like that likes to be fucked, Prospect?"

Shane's eyes moved from the girl to Wolf.

In a flash, Wolf moved in, grabbed Shane by the hair and shoved him face-first down over his bike. "You bend her over, pull her hair"—Wolf paused to yank Shane's head back, then bent close to his ear—"whisper dirty things in her ear, and fuck her like you mean it." Wolf began thrusting his hips into Shane's ass as his brothers began howling with laughter.

Red Dog jumped in on the action. Mimicking a high-pitched female voice, he taunted, "Ooww, Shane, don't stop. It feels so good. Harder, Shane, harder."

Cole finally saved Shane from his torment by pulling a five-dollar bill from his hip pocket. "Here, Prospect. I want a shot waiting on me when I get inside."

Wolf let the man up and shoved him toward Cole.

Shane took the bill and looked down at it, protesting, "Five bucks doesn't go very far in this town, VP."

Cole raised his brow. "Neither does a prospect with two broken legs."

Shane shoved the bill in his hip pocket and moved inside amidst more laughter.

Crash lifted his chin toward a bike moving up the other side of the street, drawing everyone's attention. "Check out the chick riding the bobtail chopper."

The guys all turned to check her out. Wolf's eyes swept over the bike, and then moved up to the girl. As he stared at her face as she moved past, realization dawned that he recognized those features, that hair, and that Goddamned body.

Holy shit.

There was suddenly a disconnection between his brain and his mouth, because he couldn't manage to say a word. There was only one thought running through his head. Jesus Christ. What the fuck was *she* doing here?

But leave it to Green to fill in the silence.

"Wait a minute, was that…Crystal?"

"She riding with those guys?" Mack frowned.

Wolf's gaze quickly snapped to the four men riding with her. The first thing he noticed was that they weren't wearing patches and were obviously not with any club. The second thing he noticed was that they were all young and good-looking.

"Fuck, that's Jameson O'Rourke," Red Dog observed.

"No shit." Green made a move like he was about to whistle and wave to her. Wolf grabbed his forearm in a tight fist, stopping him.

"You know about this?" Crash moved in to ask Wolf.

He shook his head although he wasn't exactly sure which part of *this* he was referring to. The part about Crystal riding a bike down fucking Main Street at Sturgis, the part about how she'd ridden down that street with four other men, or the part about her being with a famous tattoo artist.

"Didn't you say she told you in Vegas she was working

241

at a shop?" Cole asked, his eyes following the bikes as they rolled farther away.

"She told me she worked the front desk for a tattoo shop, but I didn't know it was his."

"Pretty cool." Green grinned. "Maybe we can go get his autograph."

Wolf glared at him. "Maybe we can stay the fuck away."

Green's gaze sliced to Cole, and then back to Wolf. "Yeah, okay. Whatever."

"This gonna be a problem?" Cole asked, his eyes drilling into Wolf's.

"There's gonna be half a million bikers here. I'll probably never run into her again," Wolf replied.

Cole eyed him like he didn't buy a word of it. "Yeah, and you know exactly where to find her. *His shop.*"

Crash looked between Cole and Wolf, and Wolf was sure Crash remembered everything he'd told him that night he'd ridden over to Crash's loft and laid into Shannon. The night when he'd told Crash he was letting Crystal go.

"He'll be fine," Crash assured Cole, his eyes on Wolf. Then he put his hand on Wolf's shoulder and gave it a little shake. "Won't you, Brother?"

"Yeah. Sure."

They all moved toward the bar, but Wolf couldn't help glancing down the street one last time. Two thoughts kept repeating over and over in his head like a chant. The first was that she was riding. Crystal was fucking riding… and she looked hot as hell on that bike. The second thought had his heart racing. She was here. In Sturgis. She was *here!* Holy fuck.

***

Crystal tossed her pack on the faded chenille bedspread of the wrought iron double bed. The guys were letting her have the one bedroom apartment above the storefront shop all to herself while they all crashed in the tour bus parked in the back alley.

She moved to the window overlooking Main Street and pulled the curtain back. She had a perfect view of all the action. She could almost imagine how loud it was going to be. The rumble of bikes moving up and down the street would be keeping her up all night, she was sure.

A small smile pulled at her mouth. Even so, *holy hell*, it was exciting to be here. She'd never been to anything like this. Sure, she'd ridden with Wolf. Many times. But never on club business, never on a run, and never to a rally.

She bit her lip as thoughts of him filled her head, and she wondered if he'd be here, wondered if the club was here, and if they were, if she'd ever run into any of them.

Dropping the curtain, she turned to her pack and pulled out her clothing to hang in the small closet. It was mostly tanks or tiny spaghetti-strap tops, so they didn't take up much room. Then she pulled out the flannel shirt she had buried at the bottom, the one that belonged to Wolf. The one she'd driven off with that morning when they'd last seen each other.

She lifted it to her face, inhaling deeply. It barely carried his scent any longer, but she liked to imagine she could still breathe him in. She couldn't count the number of nights she'd curl up in bed with his shirt wrapped around her, missing him terribly and wondering if she'd made a mistake that day when she told him to let her go.

The sound of the back door opening drew her attention.

"Crystal, you in here?"

She glanced through the open bedroom door to see Max poking his head in. "I'm right here."

His eyes moved to her. "We need your help setting up downstairs. We've got a shit-ton to get done before we open tomorrow."

"I'll be right there."

He backed out and closed the door.

Hanging the flannel shirt carefully on the bedpost, she quickly unpacked the rest of her things and hurried downstairs to get to work.

CHAPTER TWENTY

The Evil Dead MC's Sturgis campground was located on forty-four acres halfway between Sturgis and Deadwood. The club had purchased the property back in the eighties. It was private, secluded and, most importantly, away from the crowds and law enforcement.

Toward the back of the property there was a large steel building the club had put up about ten years ago. It was a huge open space, not much more than a place to get out of the weather when it rained. Most of the time, the members crashed out under the stars with just sleeping bags.

As dusk fell, they had a fire going on some cleared high ground. Wolf stood with Crash, Cole, and Mack about fifty feet away from it. The Birmingham, Gulf Coast, and New Orleans Chapters had all just rolled in, having ridden up together. The men watched as the new arrivals parked their bikes in the gravel lot beside the big shed.

Ambling over, Butcher, the Birmingham Chapter

President, greeted Mack with a handclasp, pulling him in for a chest-bump and back-slap. His VP, Shades joined them as well.

The men from Chapters from opposite sides of the country greeted each other with back-pounding hugs and great enthusiasm, truly happy to see each other. The times they were able to meet up being few and far between.

"How was the trip?" Mack asked.

"Long. Fourteen hundred Goddamn miles."

Cole grinned. "Same for us, Brother. It's fourteen hundred miles from San Jose, as well."

"So you feel my pain?" Butcher grinned at him.

"Damn straight," Cole agreed.

"You ready for a beer?" Mack asked.

"Hell yeah," both Butcher and Shades replied at once.

The men all chuckled.

Cole let out an earsplitting whistle. "Hey Prospect, bring a couple bottles of beer."

Wolf twisted to look as one of their prospects, Jake, ran to obey.

Butcher eyed the prospect's retreating back as the man moved to do his VP's bidding. "So, how many prospects are you patching in this trip?"

Mack's eyes followed Butcher's. "Two. Jake and Shane. And you?"

"One. 12gauge." Butcher lifted his chin toward a prospect over near their bikes.

Mack nodded.

"Maybe next year we'll have more. Right, Shades?"

Butcher asked, turning to his VP.

Shades nodded. "Gulf Coast is prospecting three. Everything goes well, they should be patching in by the next Sturgis meet."

Mack nodded again. "Good to know. Heard about your trouble down there."

"We handled it." Shades met his eyes.

Mack grinned. "I heard that, too."

"Made for a good story. Ax and all," Cole elaborated, folding his arms and grinning.

Shades grinned back with a shrug. "Hey, a man gets real cooperative when you start discussing how to dispose of his body parts."

Crash gave Shades a sly look. "Yeah, I bet they shit their pants."

"What can I say? I have expert motivational skills," Shades replied with splayed hands.

"That you do," Butcher agreed as the men all chuckled. Then he added in a more serious tone, looking at Mack, "Heard you've had some trouble in Cali."

Mack nodded. "That we have."

"You know who it is?"

"Got several possibilities. We're still looking into it."

Butcher nodded. "You need any help, you let me know."

Mack nodded. "Will do."

***

After chatting with members of the other Chapters for a while, Wolf moved to sit by the fire next to Red Dog. He lowered himself to the ground, leaning back against the log

Dog was using as a backrest.

"How's it goin'?" he asked.

Red Dog had a stick in his hand. He pulled a toasted marshmallow from the end of it, and then smashed it between two graham crackers and some chocolate. "Just peachy."

"What the hell are you doing?" Wolf asked with a frown.

"Makin' s'mores. Want one?" Dog offered the stick to Wolf, who shook his head.

"What are you, *twelve?*"

"S'mores are fucking fantastic. Don't gotta be twelve to enjoy one."

Wolf's eyes dropped to the bag of marshmallows at Dog's side. "Is that what you had in that bag from the quick-rip mini-mart earlier?"

Dog grinned. "Maybe."

Green leaned back against another log, took a long toke off a joint, and stared up at the night sky. "Look at all those stars, man. They make you feel so insignificant." Then in classic Green fashion, he switched topics out of the blue. "When I die, I want one of you to go to my funeral dressed like the grim reaper. Don't say anything, just stand there."

Wolf looked over at Dog. "Is he high?"

"Yup." Then Red Dog popped another bite in his mouth, licked his fingers, and replied, "Everyone at my funeral gets a stun-gun. The last one standing gets all my stuff."

Wolf chuckled, taking a hit off his long-neck bottle of beer.

Crash and Cole ambled over and sat down on the end of the log.

"Got an announcement to make, boys," Crash proclaimed.

All eyes turned toward him.

"Shannon and I are gonna have a baby."

Cole slugged him in the arm with a big grin, just as surprised as the rest of them apparently. "Congratulations, Brother."

Green sat up and passed him a bottle of Jack. "You knocked up your ol' lady? Good job, bro."

Crash accepted the bottle and took a slug of the whiskey with a sheepish grin as the rest of the men toasted with shots and ribald comments about his prowess as a man.

Green sat back, crossed his legs at the ankle, and admitted, "So far, my only accomplishment in life has been *not* having kids."

"Yeah, Green, and society is really grateful," Red Dog replied toasting another marshmallow over the fire.

Cole looked over at Crash. "Let me give you some advice on dealing with a pregnant woman."

"This should be good," Wolf put in with a grin at Crash, taking a slug from the bottle of whiskey being passed around.

"Unless you are physically dying, and I mean shot six times and about to pass out from blood loss, do not, I repeat, do not complain about any of your ailments. Any gripes you have about being tired or achy will *not* be met with sympathy, Brother."

The men all chuckled.

Cole continued. "And keep your place stocked with lots of alcohol."

"She can't drink," Crash protested, giving him an arch look.

Cole eyed him back with a sly grin. "No, but trust me, *you're* gonna want to."

Another burst of laughter from the men could be heard.

"And when she gets to the third trimester, just resign yourself to letting her have control of everything. The TV remote, the car radio, the bank account—"

"Your balls," Red Dog added with a grin.

"Shit," Crash whispered worriedly and took another slug from the whiskey bottle Wolf passed back to him.

Wolf grinned at the jokes along with all his brothers, but he couldn't help it when all the talk of babies and pregnant women had his mind drifting to Crystal. He stared into the fire. He was happy for Crash, make no mistake, but the illustration of what Crash and Shannon had and their happiness was a sharp reminder of all he and Crystal had lost. And perhaps, if he was being honest, it made him jealous of all that Crash had with Shannon. All that Cole had with Angel, as well.

Maybe, for the first time, he was beginning to realize he wanted that, too.

And Crystal was here. So close. So fucking close. It had him wondering if there was such a thing as fate. And maybe, just maybe, fate was giving him another shot.

CHAPTER TWENTY-ONE

The afternoon sun shone down on the campground. The full-patched brothers of all the attending Evil Dead MC Chapters were lined up in two rows, facing each other, gauntlet style. Typically, the Chapter Presidents stood at one end, their VPs at the other, along with the prospects currently about to be patched into the brotherhood.

There was only one prospect left to run this year's Gauntlet.

Mack stepped forward, a leather cut with a full three-piece patch on the back fisted in the hand at his side. At the other end, Cole put a hand on Shane's shoulder and shoved him forward a step.

Mack grinned and held up the last cut. "You want this, Prospect? Come and get it."

Wolf looked from his President to Shane, and his hand tightened into a fist. He fully intended to get his last swipes in at the man. Wolf watched as Shane's eyes swept up one side and down the other of the gauntlet of men he was expected to run in order to get his cut—a cut Wolf knew only too well a man would do anything to get, especially after the year of hell the club had already put him through.

Wolf had been were Shane was standing once. He knew the feeling Shane was experiencing at this moment: wanting that cut so bad you'd do anything for it, knowing that before you reached it you were going to receive the beating of your life, knowing that before it was done, you'd be crawling the last dozen feet. Not for a second did you let any of that deter you from getting your hands on that fucking cut.

He looked at Shane's face. Yeah, he felt it. And he wanted that cut badly.

Wolf grinned. *Come and get it, indeed, boy.*

Shane gritted his teeth and bolted forward. The brothers didn't let him get ten feet before they were on him, every one of them throwing a punch. They tossed and shoved him back and forth between the lines like a pinball. By the time Shane reached Wolf, who was standing fifteen feet from Mack, he was staggering.

Red Dog, who stood across from Wolf, grabbed hold of Shane and shoved him toward Wolf.

"Last shot, bro, have at him." Dog chuckled.

Wolf hit Shane square in the jaw with a roundhouse punch that took him to the ground. Once Shane was down, Wolf kicked him in the ribs. Shane crawled toward Mack, and that last fifteen feet took forever as Shane received kick after kick amid shouts from the club ordering him to get on his fucking feet.

Shane made it to Mack who held the cut high above his head and growled down at him, "I don't give cuts to men that grovel in the fucking dirt, Prospect."

Shane staggered to his feet, and then, staring Mack dead in the eye, he grabbed for the cut, jerking it from the man's tight hold. When he got it free, he swayed.

Mack grinned, grabbing him by the biceps to hold him up and grunted, "Congratulations, *Brother*."

The significance of being called Brother for the first time wasn't lost on Shane. He grinned through his split lip, blood coating his teeth and running down his chin. His eyes were already beginning to swell shut like a prizefighter after going ten rounds. Mack pulled him in for a back-pounding hug.

When Mack released Shane, he looped his arm around his shoulders and turned him to face the club. With all joking aside and in all seriousness, he looked down at Shane. "Always keep the heart of a prospect and look for ways to make your brother's lives better. Your brothers and club are lucky to have you."

Shane nodded. "I'm lucky to have all of them, too."

"You're a brother, first, last, and always," Mack pronounced.

Shane grinned. "Evil Dead, first, last, and always."

Crash stepped up, having a special connection with Shane since he'd sponsored him. Mack released him as Crash took Shane's face in his two hands and grinned at him.

"Loyalty means I've got your back, Brother, whether you're right or wrong. If you're wrong, you better believe we're gonna talk about it later."

That got a laugh from the brothers.

Crash pulled Shane in tight for a hug. "Love you, Brother."

"Dog pile!" Dog shouted as they all swooped down to pile on the hug.

CHAPTER TWENTY-TWO

The boys entered their third bar of the night. Taking the prospects out on their first night as full-patched members to celebrate was a club tradition. The older members took that responsibility seriously.

Wolf moved up to the bar as his brothers crowded around. Crash sidled up next to him. The place was packed, and it took several minutes to get a drink. When they all finally had one, they made several toasts to their new brothers.

Afterward, Green leaned over to Jake and put his arm around him, leaning in to shout in his ear over the crowd noise and music, "Let me give you some advice about women, now that you've got your patch."

Jake grinned at his new brother, who was already quite shit-faced. "What's that, Green?"

Green got a shit-eating grin on his face and proclaimed

in a sloppy drunken whisper that was really more of a shout, "If you lick them, they will come."

Jake, who was just taking a hit off his bottle of beer, almost snorted it out his nose. When he recovered, he looked over at his new brother. "Good to know, Green."

Green nodded and rubbed Jake's head. "I love you, man."

"Love you, too, bro."

Then Green moved over to Red Dog and threw his arm around him.

Dog looked over at Green. "You tell me you love me, and I'll knock your lights out, you drunk motherfucker."

Green just gave him a drunken grin. "I'm a lover, not a fighter."

"Bull*shit*," replied Crash, having fought the man in the cage on fight night on more than one occasion.

Undeterred, Green continued talking to Dog. "You and me go together like Assault and Battery."

Wolf chuckled. "More like Asphalt and Road Rash."

Dog shoved Green away. "Get off me. Go find some dumb blonde to bother."

Green wandered off.

Wolf grinned and commented to Dog, "He likes you."

"Well, I *am* a good time."

Jake looked over at Shane and said with a grin as he raised his beer to his lips, "It's very possible that our brothers have undiagnosed mental disorders."

Red Dog corrected him. "Our brotherhood is built on a solid foundation of alcoholism, sarcasm, inappropriateness, and shenanigans. And don't you forget it."

Shane held his bottle up. "Amen. To brotherhood."

The rest of them clinked bottles.

Dog moved in to stand on Wolf's other side. "I'm halfway through this beer. Time to order another."

Crash agreed. "You put your order in now, you might get it about twenty minutes after you run out."

Dog laughed at him. "That's Sturgis for you. Which is why I always bring my own."

They watched as Dog pulled a flask out of his pocket.

"Well don't hog it all. Pass it here," Wolf insisted. Dog passed it to him. Wolf took a long pull, then passed it back, noticing Dog's eyes were on something across the bar.

Dog leaned on his folded arms, elbows on the bar and looked at Wolf. "So, you and Crystal—"

"There is no 'me and Crystal', Dog. We're over. We've been over."

"You sure about that?"

"Pretty sure, Dog. Why?"

Dog took Wolf's jaw in his hand and turned it in the direction of the other side of the bar. "Then I guess this won't bother you."

Wolf looked over to where Dog aimed his gaze. There, across the bar, up on a bench was a girl dancing to the old Creedence song currently blasting through the bar and singing along at the top of her lungs. Not just any girl. It was Goddamn Crystal.

His eyes swept over her. She was wearing low rider jeans torn at the knee, a big belt, and a white long sleeve top emblazoned with the words *Mama Tried* clearly referencing an old Merle Haggard song. The top was scooped, showing a swell of cleavage, and fell just short of the belt, teasing with an inch of skin. Her long dark hair swung down her back as she moved.

Wolf watched in stunned amazement as she lifted her arms over her head, her body undulating to the music, her hips rocking, hypnotizing every man in the place.

Ho-lee fuck.

"Yeah, you're over her all right. Like hell."

Crash looked over Wolf's head to Dog. "And the wall of denial comes crashing down."

Dog replied back, "Yeah, with a boom."

"Fucking hell," Wolf muttered, realizing all over again just what he'd lost.

Suddenly Dog was leaning in to shout in his ear, "You let *that* go? Were you fucking high?"

"Apparently," Wolf muttered.

"I'm not sayin' you're stupid, but man, you make some really bad decisions, bro," Crash advised.

"Rub it in, why don't you?"

"I don't have to. She's doing a damn fine job of that all on her own."

"She sure knows how to serve it up, don't she?" Dog muttered, his eyes on Crystal.

"The way you did her, bro, you deserve it. Every twist," Crash told Wolf.

"Goddamn, she knows how to gut me," Wolf whispered in a voice thick with torment. "Why the hell did we have to pick this bar?"

"Sorry Wolf, but you don't get to choose off the Karma Menu, you just get what's coming to you."

Dog grinned, continuing the torment. "Confidence is the sexiest thing a woman can wear. Followed closely by a spectacular push-up bra. Which that is, I might add."

Crash chuckled, taking in Wolf's furious look. "Is this where the thunder claps and the sky turns black?"

"I think so, bro," Dog replied with a grin.

***

Crystal looked over the heads of the crowd from her place up on the bench. When she'd been getting squished by the crowd, Max had suddenly lifted her up by the waist, onto the bench near the window. Then of course she had to start dancing when her favorite Creedence Clearwater Revival song started playing. Well, that and the fact that she'd had a couple of shots and had been having such a good time with Max and Liam. Now, as the song ended, and her eyes scanned the crowd, she stopped dead in her tracks.

Holy crap. The Evil Dead MC. Not just the MC, but the San Jose Chapter.

Out of all the bars in this town, out of the half a million bikers in this town, out of all the MCs roaming Sturgis this week, they had to show up here. *Now*. On the one night she had a chance to get away from the shop and actually take in the whole Sturgis scene.

Of course, she'd known there was a possibility they'd be in Sturgis. Okay, more than a possibility. She was well aware that Wolf's club made the trip every year. It was their national meet. Every Chapter across the country sent members.

But she'd hoped with as big a rally as Sturgis was that she'd never cross paths with any of the members from San Jose.

Apparently that dream was shot to hell.

Not only were they here, she had absolutely no hope of hiding in the corner and hoping they wouldn't see her. After that dance on the bench, they'd definitely noticed her. Hell, half the bar had noticed her.

Crap. How stupid could she be? Why had she done that? Then it hit her.

She had no reason to hide. She had nothing to be ashamed of. She was a grown-ass woman. If she wanted to cut loose and enjoy life, then she'd do it. Anyone who had a problem with it could go to hell.

Except she really wasn't up to a confrontation with Wolf, even though they hadn't ended on a completely bad note. He'd let her go, like she asked. He'd told her he was sorry for how he'd treated her. He'd told her if she ever needed anything, he'd be there for her. So maybe she was overreacting, blowing this way out of proportion. After all, those guys were all still important to her.

"Crystal!" She heard Red Dog bellow out, and she picked him out of the crowd, which wasn't hard. Before she knew what she was doing, she jumped down and moved across the floor, running to jump in his arms.

"Dog!" She hugged his neck.

"Hey, cupcake. How's my baby girl?"

She pulled back to smile at him. "Good. Real good."

He smacked her ass. "Saw you dancin' up there. Way to shake your money-maker."

She blushed, burying her face in his neck. "Oh God."

He murmured in her ear, "Also saw you ridin' down Main Street the other day. Why didn't you tell us you'd be here?"

Her head pulled back and her eyes moved over his head, past all the other members to connect with Wolf as he stood at the bar, hanging back, giving her space while the rest of his brothers moved in to greet her.

She shrugged. "You know."

Dog's face sobered. "Yeah. I know. Doesn't mean you had to run off like you did. Doesn't mean the rest of us don't miss you."

He set her down.

"I'm sorry, Dog. You're right. I should have stayed in touch." She ran her hand down his cheek. He grinned, pulled her palm to his mouth, and kissed it.

"Glad to see you, sweetie."

Then suddenly she was swept up into Cole's arms. "Hey, kiddo. It's good to see you. And where the hell did you learn to ride?"

She grinned and shrugged. "My bosses."

Cole's eyes lifted across the bar to the men she'd been standing with. "That them?"

She nodded. "Yes."

Then Crash was hugging her tight and murmuring in her ear. "Hey, babe. You doing okay?"

The concern in his voice had her wondering if he knew something. If Wolf had told him anything, and if so, just exactly what that had been. Her eyes moved over Crash's shoulder to meet Wolf's eyes again. He looked away, almost guiltily, and she knew that he had. But what? The baby? The suicide attempt? All of it?

She pushed out of Crash's arms and put on a fake bright smile. "I'm fine, Crash. How's Shannon?"

Crash grinned. "She's good. Real good. You should call her."

Crystal nodded. "I will. I miss her."

"She misses you, too. Why don't you come for a visit?"

Again her eyes slid to Wolf where he leaned against a corner of the bar. "I don't know."

Crash followed her gaze then turned back to her. "Go say hello."

Her eyes flicked up to Crash, who gave her an encouraging smile and a gentle shove on the small of her back.

She really didn't remember walking across the twenty feet that separated them, she just found herself standing in front of him. "Hey, Wolf. How are you?"

Their eyes met as he moved in for a hug. Didn't he realize what being in his arms again was doing to her? Hell, she was coming undone, unraveling right on the spot. All those feelings she'd tried to bury came rushing to the surface and threatened to bubble over. They held each other for a long moment, and then he stepped back, forcing her to take a deep breath and get it together.

Their eyes met, and she wished he'd look off somewhere instead of searching her gaze as if he could see every feeling she tried to hide.

God, why did he have to look at her that way, why did he have to make her want him?

It was all there again, the desire, the hunger, the need, like it'd never been gone. It just flamed right up, blazing as strongly as ever.

Then suddenly Shane was there, standing at her side. She turned, looking up into his grinning face. He spun, showing her the back of his cut.

"Check it out, Crystal. Full patch."

Her eyes fell to take in the full three-piece patch, and she grinned, truly pleased for him. "You got your patch!"

He turned, and she gave him a hug. "Me and Jake, both."

She pulled back to smile up in his face. "That's great. I'm happy for you." Her eyes moved past him to search the crowd. "Where is he?"

"He's here somewhere. Probably hitting on some chick." Then she watched his eyes move over her shoulder to Wolf. And then he was taking her hand and pulling her along. "Dance with me."

As he pulled her through the crowd, she glanced back at Wolf to see his eyes on her. He looked pissed, but there was nothing he could do about it anymore. Shane was no longer a lowly prospect that he could push around.

They got to the tiny dance floor in the back corner of the bar, and Shane pulled her into his arms. They rocked slowly, and then he dipped his head to her ear.

"Bet this is pissing him off big time."

She pulled back to look at Shane. "You mean Wolf?"

He nodded. "Gotta admit, it feels good not to have to take his shit anymore."

She noticed for the first time, in the colored spotlights of the dance floor, the bruising on his face. Her hand moved up, her thumb brushing over his cheekbone. "You're hurt."

"Nah. I'm okay."

"You were in a fight?"

"Let's just say they make you earn this cut, right up to the second they give it to you."

"Oh." She didn't know what to say to that. She knew that because of her, the bad blood between Wolf and Shane had made it all the worse for him. He'd taken more than his fair share of abuse, at least from Wolf. More than his buddy, Jake had to take. She looked up into Shane's eyes. "I'm sorry."

"For what, darlin'?"

"I probably made it worse for you, I mean, when I came onto you that first night, trying to make Wolf jealous. That put you on his radar. I'm sure he put you through hell for it."

Shane studied her a moment.

"Yeah, I'm not gonna deny it, he did. But that's over now. Ain't a damn thing he can do about it anymore. I gotta say, a little payback would be nice." He grinned down at her. "You want to help me out with that?"

"Payback?"

"Yeah, surely you wouldn't mind getting a little of that yourself." When she didn't answer, he grinned and suggested, "Let's show him what he's missing; show him what he can't have."

Before she could reply, he dipped his head and brushed his lips against hers. It was a soft kiss, not aggressive, not assertive, more seeking, testing the waters to see if there were any feelings reciprocated on her part.

Shane was a good man. If she took up with him, he would be kind to her, treat her right. She knew that, but the feelings just weren't there. They'd hooked up once, in secret, and Crystal had enjoyed it. But she had known if Wolf had found out, he would have made sure Shane never got his patch. Crystal knew, even then, that getting involved with her would be the end for Shane, so she'd pushed him away. The last thing she wanted was to be the reason he didn't get his patch. She liked Shane. He was sweet. But... it wasn't enough.

Shane pulled back to look down at her and smiled. "You're still hung up on him, aren't you?"

She studied his eyes. God, she was. So hung up on him it was insane. Shane must have read the truth in her eyes, felt it in her kiss, because he didn't say anything more, just pulled her into his arms. She rested her head against his shoulder, wishing she could feel for Shane the way she felt for Wolf.

It would make things so much simpler.

***

Wolf stood at the bar, his eyes on the couple dancing. He knew he should look away. Why torture himself like this? But he couldn't tear his eyes from them.

He felt Crash move in to stand next to him.

"That's gotta hurt."

Wolf knew Crash was referring to him having to watch Crystal in a brother's arms and not being able to do shit about it.

"Yeah," was all he could muster.

"She's nobody's ol' lady yet, in case you want to give it another shot."

Wolf shook his head. "I jerked her around so many times."

"Yeah, you did. Doesn't mean a man can't change."

Dog moved in on Crash's other side and put in his two cents, like Wolf needed anymore ribbing from his brothers.

"That right there is a girl on a mission."

"Yeah, a mission to show Wolf what a fool he is," Crash replied.

Dog chuckled. "That's not hard to do."

"Okay, boys, enough. I get the picture, I'm an idiot."

"Yup."

"No arguments here."

Crash looked over at him. "So the question is, what are you gonna do about it?"

When Wolf refused to rise to the bait, Dog pressed it home. "If you had any balls, you'd go over there and cut in on that dance."

Wolf looked over at him. "Oh, you'd just love to see that fistfight, wouldn't you?"

Dog shrugged with a grin. "Maybe." He waited half a beat before adding, "You gonna just stand here like a pussy? Makes me ashamed to call you Brother."

Crash leaned in to taunt, "Time to step up to the plate there, A-Rod."

Wolf tossed his drink back, slammed the glass on the bar, and turned to stalk toward the dance floor. He could hear his brothers laughing in his wake and Dog bellow out, "Gangway. Dead man walking."

Christ, the things his brothers goaded him into doing. This was probably a huge mistake, but fuck it, he was committed to it now. No turning back.

***

Crystal turned in Shane's arms as they swayed to a slow song. As they rotated around, she could see Wolf moving through the crowd toward them, his eyes on her.

"Oh God," she whispered.

Shane looked down at her with a frown and turned to follow her gaze.

"Please don't fight," Crystal blurted out, knowing what was going to happen when she felt Shane stiffen in her arms.

His eyes returned to her. "My days of backing down to Wolf are over, Crystal."

"Please, Shane," she begged and watched his jaw clench. He was struggling with caving into her request, and she knew just how much that would cost him.

"I've waited a long fucking time for this day, Crystal."

"I know, I know you have, I'm just asking you not to throw the first punch."

Then Wolf was upon them. Crystal's eyes moved between him and Shane. And then Wolf shocked the hell out of her by actually being cordial.

"Mind if I cut in, Brother?" Then he *truly* shocked her by asking, "Please?"

Shane must have been just as shocked. His eyes flicked down to her as if he were asking if that was what she wanted. She nodded, and then he released her as Wolf moved in.

She felt Wolf's hands settle on her waist, his palms hot on her bare skin. Hesitantly she slid her hands up his cut to encircle his neck. He pulled her closer, until they were brushing up against each other.

She looked up to see his dark eyes' intent as he stared down at her. What the hell was he doing? Why was he putting them both through this? His eyes dropped to her mouth, and she couldn't help but do the same. She studied those lips of his and could think of nothing more than tasting them again.

She wasn't sure if he dipped his head, or if she lifted hers, but suddenly their mouths were only an inch apart. She didn't know how long they danced like that, tempting fate, perhaps each seeing how long the other could last before they closed that last inch. Was it a minute? Ten?

They moved in a slow circle, the noise of the crowd and the music fading away until it was as if they were the only two in the room. She could feel his breath, and she was sure he could feel hers. Neither of them said a word. It was almost as if they were cast in a spell neither of them wanted to break.

"I guess I should have seen this coming."

She knew he was referring to the attraction between them, the powerful pull that seemed to draw them together.

But how could he have foreseen them running into each other? He couldn't have known she'd be here in Sturgis. Her brow furrowed and she whispered, "What? Seen this coming...how?

"From when I saw you the other day."

"You saw me?"

He nodded. "Saw you ridin' up Main Street, bold as brass."

"Oh."

"Yeah. Oh."

Her eyes moved up to his, searching between them. His dropped again to her mouth.

"You waitin' to see how long it takes me to close this last inch?"

She swallowed, but didn't answer. Did she want that? She did, but...

"Once your lips touch mine, girl, it's over. You know that, don't you?"

"Wolf, what are we doing?" she whispered.

"Playing with fire. Seems we've both got a thing for that."

"Maybe we're just asking for trouble."

"I asked myself that same question. You come up with an answer?"

She shook her head. Then suddenly he was stepping back, grabbing her hand and pulling her through the crowd. He took a right turn and led her down the hallway to the restrooms. A moment later, he had her backed against the wall.

"I ain't playin' games, Crystal."

"What are you doing?"

He searched her eyes before he answered. "I don't fucking know. I just know this happens every time I lay eyes on you. I've come to realize it's always gonna be that way." He paused to tuck a lock of hair behind her ear, his eyes following the movement. "When I saw you ride past on that bike? Hell, I thought maybe it was fate, comin' back around to give me another shot. Give us another shot."

"Wolf."

"Am I wrong? Am I the only one who can't let go?"

"No," she whispered, looking down.

"There was a time you couldn't get enough of me. Did I kill that?"

She shook her head, and he brought his hand to her chin, tilting her head up, bringing her eyes to his.

"Crystal?"

She wasn't sure what his question was, but a moment later, he finally closed the space between them, his mouth coming down on hers.

They kissed a long time, and she remembered how badly she'd missed his kiss. He took his time, and he was good at it. Extremely good.

She found her hands drifting up to pull his head back down when he broke off to breathe. He let her, and her enthusiasm only flamed the fire higher. He stepped in, crowding her against the wall, pressing his hips to hers, his knee forcing her legs apart. She felt his muscular thigh rub erotically against her crotch.

Dear God, if he kept that up, he'd get her off right here. She broke free, her hands coming up to push him back enough so she could gasp in a breath. "Wolf, wait."

He didn't want to be denied. She could see it in his eyes. It was a struggle for him to back down, but he did it. For her.

"You don't feel it then? It's gone?"

She could hear the torment in his voice.

"It's not that. I still feel it."

People started coming down the hall, and then Cole came out of the bathroom. He paused when he saw them, his eyes moving between them. As he stepped past, his gaze connected with Crystal's.

"I want to see you before you cut out of here tonight."

She nodded, frowning, wondering what that was about. "Of course."

Wolf straightened, stepping back, giving her some room.

Green stumbled drunkenly down the hall, and Wolf must have given up on them having any time alone. He took her by the hand and pulled her back into the bar. The rest of the club had managed to commandeer a table, which is where Cole now sat with Crash. The rest of them stood nearby at the bar.

Wolf turned to her. "You want a beer?"

She nodded.

Cole grabbed her wrist and pulled her toward him.

"I'll keep her safe while you get it," he said to Wolf, who nodded and moved off toward the bar. Cole pulled her down onto his lap. "You okay, darlin'?"

She nodded.

"I heard about the pregnancy," he murmured in her ear.

Cole was never one to beat around the bush.

She sucked her lips in. Crap. She couldn't help wondering if he knew the rest, too.

"Babe, you should have told him," he admonished her softly.

She nodded. "You're right. I should have."

He squeezed her hip. "He would have stepped up."

"You think so?"

"Yeah. I do."

She shrugged. "It doesn't matter now."

He nodded. "Yeah. I'm sorry about your loss."

She looked down at the hands in her lap, and then met his eyes. "Thank you, Cole."

He studied her, and she knew he was trying to gauge her feelings.

"You happy now?" He lifted his chin toward where Max and Liam stood.

She twisted and caught Max's eye. He lifted his drink to her. Turning back to Cole, she saw the concern etched on his face. She nodded. "Yes. I am. I'm happy."

He nodded back. "Good. I guess. We all miss you, though."

"I miss all of you, too."

"Crystal, I want to ask you something. And I want you to be straight with me about it."

"Okay." She frowned, wondering where this was going.

"Did Mack run you off?"

She shook her head. "No, Cole. I left all on my own. I…I needed to leave. Put some distance between Wolf and me. You know?"

His hand came up to cup her face for a brief second before dropping away. "I know, sweetheart."

***

A man sat hidden deep in a corner of the bar. He'd just had another girl look at him in horror when he'd tried to hit on her. He knew his disfigured face was terrifying. He had a fucking mirror. He didn't need some fucking whore to sneer at him. He contemplated cornering the bitch in the back hallway later and showing her the meaning of the word horror, but then his attention was distracted by the flash of a patch on the back of a cut—an Evil Dead patch, the club of the man responsible for his damaged face. The man he'd sworn revenge on.

The crowd was thick, making it hard to see, but eventually a brief path cleared, revealing the man himself sitting at a table. Cole Austin, VP of the San Jose Chapter. He had a woman on his lap, and the tender way he was touching her face, she had to mean something to him.

She wasn't his ol' lady, and she wouldn't be the major payback that was part of that plan, but she'd be a start. An evil smile formed on his distorted face. She'd be a real good start.

***

Crystal watched as Wolf returned with four bottles and passed them out. Cole kicked a chair out for him. Wolf sat, took Crystal's hand and pulled her from Cole's lap to his, looping an arm around her waist. On one hand it felt awkward to be sitting on Wolf's lap, especially with both

Cole and Crash grinning at her as they sipped on their beer. On the other hand it felt so right, exactly where she belonged.

He made her feel like it was the most normal thing in the world, like there hadn't been any rift between them, like he wouldn't be riding out of town later in the week and leaving her behind.

He seemed happy, grinning to his brothers and them grinning back, like everyone was happy to have her back in the fold. But she wasn't.

Was she?

A few minutes later, she felt a presence at her side and looked up to find Max and Liam.

"Hey, guys," she said.

"You ready to head back?" Max asked with a warm smile on his face while Liam's eyes moved around the table.

She felt Wolf's arm tighten around her and saw Cole's eyes move from his brother to the two men. Crystal knew this could get real ugly real fast, and she quickly tried to diffuse it.

"Max, Liam, I want you to meet some friends of mine. This is Cole, Crash, and Wolf. Guys this is Max and Liam, two of my bosses."

Cole and Crash nodded. Wolf just stared.

"How many bosses do you have, Crystal?" Cole asked.

She smiled, trying to put everyone at ease. "Four."

Cole's brows rose. "Four? That must be a nightmare."

She tried to laugh it off. "They're great to work for. Really."

"You the ones who taught her to ride?" Wolf asked.

Crystal turned to smile up at Max. "That was Max, mostly. He was extremely patient with me."

Max grinned down at Crystal. "Our girl here is a wild one. Blastin' down the highway doin' ninety-five."

Cole's eyes narrowed at the man. "That your doing?"

"The skills? Yeah. The wild side? No."

Cole nodded, and she saw his eyes move over her shoulder to Wolf as he sat behind her. She twisted to look at him. "I really should be getting back. We start early in the morning."

Wolf held her eyes. "Where are you staying?"

"There's an apartment above the shop. I'm staying there."

"With who?" Wolf asked with an edge to his voice.

"With no one."

He lifted his chin toward Max and Liam. "And where are they staying?"

"Not with me, Wolf."

He nodded, as if that was still to be determined.

She moved to get up. "It was good seeing you all." Her eyes moved around the table. Cole's gaze went to Wolf, almost as if he was wondering what Wolf was going to do, if anything.

Surprisingly, Wolf said nothing.

"Well, see you around." She suddenly felt awkward as hell, and beat a hasty retreat toward the door, Max and Liam on her heels. They walked the two blocks back to the shop, and no one said a word. When they reached the shop, they walked around to the back alley. Max and Liam escorted her to the exterior wooden stairs that led to the second floor apartment. The tour bus was parked half a block down. They waited at the bottom of the steps until she unlocked the door and entered.

Leaning back against it, she exhaled, her thoughts drifting to Wolf. He'd let her walk away without a single word. It made her wonder if she'd misread the entire evening. Did the dance, the kiss, the things he said not mean what she'd thought?

She bit her lip, realizing how badly that hurt. God, he still had the power to slay her.

Then her thoughts turned to Max and Liam. She imagined that even now they were reporting back to Jameson and Rory about the "friends" she'd introduced them to tonight. She could only imagine the speculations that would be tossed around.

She shook her head and moved toward the bedroom. She couldn't think about that now. She needed to curl up and get some sleep.

***

"What the hell was that?" Cole drilled Wolf with a look after Crystal had left.

"What do you mean?"

Crash leaned forward. "One minute she's cuddled on your lap, the next you're letting her walk out the door. That's what he means."

Cole frowned. "Am I missing something? I mean, what I saw in that back hallway—"

Wolf cut in. "What you saw in that hallway was a

connection that time hasn't broken."

Cole huffed out a breath and shook his head. "Don't care how strong a connection you two have, it can all be washed away with a woman's tears. And the way you let her go tonight—"

"What choice did I have?" Wolf snapped.

Crash gave him a what-the-fuck look. "Who the hell *are* you? Are you not a member of this club? Because no member of my Goddamn club says those words. What the fuck do you mean *what choice did you have?*"

"She works for those guys, Crash. She told me once to let her go. You heard her yourself. She says she's happy. You want me to make a scene and cause trouble for her with her employers? Fuck up her job? How's that gonna win her back, genius?"

"So you did nothing? First time you've seen her in *how* long? Wolf, you didn't even walk her outside." Crash lifted his chin toward the door.

Wolf ran his hand angrily through his hair. Christ, he hadn't. How'd she take that?

"I fucked up?"

Cole had no problem answering his stupid question. "You want me to say it? Yeah, you fucked up, Wolf. And don't play dumb with me. You knew what you were doing. I don't buy this crap for a minute, so cut the bullshit. What the fuck is your problem?"

Wolf shook his head, leaning over the table.

"Whatever. Do what you want. I came to get drunk, not to play your damn therapist. I'm getting another beer." Cole shoved his chair back and walked off.

Crash leaned his folded arms on the table. He waited until Cole had moved away, and then he started in with his own advice with a grin. "I got no problem playin' your therapist."

"Lucky me."

"You need a woman in your life, Wolf. One who knows you. One who understands you. One who lets you be who you are."

Wolf ran a hand down his face. Crash wasn't telling him anything he didn't already know—he was describing everything Crystal already was to him.

Crash dipped his head closer, his voice quieting. "This life, this job, this club…it's not always easy. It can suck the soul right out of you. You need someone to go home to, Wolf. Someone to take away the darkness, fill you up with light. Shannon does that for me. Angel does that for Cole. If Crystal can be that for you, why are you fighting it, bro?"

"I don't fucking know."

"Yeah you do."

Wolf blew out a long breath. Yeah, he did. "I've never lived up to anyone's expectations, Crash. What if I can't live up to hers? What if I destroy everything that's good about her?"

"This more baggage your piece-of-shit father left you with?"

Wolf huffed out a laugh. "Probably." Then he ran a frustrated hand down his face, shook his head, and looked over at Crash. His brothers wanted him to cut the bullshit, fine. "Yeah, she's what I need. I know that, Crash. But what if I'm not what *she* needs?"

"What if you are?"

Wolf swallowed.

"That scares you, doesn't it? Being what she needs?"

When Wolf stayed silent, Crash shook his head in aggravation, got up, and walked away.

Red Dog strolled over, a beer in his hand. He stood and looked down at Wolf. "He rub your head and tell you everything's gonna be all right?"

"His pep talks suck."

"Yeah, he was voted most likely to depress people."

"Shut the fuck up." Wolf stood up and stalked toward the door with Dog's laughter following him out.

He shoved through the crowd. Ten feet from the door he slammed right into a member of the Death Heads MC, pushing him back into the two brothers behind him as they walked in the bar. For one of those split seconds that lasts a lifetime, Wolf and the Death Head stared with stunned surprise into each other's eyes. There was no love lost between the two clubs, in fact they were sworn enemies, and that animosity was plain in both their eyes as they glared their bitter hatred back at each other. Then the Death Head members at the man's back shoved him forward, and he came up swinging, hitting Wolf with a powerful right hook.

Wolf returned the punch causing the Death Head to stumble back. Screams erupted in the bar as patrons scattered back. The next thing Wolf knew, all his Evil Dead brothers had pushed through the crowd and were taking his back, fists flying. It was seven to three and the brawl ended with the three Death Heads lying on the floor.

"Move!" Cole jerked his chin toward the door, and his club cleared out, pushing out onto the street, knowing they only had minutes to get the hell out of there before the cops arrived and hauled every single one of them in.

The men scrambled to their bikes, and a moment later seven bikes roared off down the street.

CHAPTER TWENTY-THREE

The old wrought iron bed squeaked as Crystal rolled over to face the front window. The rumbling sounds of motorcycles passing below echoed up from the street. It was past midnight, but the sound didn't bother her. She couldn't sleep anyway, not when her mind was consumed with reliving her encounter with Wolf earlier, every moment playing out over and over in her head like an endless parade of images. The look in his eyes when he first saw her, the way he held her when they danced, the way he kissed her in the hallway, the way he looked at her as she left.

She was startled out of her thoughts by a knocking. Rolling over, she looked through the open bedroom doorway into the main room and toward the back door.

Who could that be? Jameson perhaps, coming to ask her about whatever Max and Liam had probably told him. Tossing back the covers, she strode toward the door. The top half contained a window covered with a red gingham kitchen-style curtain. She paused, pulling it aside to peer out.

It was dark, but she could make out the tall shape of a man wearing a leather cut. His arms were lifted, his hands bracing on either side of the doorframe. His head was dipped, but it lifted when the curtain moved, and his eyes connected with hers through the glass.

Wolf.

She unlocked the door and opened it just three inches, but that didn't stop him. He pushed it open and stepped inside, forcing her to step back. She watched his eyes as they swept down over her, taking in the flannel shirt wrapped around her.

His eyes flicked back up to hers, and she could read the thoughts running through his head. He knew in an instant just what wearing his shirt to bed meant, everything it revealed about how she felt about him. As she watched, his eyes roamed over her body again, sweeping down over her bare legs, exposed by the shirt that only fell to her mid-thigh.

The door clicked softly as he pressed it shut, his eyes still on her legs.

She wrapped her arms around herself, hugging against the chill night air that had swept in with him. "What are you doing here, Wolf?"

His hand lifted, and he brushed the back of his index finger over the soft flannel fabric just above her breast. "You're wearing my shirt."

She looked away. She could hardly deny it. "Yes."

"Why?"

She swallowed, but didn't answer.

"Your question… my question. I'm betting they both have the same answer."

She looked back at him then. Her heart was pounding in her chest, and it felt hard to breathe. He took a step toward her, and she took a step back. "Wolf."

He took another step. "Crystal."

She stepped back again, and he followed, like he always did, stalking her across the room until she felt the cool plaster of the wall next to her bedroom door pressed to her back.

"Tell me I'm wrong."

"Wolf."

He moved in closer, his face inches from hers and repeated his soft words. "Tell me I'm wrong."

It was then she noticed the bruising on the side of his face. Her hand came up, her fingers gently touching his cheekbone. "Wolf, you're hurt. What happened?"

"Doesn't matter. I'm fine." He moved in again.

She lifted her hand and pressed her palm to his chest, his cut cool beneath her fingers as she attempted to hold him back. "We need to talk."

"We do. But not now." His hands moved between them, his fingers closing around the plackets of the flannel shirt. With a hard tug he popped all the buttons free, sending them scattering on the floor as she gasped, excitement and erotic fear taking her breath.

The shirt fell open, revealing her bare skin all the way down to her panties. His eyes moved over her, taking in every inch.

She watched his eyes lift and move beyond her to land on the bed visible through the doorway. Then he bent and locked his arms around her bare thighs. He hefted her up, and her legs wrapped around his waist. She clutched at his shoulders, gasping in her surprise as the shirt fell back off her shoulders to hang from her elbows

He carried her into the bedroom, and a moment later she felt her back pressed to the soft sheets still warm from her body heat.

"Wolf."

His mouth came down on hers, silencing any protest she might have made. His tongue swept inside as his hands captured her head, cradling it while he kissed her, long and deep. Her hands moved to slide around him of their own volition, stroking over the patches on his cut, moving up to thread through the soft curls at the back of his neck.

She heard his groan, felt it vibrate through her mouth as he sank deeper onto her, one knee forcing her thighs apart, making room for his body to settle between them.

His mouth broke free, trailing across her jaw and down her neck. She tilted her head back, giving him better access, and his mouth latched onto the skin below her jawbone, sucking hard enough to leave a mark. Maybe that was his intension—marking her as his.

She moaned, and his body slid lower, his mouth trailing down over her collarbone, down her breastbone, and then to climb the soft mound of her breast to latch onto her nipple. As he sucked on it, his fingers closed over her other nipple, pinching and twisting. The dual sensations sent a white-hot jolt straight between her legs.

She writhed, attempting to find some relief by rubbing against him. He didn't leave her hanging, he knew what she needed and his free hand moved to give it to her, his fingers sinking into her slick folds, stroking softly. He didn't let up tormenting her nipples as he caressed with deep, slow strokes.

"Wolf," she panted, her fingers sinking into his hair, holding his head to her breast. It wasn't long before the multiple sensations coming at her from every place he touched unraveled her and she began to thrust up into his hand, meeting every stroke, drawing them out.

As her responses increased and her need ramped up, he slid two fingers inside her, his thumb taking up where his fingers had been. Now, as the points of stimulation increased by yet another, she arched, her head going back in the mattress, a long moan escaping as the orgasm roared through her.

He slid down, positioning between her legs. She'd barely recovered, and he was preparing to start again.

"Wolf, I can't..." she panted.

He just smiled at her, her words not stopping him in the least.

The scent of her arousal now hung heavy in the air.

With one soft nuzzle of his mouth, he breached and invaded her soft petals, dazzling her senses as he slid his tongue inside and electrified everything he touched, with a languorous sweep, a lingering slide. His lips brushed her again and again, and Crystal opened to him a little more. He sank deeper than before. He tasted, teased, withdrew. *No!* She needed more, and pressed up.

Wolf rewarded her with another teasing caress of his lips, which melted over her and then his tongue was diving inside in a firm and wild possession. She may have half expected it, but the slide of his tongue still blindsided her defenses.

She clawed at him. Barely breathing, dizzy with the sensation, she writhed as heat curled in her belly, her nipples tightening.

Suddenly, he retreated, leaving behind an ache she already couldn't fight. *Oh God.*

"Please," she begged, all shame gone.

"You want something, sweetheart?"

God, she'd missed him. She just wanted to feel him inside her, feel his weight on her as he lost control.

"You. Now. Please, baby."

He didn't deny her, but slid up over her, his body coming down as he brushed the hair back from her damp forehead.

He kissed her then, and she tasted herself on him. He ate at her mouth and she could feel the erection through his jeans. She realized he was still dressed, and her hands were suddenly frantic to get his clothes off, moving up to push his cut off his shoulders.

A moment later, he was off the bed. He stood next to it, staring down at her with hungry eyes as he tore his clothes off. She watched, her eyes moving over his body as he bared it to her. His broad shoulders, muscular arms and chest, his flat abs… Her tongue came out to lick her lips in anticipation.

His eyes fell to her mouth and a second later he was back on top of her. Taking his cock in his hand, he rubbed his hard length against her entrance. It didn't take long for his cock to be coated in her slick release.

He stared down at her. "I hated the way you left me at that damn motel."

She knew then that he was talking about the motel at the state-line where they'd had their confrontation. Where she'd pleaded with him to let her go. Where she'd seen the torment in his eyes as he'd done just that.

"I hated it too," she said as she writhed against him, struggling to guide him into her. He gripped her wrists over her head, pinning her on the bed.

Breathing hard, her back arched as she tried to mold her body to his.

He pulled away to look her in the eyes. His voice was ragged. "You drive me crazy, girl. And right now I'm going to fuck you hard. Like I need to punish you for that. For leaving me like that. Doesn't mean I don't love you, Crystal."

He studied her eyes.

"You gonna let me? You gonna take it like that? Like I need to give it to you?"

Looking up at the lust in his eyes, she nodded. She'd give him anything he needed. Maybe that was her downfall. He held that much power over her. Her *love* for him held that much power over her. It was so big, she could refuse him nothing.

At her acquiescence, he moved back off her. Grabbing her wrists he hauled her off the bed. Then he spun her around and with a firm hand in her back, he pushed her face-first into the bed.

He bent over her body, his chest coming down over her back as he rubbed his hard length against her entrance.

"Ask for it," he growled.

She didn't hesitate. "Fuck me, Wolf."

He plunged inside her, bringing her up on her toes. She felt him lock one muscular forearm across her pelvis. His other hand came down on the mattress near her face. His stiff arm held his weight as he thrust into her again and again, his skin slapping against hers.

She was still slick from her orgasm, but it had been a long time since she'd had sex. Since him, actually. She was tight, and she knew she'd feel the ache tomorrow after he finished with her.

She moaned and his thrusts immediately slacked off, as he reined in his assault.

"You okay?" he panted.

She nodded her head against the mattress.

"It's too much, you tell me," he ordered, his pace picking up again.

"Make me come, Wolf," she pleaded. A moment later the arm locked around her hips disappeared and his hand went between her legs. His fingers stroked, seeking out her trigger. It didn't take him long to bring her to the edge again. And when he did, she began moving against him, pushing back against every driving thrust.

"Find it, Crystal. I need you to find it, because I'm about to explode."

He increased the frantic petting of his fingers and she soared over the edge, crying out his name.

A moment later he followed her over, his hands moving to clutch her hips tightly as his body went solid.

***

"Come here, babe. I want to cuddle with you."

Crystal turned her head on the pillow to look at Wolf. Her brows rose, clearly expressing her disbelief. "You *hate* cuddling."

"I do not. I love to cuddle."

She smiled and rolled her eyes. He was so full of shit, and she felt the need to remind him. "Remember that first night we slept together?"

"Of course."

She arched an eyebrow. "Remember the next morning?"

He grinned. She'd obviously reminded him of just how clear he'd been that morning about cuddling. "You mean when you taught me the meaning of the word 'negotiate'?"

She smiled back at him, remembering clearly how she'd brought him around on that one…

Six years earlier…

"I don't do cuddling, babe," Wolf said as he pulled out of her arms and stood. He yanked his jeans on and left the room, muttering, "You got any coffee?"

Throwing a robe over her shoulders, she went in search of him. She found him at her kitchen sink, his palms resting on the edge, looking out the window. Walking up behind him, she slid her arms around his waist, her mouth pressing kisses between his shoulder blades. "Is it just cuddling you don't like or *all* touching? Cause I know you like the sex."

"I don't do cuddling, babe. I told you that."

She kissed his back again. "Is that non-negotiable?"

"Pretty much."

She pulled away, went to the fridge and opened the door. "That's gotta give you problems with the ladies, Wolf."

He turned and leaned against the sink. "What do you mean?"

She pulled a carton of orange juice out of the shelf in the door. "I mean, that's a big thing for women. And telling a woman there's no cuddling, *ever*. Baby, that's like telling a man, no blow jobs, *ever*. Like that'd fly. Not with any guys I've ever met. Hell, Jason would have been done with me the first night."

He folded his arms. "Really?"

"That boy liked his dick sucked. And I mean all the time. Two, three times a day, if he could get it." She waggled her eyebrows and smiled, then took a drink right out of the carton.

"Guess he was a lucky man, then. Not all girls are willin' to suck a man's dick, babe."

She looked at him frowning and put the carton back. "Honey, you're spending time with the wrong women."

He huffed out a laugh and had to agree. "Maybe so,

darlin'. Maybe so."

"Well, that just breaks my heart."

"Shut up and kiss me."

She held her ground and smiled. "Cuddling is important to me, Wolf. How important are blow jobs to you?"

"Babe, you serious?" His arms came uncrossed.

She crossed her arms and moved her head from side to side. "Um hmm. Guess we'll see who lasts the longest."

"Babe."

She raised her eyebrows.

"You're really bein' serious?"

"Yes, I'm *bein'* serious."

He shook his head and huffed out a breath. "Fine. I give."

"Hey, I'm not twisting your arm here." She pointed out.

He grunted out a laugh and grinned. "You're twistin' more than my arm, babe, and we both know it."

She smiled.

He grinned. "Come here, and we'll negotiate."

"I like the sound of that."

***

They smiled at each other, both reliving the memory. She had to admit, it was a sweet memory. Especially the sex and cuddling that negotiation had led to when she dragged him back to the bedroom.

Wolf twisted toward her, his elbow in the pillow, his head resting in his hand. He lifted Crystal's arm by the wrist and admired the new tattoo. "Pretty work. He do that?"

Her eyes fell to where he held her hand, and she knew he

was referring to Jameson.

"Yes."

He brought her hand to his mouth to press a soft kiss to her inner wrist. "It hurt to let you go, Crystal."

Her eyes lifted to meet his.

"Every time I'd hear someone say your name," he continued, "I'd feel the sting."

"I thought maybe you'd forget about me," she whispered.

"Impossible. With the way you make me feel, it'd take a fool to forget."

"How do I make you feel?"

"Like you're the only one who gets me. Been that way since the beginning. I remember the first time I saw you." He rubbed his thumb absently over her scar, his eyes staring off into space, lost in the memory. "Damn, baby, you knocked me off my feet."

She frowned. "When I was down on my knees picking up that broken glass?"

He nodded. "You looked up at me with those big eyes of yours, and I watched them climb my body. When they finally reached my face, and our eyes connected, damn, baby, felt it jolt through me like a fucking static shock."

She grinned. "I remember you were intimidating as hell… and then you smiled at me."

"What else could I do? You were so in awe of me," he teased.

She slugged his arm. "I was not."

"Was too."

"This is your fairy tale. Tell it how you want."

"Ain't no fairy tale. Exactly how it happened."

"In your dreams."

He dropped her hand and slid his palm to her belly. "I did think you were a dream." He leaned over to nip at her earlobe and whispered, "And now that you can ride, you're a biker's wet dream."

"Oh, really?"

"Wasn't a man standing on that curb when you rode by on that bobbed-tail chopper of yours who wasn't thinking it."

She searched his eyes "You like that I can ride? I thought you'd hate it."

"You looked hot as hell on that bike. Doesn't mean I still don't want you on the back of mine. That's where you belong."

"Is it?"

He nodded. "If it's where you want to be."

She stared at him, the words stalling in her throat.

At her lack of reply, he rolled to his back and pulled her against him, wrapping her in his arms. "Let's get some sleep."

She cuddled against him, turning his words over and over in her head. Did they mean what she thought they did? And if they did, is that what she wanted?

***

Wolf woke when his cell chirped. He reached out to the nightstand and shut the alarm off, squinting against the dim light coming in through the window. It was barely dawn, but he needed to get back.

His eyes moved to Crystal.

He knew she still worried where this was going. He was a long way from winning her back, but last night she'd let him in her bed, and that was a hell of a start.

He slipped from between the sheets and quietly dressed.

When he was finished, he stood looking down at her. He leaned over a fraction, not wanting to wake her, but needing one more touch before he left. One hand softly brushed over her hair as he gazed down at her. Then he dropped his hand and moved quietly toward the door.

***

Crystal's eyes slid open as a soft *click* sounded through the stillness of the apartment. She'd been awake. She'd heard him moving around the room, getting dressed, making his escape before he had to face her in the light of day. Like he always did.

Her eyes pooled.

It was just more of the same. Nothing had changed.

He'd gotten what he wanted, and then he left.

CHAPTER TWENTY-FOUR

The brothers stood in the metal shed, a large roll-up door was open to reveal the downpour outside.

Wolf leaned one hand on the doorframe and gazed up at the dark sky, muttering, "Shit weather."

Crash stood next to him, his arms crossed and his booted feet in a wide stance. "Wouldn't be Sturgis if it didn't rain at least part of the week."

"I guess."

Shades, Ghost, and JJ from the Birmingham Chapter also stood watching the sky.

Shades looked over at Wolf. "Heard you boys had a little run-in with the Death Heads last night. Sorry we missed the fun."

Crash grinned back at Shades, answering for Wolf. "Lasted about two minutes. You didn't miss much. They just happened to walk into the wrong bar. Have you boys had any trouble with them this week?"

"Not so far," Shades answered.

"But the week's not over. There's still hope," Ghost offered with a grin and a waggle of his brows.

"Where'd you guys end up last night?" Wolf asked.

"We took 12Gauge over to a couple bars in Deadwood. Slightly less crowded." Shades grinned.

Crash and Wolf nodded.

JJ eyed the sky and complained, "This rain is sucking the fun out of the day I had planned."

Ghost twisted to look at him. "That's right, you were all set to get your club tattoo today, weren't you?"

Shades looked over at him with a grin. "Has it been two years already? Huh. Seems like just yesterday you were runnin' that gauntlet."

Under the club's National Bylaws, number ten to be exact, no member could get a club tattoo until he'd been a full patched member at least two years. He also had to be accompanied by two other tattooed brothers when he got the ink.

"Two years today, VP."

"Well, hell, let's go get it done. Ain't gonna let a little rain stop you are you? Or are you afraid you'll melt?" Ghost grinned at him.

JJ looked at him hopefully. "You'll go with me? I need two brothers, and in this weather I figured there was no chance of convincin' anybody to ride into town."

Shades grinned over at him. "I ain't afraid of a little water. Besides, it looks like it's easing up."

"Damn. Thanks guys. That means a lot."

Shades looked over at Crash. "You want to tag along?"

Crash shrugged, taking in the lightening sky on the horizon. "Beats the hell out of standing around here. I'm game."

"Hell, count me in, too," Wolf replied, dropping his arm from the frame.

The five men moved toward their bikes.

***

Crystal stood at the window of the shop, staring up at the rain. It had started pouring a couple of hours ago, and the town had pretty much emptied out, including their shop. About twenty minutes ago, the film crew had wrapped up and left. Thank God.

Not that it wasn't a great opportunity for Jameson and the boys, but having them underfoot was tedious. They were constantly in the way. Not to mention every time a customer realized they'd be filmed—and had signed the required paperwork—somehow the tattoo process took twice as long. They dragged their feet over picking a design and really played up to the camera, causing the whole process to drag out.

"You think it's going to let up anytime soon?" Max asked, peering out the window.

"Hard to tell. Radar doesn't look good," Jameson replied, standing next to him.

The distant rumble of a hoard of bikes could be heard coming down the street.

"Well, the rain's not keeping everyone from riding."

They all watched as five bikes slowed and then backed into the spots in front of the shop, their back tires to the curb. The Evil Dead MC patches on the back of the riders' cuts were clearly visible. Three of the bottom rockers read Alabama. Two of them read California.

Crystal straightened, whispering, "Oh shit."

Jameson's eyes darted to her, then over her head to Max. She saw them exchange a look and could only imagine that Max had reported back to Jameson all about their night out and running into the MC at the bar.

"Uh, maybe we should close up," Max mumbled to his brother.

***

Wolf and Crash exchanged a look when they realized which tattoo shop their brothers had picked.

Wolf dropped his kickstand and threw his leg over the bike, turning to look up at the place. He pulled his daylight KDs off and wiped the water from his face.

Crash exchanged a look with Wolf. "You gonna be cool with this?"

"Yeah. Its fine, Crash. We talked."

"You do more than talk?" When Wolf didn't reply, Crash had his answer. His voice dropped to mutter in a disappointed or perhaps warning tone, "Brother."

"You were right. What you said. All of it."

Crash let out a sigh. "She gonna be good with us showing up here?"

Wolf moved with the rest of them towards the door. "I guess we're about to find out."

***

Jameson looked down at Crystal, and she could see the concern etched on his face. But it was way too late to lock up. The MC was already coming through the door. Their broad, leather covered shoulders filled the small shop. They were dripping wet, rivulets of water running off them to puddle on the floor.

Crystal's eyes ran over the men. Three of them she'd never seen before, but the other two she recognized well enough. Crash, with his gorgeous smile aimed right at her, she couldn't help but smile back at him.

Then her eyes moved past him to Wolf, the last man through the door. He looked at her with a serious expression, and then the corner of his mouth pulled up, and he winked.

"Got a customer for you, Superstar," Shades announced, pushing JJ forward.

Jameson looked from Shades to Crystal, almost as if he was questioning whether she wanted him to get rid of these men. Not that it would be an easy task, but if she knew Jameson, he'd make the attempt if it was what she wanted. He'd go up against five of them for her.

Shit, she couldn't let him do that. The last thing she wanted was a fight. And to be honest, she wasn't sure how she felt about them showing up. A part of her wanted to see Wolf again, but like this? She couldn't think about that now. She had to diffuse the situation, because Jameson was just standing there, and the biker was starting to narrow his eyes at him, not liking his hesitation one bit.

"There a problem?" he asked with a growl.

"No, not at all. I'll get the paperwork," she murmured and moved toward the counter. "Please, gentlemen, this way."

The biker eyed Jameson, and then turned toward the counter, shoving the younger member ahead of him.

As Crystal shuffled through the papers at her station, searching for a consent form, the stern biker with the VP patch on his right chest was making her nervous as hell. Crash leaned his elbows on the counter and grinned down at her.

"How's it going, Crystal?"

The man with the VP patch looked over at him. "You know her?"

"Crystal used to run the bar at our clubhouse."

"That so?"

"Crystal, this is Shades, VP of the Birmingham Chapter. Shades, Crystal."

The man smiled then, and what a smile it was. "Ma'am. Pleased to meet you."

"You, too," she replied, giving him a nervous grin.

"Think you can relax now, darlin'?" he asked as he turned up the charm.

"Of course." She handed the paperwork to the other man. "Sign here and here, please."

Shades grinned at Crash, and then stepped away from the counter.

Ten minutes later, Jameson was at work on a full back tattoo, working off the design on the club's cut. Jameson was a fast worker, but even so, she knew that it would take several hours to complete a tattoo that size.

They had a couple more customers that Max and Liam took care of, but in comparison to a normal day, they were pretty dead. The rain was keeping most people away. It varied off and on from a downpour to a drizzle and back again. Classic Sturgis, she was told.

***

As the afternoon wore on, Jameson was getting close to finishing JJ's club tattoo. Wolf had to admit, the man had talent. His lining was perfect, and his shading was flawless. Wolf stood with his back against the wall, one booted foot raised and propped against it. His gaze moved to the right. Crystal sat at her station, trying to look busy, while he and his brothers loitered around waiting for JJ's ink to be finished. *Trying*, being the key word. It was like she was trying to ignore him, and he'd had enough.

Dropping his booted foot with a thud, he pushed off the wall and strolled toward her. Her big eyes widen when she saw him coming. His hands landed on the counter. "Can you take a break?"

One of Jameson's brothers, who'd been sitting at his station nearby, walked over. Wolf had been introduced to the man, but for the life of him, he couldn't remember his name.

"Go on, Crystal. I'll cover the phones."

"You sure, Max?"

Max. That was his name. Wolf looked over at him. "Thanks, man."

Max nodded, and Wolf watched as Crystal rose and moved toward the front door. They stepped out onto the boardwalk with its overhanging roof. Crystal took a few steps away, her eyes on the distant mountains visible at the end of the street.

A group of brave riders rode up the street, a fine mist of rain spraying up from the tires of their big bikes. Wolf watched as Crystal hugged herself, her hands rubbing up and down her bare arms, exposed by the tank top she wore.

"You cold?"

"I'm fine," she said over her shoulder.

"Crystal, what's wrong?"

"Nothing."

"You're acting like you don't know me. Like we're strangers."

She shrugged. "I don't know what you're talking about."

Wolf blew out a breath. Women always denied when something was wrong, and it was always up to the man to play twenty questions trying to figure it out. They always thought you were supposed to know what it was. Perhaps he did, at least this time.

"Last night you said we needed to talk."

She nodded.

"I put you off. I'm sorry, I shouldn't have done that. But, damn girl, I get around you and the last thing I want to do is talk."

She remained quiet, her back stiff. If he wanted to get anywhere, he was going to have to do better than that.

"Can we talk now? Please?"

She shrugged.

Well at least she wasn't walking away. The wooden

boardwalk shook as four pairs of booted feet stomped out the door. Wolf twisted to look behind him. His brothers were moving toward their bikes. Apparently the tattoo was finished, and they were ready to roll. Four pairs of eyes glanced in his direction.

"You comin'?" Crash asked.

Wolf lifted his chin. "You go on. I'll be a while."

Crash nodded.

The rain had slacked off to a light drizzle. Wolf waited while four Harleys roared to life and pulled out. When they were gone, he turned back to Crystal.

"Go ahead. Talk," she bit out, her back still to him.

Okay. Guess he was going first. And it appeared what he had to say to her, he'd be saying to her back. He blew out a breath. Maybe that was for the best, because he was about to bring up the other women in his past, and he had a feeling she wasn't gonna like it.

"I've been with a lot of women, Crystal." He watched her arms tighten around her.

"That's nothing new, Wolf."

"Let me finish."

"Fine."

"You never asked me for anything, Crystal. Not a damn thing. Those other women, all they did was want shit. Expensive shit. Shit I sometimes could give them, more often not. But they never had a fucking problem asking. Always wanting shit. Always expecting shit." Then he softened his tone. "But, you? You never did. Not once."

"No, I didn't." She shrugged. "Maybe I should have."

She still just stood there, cold as ice, and it was beginning to piss him off. He felt the distance between them growing, and he didn't like it, so he moved in close, wrapped his arms around her and pulled her against his chest. Time to cut through all the bullshit. Time to man up and get real. He asked softly, "What do you want?"

Silence.

Then she responded quietly. "You know what I want. You. All I ever wanted was to be with you, to know you loved me. I never needed all that other material stuff, or empty promises. I never needed any of it. I just needed you."

"Me." It sounded so simple. But it was far from it. His mouth at her ear, he whispered, "And when you look in the future and you have me, what do you see?" He felt her swallow and saw her suck in her lips, and he figured she was gathering the courage to answer, to give him the truth. When she hesitated, he coaxed, "Tell me, sweetheart."

"I see a house with a white picket fence and a table full of kids."

Jesus Christ. He was wrong when he thought she didn't ask for much. Hell, she wanted it all. "A tableful?" he croaked.

At his response, she stiffened in his arms and tried to pull away, but he held tight. He cleared his throat and asked, "How big a table?"

His fear must have shown through to her, and apparently he'd pissed her off. At least, he hoped her response was just a pissed off jab to get back at him.

"A big table. Big enough to seat eight people."

"Christ, babe, you…" He swallowed. "You sayin' you want six kids?"

"Yup." She threw the response at him like a challenge. Jesus Christ, six kids. "You serious?"

"Yup." There it was again, that short, chopped-off word, bitten out the way only Crystal could do it.

"How about the standard two?"

"Nope. Six."

"Three?"

"Nope."

"Four?" How the hell did he just end up negotiating the number of kids he'd give her? Had he lost his fucking mind? When she stayed quiet, as if she was considering his offer of four, he panicked and backed away, his arms sliding from her. She whirled, her eyes searching his as he stepped back, his hand running over his face. At the look on her face, he knew he'd better fucking say something because he could tell she was about to bolt. "I suppose you want girls?" He shook his head, not waiting for her response. "I'm a boy producer."

"You can't know that."

"Yeah. I can. Cause God wouldn't be so cruel as to give a guy like me girls. Hell, not after the way I've…" He broke off, shaking his head.

"Relax, Wolf. I don't want girls. What would a tomboy like me want with girls? I'm not exactly the girly type."

A half grin pulled at the corner of his mouth. "You can be. I've seen your girly bedroom. I've seen your sexy lingerie, and on occasion I've seen you all dolled up. The other girls have got nothing on you, babe."

That got a smile from her, but she didn't respond, just slid her hands in her back pockets and looked off into the distance.

"Boys, huh?"

She nodded, still not looking at him.

His phone went off. Her eyes came to his as he pulled it from his pocket and put it to his ear. "Yeah?" His eyes flicked to the horizon as he listened and then replied, "Right."

When he disconnected, she was still watching him. Waiting. Expecting.

Shit.

"I have to go. But I want to finish this conversation. Okay?"

She nodded. "Sure."

He moved to her and took her in his arms. Dipping his head he locked eyes with her. "I'm not saying no. I just…I just need time to figure some shit out."

She nodded. "Sure." There it was, that word again. She sounded agreeable, but he could feel her pulling away on the inside.

"Babe—"

"Go. It's fine. I've got things to do, and so do you, obviously. It's not a big deal." She pushed out of his arms, but he pulled her back.

"It *is* a big deal. I meant what I said. I want to finish this conversation."

She looked up in his eyes, and he saw a hint of belief in hers. "Okay."

He nodded. "Okay."

He kissed her. Just a soft press of his lips to hers, and then he moved off the porch and strode to his bike. He had a lot to think about and right now blasting down the road with the wind in his face would help clear the bullshit out of his mind. It always helped him think clearly.

CHAPTER TWENTY-FIVE

Crystal walked out the back door with the trash bag and headed across the dark alley to the dumpster. It was closing time, and this was the last chore she had left. She'd just tossed the bag inside when she was grabbed from behind, a cloth slammed over her lower face. She breathed in a sickening chemical, and she wanted to gag. Struggling, she fought against her attacker, but it was no use. He was too big and too strong.

The last thing she saw as everything went foggy was a dark panel van, its side door already slid back, open and waiting.

***

Wolf rode up to the front of *Brothers Ink*. The lights were still on, but he knew they were closing soon. He'd texted Crystal earlier that he would be coming by to finish that conversation they'd started. Climbing off his bike, he stepped up on the boardwalk and entered the shop. A little bell jingled above the door, and four heads turned his way. None of them were Crystal's.

"We're closed," Jameson called out to him.

Wolf's eyes searched out the man, finding him standing by the back station.

"I just came by to see Crystal."

Jameson eyed him up and down. It had been clear when they'd been in the shop yesterday that the man hadn't wanted them in the place. Wolf had no illusions that it was because they were bikers, hell the town was full of them. Nor was it the colors on his back that gave the man pause. This was personal. His dislike was all about Wolf's interest in Crystal.

Jameson came to stand in front of him, his arms folded, blocking his path.

"You the one she met up with in Vegas?" he asked, throwing Wolf for a loop. How the hell did he know about that? Did she tell him? Had she told him everything?

"Yeah. I am."

"Didn't you already do enough damage?"

Wolf straightened, his jaw clenching. "She here or not?"

"She's out back, taking out the trash." Wolf's eyes moved to the brother that had spoken up. It was the one called Max. Wolf nodded once, his eyes returning to Jameson. They glared at each other for another moment before Jameson finally stepped aside.

Wolf strode through the shop to the back and flung open the back door. Stepping out, he slammed the damn thing. Motherfucker. No man was going to keep him from seeing

Crystal. He glanced around and saw the dumpster across the alley, but no Crystal. The hairs on the back of his neck stood up, that strange warning feeling he had tingling down his spine. He was about to look down the alley to the right, his hand already reaching for his weapon, when his head exploded in pain, and everything went black.

CHAPTER TWENTY-SIX

Wolf came slowly to consciousness and found himself strung to a tree, his arms stretched over his head and his boots a foot off the ground. His cut and shirt had been stripped off of him and sweat ran down his chest. It was dark, but there was a campfire burning a few feet away, its heat radiating over his skin and casting him in its golden light. It was quiet except for the crackling of the fire and the creaking of the thick rope he hung from. Then he heard rustling and struggling, and his eyes focused into the darkness and shadows on the other side of the fire.

A man on top of a woman. He strained to focus, his mind still fuzzy, and his head aching from the blow he'd taken to the head. Then he saw the DK cut and Crystal's long dark hair. She was struggling.

"Get off me," she pleaded.

"You're a little spitfire, aren't you?" a man's deep voice

growled. "That's okay. I like a little fight in my women. It's so much more fun when I break 'em."

Taz. Motherfucking *Taz.*

Wolf recognized his voice, the sick bastard. Taz was a member of the Devil Kings MC. One of the nastiest Wolf had ever come up against. He was a sick son-of-a-bitch with a mean streak, especially where women were concerned. And he had Crystal pinned on the ground.

A sick feeling rolled in his stomach, and all Wolf could think about was getting Taz's attention off Crystal, and the only way to do that was to get it on him.

"You mother*fucker*. Why don't you come over here and show me what a tough guy you are? Come over here so I can spit on that fucking DK cut of yours!"

That got the man's attention. He lifted off Crystal.

"Well, look who woke up."

Taz staggered to his feet, grabbing up a bottle of whiskey and taking a slug. He moved toward Wolf, and the flames illuminated his face. Wolf saw his milky eye, the drooping eyelid and left side of his face where it looked like his cheekbone had been caved in, which made the left side of his mouth droop as well. Taz was a very good-looking guy. At least, he was *before* Cole beat him half to death one night. None of them had seen Taz afterward, but obviously the beating had caused permanent damage.

"You're one ugly motherfucker now, Taz. Bet the girls puke when they get a look at your face."

Taz let out a sick laugh. "Well when I get done with you, pretty boy, no woman's gonna look twice at you. I'm gonna cut you up so bad, they'll run screaming."

Wolf watched as Taz pulled a knife from the sheath at his hip and moved closer. Wolf's eyes lifted over his head to meet Crystal's terrified gaze. He tried to will her to run with a look, dying inside because he wanted to shout it to her, but couldn't without tipping off Taz. Then he heard a chain rattle and saw the glint of metal and realized her ankle was chained to another tree.

Jesus Christ, no.

Wolf's eyes searched the site, trying to come up with a way out of this as he hung there, swinging slightly with every twitch of his body. His arms and shoulders burned like they were on fire from supporting his weight. His only thought was that if he could get his legs around Taz's head, maybe he could choke him out. But first he'd have to kick that knife free and hope that Taz didn't have another weapon on him. Even if Wolf did manage to choke him out until the asshole passed out on the ground, that would only leave them a few moments before he probably came around again. And Wolf was strung up, and Crystal was chained to a tree. Where would that leave them?

The knife flashed out, slashing across Wolf's abs, and a searing pain exploded through him. He hissed in a breath, determined not to scream. He mustered all his strength and kicked out trying to knock the knife from Taz's hand, but hanging there like a pendulum, he just didn't have the force he needed.

Taz laughed his maniacal laugh and slashed again and again. Wolf tried to defend himself with his legs, but soon they were slashed over and over as well. He could hear Crystal's screams over Taz's laughter. Finally, Wolf realized Taz had stopped slashing, and Wolf now hung there, swinging, blood pouring down his chest and legs.

Then the knife came flickering into his line of sight a moment before a searing slash cut across his jaw. This time Wolf couldn't hold back the scream of pain.

Taz chuckled. "Now we're getting somewhere."

Crystal screamed, begging him to stop. Taz ignored her.

"Bet you're wondering what this is about. Wondering why I got you strung up. Now I'll admit there ain't no love lost between our clubs. But this isn't club retaliation. This is personal."

"Personal? What'd I do to you?"

Taz bobbed his head from side to side as if mulling his answer over. "Not exactly what *you* did, more like your VP. But I know you were there the night he did this to my face."

Wolf watched him point to the left side with the tip of his knife.

"I think I owe him a little payback."

"Is that what this is? Payback?"

"Your VP's a hard man to get close to. He's always surrounded. Always got guys on him." Taz grinned. "But I have my ways of hitting back. Like burning that fucking whorehouse to the ground."

"That was *you*?" Wolf bit out against the pain.

"Yeah. Didn't see that coming, did he? Your VP thinks he's so fucking smart. He ain't so smart."

Wolf tried to laugh, but fuck if it didn't hurt like hell.

"And yet, you haven't been able to get near him."

"Well…if I can't get near your fucking VP, I'll just have to take my revenge out on you, won't I?" He shrugged. "I figure one Evil Dead member is as good as the next. Right?" When Wolf stayed quiet, Taz continued taunting him. "What's the matter, cat got your tongue? Maybe I should cut it out for you."

He let out a maniacal laugh again, and Wolf gritted his teeth, his body shuddering with pain.

"Not such a tough guy now, are you? I'll let you in on a little secret… When I'm done with you, I'll send your brothers a message letting them know where to find your body. Maybe I'll tack a note to you. Tell Cole that this is what I plan to do to his wife."

Taz began his slashing again.

Wolf didn't know how much longer he was going to be able to last without breaking. Then, as if heaven-sent, Taz's cell went off. Taz pulled it from his pocket, snickering at Wolf. "Don't go anywhere." Then he put the phone to his ear. "Yeah?"

Wolf's eyes lifted to Crystal's, wishing he could hold her one last time. He didn't want to give up, but fuck, he didn't see a way out of this. Then miraculously, Taz stepped away, crossing the campsite to the other side and stepping around the side of the panel van that was parked twenty yards away.

Crystal was already as close as the stretched chain would allow. Wolf looked at her. There were tears streaming down her cheeks, reflected in the golden firelight.

"Wolf," she whispered brokenly.

"Crystal." Wolf grimaced against the pain and tried to smile for her. "We never got to finish that conversation, baby."

"We don't need to, Wolf."

He nodded and tried to take the emotion out of his voice, knowing the only help he could give her now was to talk her through this and give her whatever strength he could that way. He continued in as calm a voice as he could muster, "You've got to talk him into taking that chain off you."

"He won't." She shook her head.

"Baby, it's your only shot at getting out of here. Come on to him."

She looked toward the van.

"Look at me, Crystal." When she turned her tear-streaked face back to him, he continued, "You do whatever you have to do. Do you understand me?"

She nodded.

"And when you get free, you run."

"I'm not leaving you."

"You have to. You run, and you don't look back. Promise me, baby. Promise me," he pleaded with her.

She shook her head. "I...I can't. Don't ask me to leave you. He'll kill you."

"He'll kill us both. It's my fucking fault you got dragged into this MC bullshit. He's gonna kill me. But don't ask me to watch him kill you, too. That's his plan—to make me watch him hurt you, and then kill you. He's just playing with me now, baby, making sure these cuts aren't deep enough.

He doesn't want me to bleed out too quickly. That'd ruin his fun."

"Wolf, I love you. I can't leave you."

"I love you, too, baby. Always have. And I'm so sorry. Christ, there's so much shit I'm sorry for. But you gotta listen to me now, Crystal. Promise me. You get free, you run. Promise me."

She just started crying harder.

Wolf could see Taz coming back.

"Don't let him see you cry, baby. He feeds off that shit. That piece-of-shit is not worth the satisfaction."

She looked up at him through her tears, and it broke his heart.

"Baby, you can do this. You've got to stop crying. Pull yourself together, sweetheart. I need you to be strong for me. Can you do that?"

She sniffled and wiped her face. Then she took a deep calming breath, and Wolf watched her try to get herself under control. It was almost as if a mask came over her face, hardening her resolve, and Wolf saw her strength return.

Taz walked back over. He took another hit off his bottle of whiskey.

"Can I have some of that?" Crystal whispered, drawing his attention.

Taz moved to stand over her. "Maybe, you ask nicely."

She was sitting on her knees, her feet tucked under her, looking up at him. Sliding her palm up his thigh, she asked, "Please?"

Wolf watched as Taz grinned down at her, then he took

her chin in a hard grip and yanked it up. He brought the bottle to her mouth and tilted it, pouring some down her throat. She gulped, trying to keep up with the stream. Finally, he loosened his grip on her jaw, and she coughed and sputtered, pulling back.

Taz let out a chuckle, but Crystal surprised him by tightening her hand on his thigh, squeezing. Wolf could see Taz's eyes flicker with heat and his grin fade. Crystal stared up at him, completely submissive, her other hand reaching up to stroke up his other thigh, moving slowly toward Taz's belt buckle. He stood there, unmoving, allowing her touch.

Wolf watched intently, hating to see this, his stomach turning at the thought of Crystal having to suffer that man's touch, but knowing in his heart, it was the only chance she had—her sexuality was the only weapon available to her. And if he was being honest, it was a longshot that Taz would let her free, no matter what she did.

Taz took a half step closer to Crystal, and hope soared in Wolf. *Maybe, just maybe.*

Taz took another slug of the whiskey bottle he still held in his hand, and Wolf said a silent prayer that Taz was just drunk enough to let his guard down.

Wolf hung there, swinging slightly, the rope creaking. He tried to hold himself completely still, wanting to give Crystal what might be her only shot, not wanting to draw attention to himself for fear the spell Crystal was casting over Taz would be broken. His skin was on fire, searing pain from a half a dozen slashes burning through him, making his muscles tighten and clench. He wanted to close his eyes

WOLF

against the pain, but he couldn't look away from Crystal, not for a second.

Wolf heard the clink of the buckle opening under her nimble fingers. He watched as Taz lifted his free hand and threaded his fingers through her hair, his fist closing tightly. She fumbled with his zipper, pulling his cock out.

Then Wolf silently swore as Taz pulled the knife from the sheath at his hip where he'd jammed it when his cell had gone off, and he tossed it well out of Crystal's reach. Goddamn, there went possibly her only chance. Wolf didn't think for a minute she'd be able to overpower him. Taz outweighed her by eighty pounds at least. Eighty pounds of solid muscle.

Crystal took him into her mouth, and began to give him a blowjob. Wolf gritted his teeth at what she was forced to do. As minutes passed, she began working him at an ever increasing pace. It wasn't long before the whiskey bottle was slipping from his hand, so that he could bury his fingers in her hair, controlling her movements with two fists pulled tight in her tresses. He fucked her mouth, his pace increasing. Finally, he came with a bellowing grunt, staggering a step as the strength drained out of him.

In a flash, Crystal had both hands curled around his waistband, fists wrapped tight around his belt, pulling him off balance and down to the ground at her side. Her right hand grabbed up the discarded liquor bottle, and in an arcing swing, she brought the bottle smashing down on Taz's head with a loud crack. He went limp instantly, and she began frantically digging through his hip pocket. She came up with the key and undid the padlock to the chain around her ankle. When the chain fell away she was scurrying across the ground in a flash, scrambling for the knife. Then she was staggering to her feet and moving toward Wolf. She reached for the rope strung diagonally and tied off at the tree trunk. She began sawing quickly through its thickness.

Wolf swung slowly as she sawed.

"You did good, baby. But you should run. You're wasting precious time on me."

"I'm not leaving you. We're getting out of this together."

They heard a groan from across the campsite. Taz stirred.

"Baby, he's coming around. Please, just save yourself."

Crystal sawed harder. She was only halfway through the rope that was as thick around as her wrist. But it was enough, because a moment later the rope snapped, and Wolf crashed to the ground. He groaned with the pain that shot through him at the impact. Crystal was on him a second later, trying to gather him in her arms, but he could see beyond her that Taz was staggering to his feet.

Wolf stuttered out frantically, "Get his gun, baby. Bring it to me. Hurry."

It was lying across the campfire on top of Wolf's cut. Crystal scrambled across the campsite and returned to Wolf with it. He took it from her, grabbing it in his hands which were still tied at the wrists. He lifted his arms, pain searing through his abdomen with the movement, and aimed at Taz.

Bam. Bam. Bam.

Taz's body jerked three times and slid to the ground.

Then before Wolf could say anything, the world faded to black as he lost consciousness from blood loss.

CHAPTER TWENTY-SEVEN

"Wolf! *Wolf!*" Crystal cried, trying to shake him. "Oh God, please don't let him die." She took the gun, shoved it in her waistband, and then ran to the van. Fumbling with the keys in her shaking hands, she managed to get it started and drive it across the campsite, stopping next to Wolf. Throwing open the cargo doors, she dragged Wolf over and somehow managed to roll his body inside, throwing the long thick rope around his wrists in with them. She jumped behind the wheel and tore out of there. The van bounced as she hit the highway, but when she looked back at Wolf, he was still unmoving.

"Oh, please God, let him live," she prayed as she tore down the highway. After several tense moments of hearing nothing but the roar of the engine and the tires on the pavement, she turned back to Wolf and yelled at him, "You can't die on me now, Wolf. Not after all this. Baby, please, talk to me." He didn't respond, and she pressed the accelerator all the way to the floor as she sped toward the only place she could think to take him—the Evil Dead's campsite. It wasn't too far, and they'd know what to do. They'd help him. If only she could get there, everything would be okay, she told herself over and over. Cole would make everything okay. He'd take care of this. He wouldn't let Wolf die.

She just had to get there, and everything would be all right.

"You're going to be okay, Wolf. We're almost there, baby. Just a little farther. Hang on, baby." She kept talking to him. In her mind, as long as she kept talking to him, he would be okay. "I see it, Wolf. We're almost there. You're gonna be okay. You're gonna be okay. You're gonna be okay. Everything's gonna be okay."

She flew into the camp, brothers scattering out of her way to avoid being rundown. When she came to a lurching halt, half the camp was running toward the van. She stumbled out and ran smack into Red Dog's arms. She was covered in Wolf's blood from having dragged him to the van.

"Crystal. Jesus Christ. What happened?" He caught her to him.

"It's Wolf. Taz almost killed him. Please. You have to get him to the hospital. He's bleeding so badly. Oh, God. There's so much blood. You have to help him," she pleaded brokenly, clutching at Dog's arms.

"Baby, calm down."

The other brothers were already scrambling into the van.

Crash yanked his shirt off and pressed it to one of the deeper cuts on Wolf's leg.

"Did he cut the femoral artery?" Green asked, leaning in and peering over Crash's shoulder.

"I don't think so, he'd be dead already."

Cole growled, "We need to get him to the hospital."

Mack shouted, "I got this." He jumped in the driver's seat.

Crash lay on the van floor holding Wolf, trying to stem the blood flow. Cole's eyes connected with Mack's through the sliding cargo door. "There's gonna be questions."

"I said I got it. Move!"

Cole slammed the side door, and the van sped off into the night.

Crystal watched it barrel down the highway toward town, her brain catching up with the action. "Wait, I want to go with him. I need to be with him."

Cole turned toward her, his eyes sliding over her tangled hair and blood drenched clothing. "Are you hurt?"

She shook her head. "It's all Wolf's blood. None of it is mine."

He nodded. "Good. I'll take you to Wolf, darlin'. I promise. But first you're gonna lead us to Taz."

"Wolf shot him," she replied, confused.

"Then his body shouldn't be hard to find," Cole snapped, then turned to his men. "Red Dog, Green, let's go."

CHAPTER TWENTY-EIGHT

Crystal led them back the way she'd come. Riding until she saw the flicker of a campfire off in the distance about fifty yards from the road. "Here. Turn here," she yelled over Cole's shoulder, as she sat on the back of his bike. She pointed toward the fire.

Cole, Red Dog, and Green went off-road. They pulled to the campsite, drawing their guns as they dismounted. Cole shoved Crystal behind him. Four sets of eyes scanned the campsite. No Taz in sight.

Crystal peered around Cole's shoulder, her eyes scanning around the campsite, searching the area where Taz had been before they left. "He's gone," she stuttered, unbelieving.

Red Dog stood next to the tree where Wolf had been strung up. The cut and frayed rope tied off to the tree trunk still lay on the blood-soaked ground. "Jesus Christ. Look at all this blood."

Cole turned to Crystal. "Where was he when Wolf shot him?"

Crystal stared up at him, half in shock.

"Show me," Cole snapped.

She pointed to the area, and Cole bent to look at the bloody trail that led away into the trees. He stood, motioning with two fingers for Dog and Green to follow him. They quietly followed the trail, guns drawn, and not fifty yards into the undergrowth, they found him.

"Going somewhere?" Cole asked a surprised Taz, who glared up at him and then huffed out a laugh as he kept scrambling back, his boot heels digging in the dirt and inching him along in a pathetic trail.

"Did you see what I did to your guy?" Taz grunted out in pain. "It was really you I wanted strung up in that tree. *You* I wanted to fucking slice up. For what you did to my face. I wanted to make you pay for it, you son-of-a-bitch." He laughed and grunted in pain again. "But I guess I'll have to settle for the fact that every time you look at your *brother's* scarred up face, you'll be reminded that *I* did that to him, and that it was meant for *you*. He took your punishment for you. You gonna be able to live with *that*?"

"Shut your fucking face, asshole," Cole growled. Then he raised his gun and emptied his clip into Taz, watching his body jump and jerk as each shot plowed into him. He didn't stop until he'd fired every one of the fifteen rounds, and there was just a clicking noise as he continued to pull the trigger over and over.

"Cole. You're empty, Brother," Red Dog whispered quietly from behind him.

Cole stared down at the man who had haunted his life for years, all the way back to when Angel had first come into his life, his chest sawing in and out with his ragged breathing. It was over. That sadistic son-of-a-bitch would never again torment anyone.

Green held out his gun to Cole. "Here, use mine."

That broke the tension, and Red Dog slapped him on the back.

Cole let out a deep cleansing breath, the weight of his hatred rolling off him.

Red Dog's hand on his shoulder tightened. "You know all that garbage coming out of his mouth was bullshit, right?"

Cole looked back at him, but couldn't bring himself to agree. His eyes dropped back down to Taz's lifeless body, and he ordered, "Bring some guys back and bury his body where no one will find it."

Green and Dog both nodded wordlessly.

"And bring me his cut."

"You got it, Brother. He got off too easy."

"I'd have strung him up from that fucking tree and tortured him all night, but I don't have a another minute to waste on this piece of garbage. We need to get to the hospital."

Cole turned and headed back to the campsite and Crystal. She stood with her arms wrapped around herself, her body trembling. He figured shock was starting to set in. He took her in his arms, holding her tight, his hands rubbing up and down her back. "He's dead, sweetheart."

"I heard so many shots. Are you all okay?"

"That was all me."

"Oh."

Cole glanced around the campsite. "What did you and Wolf touch? I need to know everything you put your hands on. We can't leave any traces of either of you being here."

"But all that blood. Wolf's DNA…"

"We'll bury the blood soaked dirt. What else?"

She pulled the gun from her waistband, and Cole took it from her, shoving it in his own waistband. "What else?"

She glanced around. "The keys, the van, the knife—it's still in the van, I think. Umm." Her eyes fell on the whiskey bottle, its glass shining in the dying embers of the fire.

"The bottle." She pointed and Cole's eyes followed, seeing it lying on its side in the grass.

He pushed away from her and moved, bending to pick it up. "What else?"

She pointed to another tree at the other side of the fire. "The chain."

That got Cole frowning, his eyes searching the ground. They fell on the thick chain and padlock. Jesus Christ. "He used that on *you*?"

She nodded. "It was around my ankle."

Cole's jaw clenched, wishing again he had the time to string Taz up and make him pay for all this shit as he gathered the chain in jerking movements. He paused, turning toward Crystal, his shoulders slumping under the weight of what had happened here. "How the hell did you both get free? I mean, Christ, Wolf's strung up to that tree, you're chained to this one..."

Crystal hugged herself. "Wolf talked me through it. I was getting hysterical. Taz got a call on his cell and walked off to take it. That gave us a few minutes to talk. Wolf calmed me down. Got me focused. Told me what to do."

"And what was that?"

"He told me I had to use the only weapon I had. Sex."

"Shit."

Crystal straightened. "I did what I had to."

"Darlin'." Cole didn't know what to say.

"I gave him a blowjob, and when his guard was down, I pulled him off balance and to the ground. And then I hit him with the bottle. Got the keys and freed myself. Wolf wanted me to run, to save myself. But I couldn't do that. I would never have left him."

She said the words loudly, as if she needed to convince him. Cole reassured her that wasn't necessary. "Crystal, I know you'd never leave him."

"By then Taz was coming around. I got the knife and started cutting Wolf down. He kept telling me to leave him and go. I thought I'd never get through that thick rope, but I kept sawing at it until it frayed and snapped. I brought the gun to Wolf, and he shot Taz three times."

Cole nodded.

"That's when Wolf passed out. I drove the van over to him and got him inside. I don't know where I had the strength to do that. Adrenaline I guess." She started shaking.

Cole approached her and put an arm around her, pulling

her to him. He pressed a kiss to her forehead. "You did good, Crystal."

She hugged him. "He can't die, Cole."

"He won't, babe. He's strong." Cole glanced around. "You touch anything else?"

"That's it."

"You sure?" His arms fell to her upper arms and pushed her back, looking down at her face. "You gotta be sure, darlin'."

She nodded. "I'm sure."

"Okay. Let's get out of here." Her eyes moved to Dog and Green in the woods. "They'll be cleaning this up all night. Let's get you to the hospital and your man."

She nodded, and they moved toward the bike.

CHAPTER TWENTY-NINE

Cole sat on a vinyl couch in the hospital waiting area. Crystal was snuggled against his chest sound asleep, her legs tucked under her. She'd finally given in to exhaustion after sitting up with Wolf all night. He'd yet to regain consciousness.

Cole felt his cell vibrate and slid his hand in his pocket to retrieve it. Looking at the screen, he smiled and put it to his ear, answering quietly so as not to wake Crystal.

"Hey, babe."

Angel spoke in his ear. "How's Wolf?"

"He's still unconscious. They repaired all the damage and gave him blood. They're watching him closely. They want to make sure he doesn't have any organ damage from the blood loss. His blood pressure is still pretty low. They're giving him something that's supposed to help with that. Now we just wait, I guess."

"Please tell me he'll be okay, Cole."

"He's a fighter. He'll pull through this, Angel."

"Okay," she said in a soft voice.

"How are the kids?"

"Fine. They miss their daddy."

"I wish I could say I'll be home soon, but I'm not leaving until we can bring him home with us."

"I know, honey. I wouldn't expect anything less. How is Crystal doing?"

"She's asleep on my shoulder at the moment. She finally passed out about twenty minutes ago."

"I should come up there and be with her. She probably needs another woman right now."

"Baby, she's fine. I'm taking care of her. All of the boys are."

"Are you sure? I could catch a flight and be there in a few hours."

"Angel, she'll be okay."

"All right, honey."

Just then Cole looked up to see several men in Evil Dead cuts troop into the waiting room that was already crowded with brothers. It was Shades and a couple of his guys, a big one named Griz, and a guy built like a brick house named Hammer.

"I gotta go, babe. Love you. I'll call you later." Cole disconnected and slowly slid from beneath Crystal, lowering her gently down on the couch. She didn't wake.

He stood and clasped hands with Shades. They bumped shoulders and slapped each other on the back.

"Heard about your guy. How's he doing?" Shades asked.

"He was sliced up pretty bad. Lost a lot of blood, but he's hanging in there."

Shades nodded, his voice low. "Any idea who did it?"

"A DK," he replied quietly.

"No shit?"

Cole nodded. "A sick motherfucker out of Cali named Taz. Went nomad a couple years ago. I've had several run-ins with him over the last few years."

"Hell, let's go get him," Shades offered.

"Already taken care of."

Shades nodded, understanding Cole's unspoken message. "Good."

Cole noticed the frown on Shades' face and knew there was something he wasn't saying. "What?"

Shades eyes moved to the two uniformed officers who'd been posted down the hall. Mack was right now down at the station giving some bullshit statement about an attempted robbery by a masked man. Cole wasn't sure how long that was going to fly. Cole's eyes followed Shades', and then returned to him. "Shades?"

"Look, you've got enough on your hands—"

"Yeah, and my patience is about shot, so just fucking tell me."

"We've got a guy missing."

"What do you mean 'missing'?"

"Didn't come back to camp last night. Haven't been able to reach him. He's not answering his cell. It just goes straight to voicemail and about an hour ago, it stopped doing even that."

"Maybe the battery died."

"Yeah."

"You don't buy it? He's not just off fucking some pussy?"

Shades shook his head. "He'd have found a way to check in."

"You're worried it's connected to this?"

Shades shrugged. "Strange coincidence."

Cole shook his head. "It's not related. Taz...he was acting alone. It was a personal grudge."

Shades nodded, but Cole could see the wheels turning in his head as he tried to figure out an explanation.

"Have you had any other trouble I don't know about?" Cole pressed.

Shades shook his head. "If it's not the DKs making a move against us...I don't know, there's been some shit going on with the Death Heads, but nothing we've been connected with."

"What shit?" Cole asked, frowning. This was news to him.

"Rumors mostly. Nothing I can confirm or pin down. But they had some kind of agenda this week. They've been all over town. Not just making their presence known, it was almost as if they were hunting something or someone."

Cole nodded. They had been acting odd. Not in their usual way. What the fuck was up with that? "So, who's missing? What's his name?"

"Ghost."

Cole nodded. He'd met Ghost the last time he was in Birmingham, and again at the campsite at the beginning of the week. He was a good man. "You want some of my guys to help you find him?"

"Nah. He'll turn up. Keep me in the loop on Wolf, yeah?"

Cole nodded. "Will do."

Shades and his guys left.

As they moved down the hall, they passed Red Dog and Green walking in.

Cole's eyes connected with them as they approached. His eyes swung down the hall to make sure the officers were still occupied, before he turned back to ask in a hushed voice, "Everything go okay?"

Dog nodded. "Found something."

Cole frowned wondering what the hell else could go wrong. "Yeah? What's that?"

Dog held out his fist, obviously holding something that he wanted Cole to reach out and take. Cold extended his hand, palm up, half-afraid at what Dog was about to drop into it.

Dog opened his fist and something cold and metallic fell into Cole's waiting palm. He looked down.

Two silver rings. Two Evil Dead rings. The two rings that were missing off Digger and Weed's bodies.

Holy fuck.

Cole's eyes darted up to bore into Dog's. "Where the hell did you find these?"

Red Dog's brows rose meaningfully as he delivered the

news. "Pocket of Taz's cut."

"That son-of-a-bitch," Cole hissed, trying to contain his rage in the quiet hospital waiting room.

"Exactly. Makes me want to dig him up and kill him all over again."

Cole quickly shoved the rings in his pocket, glancing again toward the officers.

"You think the DKs put out that hit?" Green asked quietly.

Cole shook his head. "Doubt it. Big Ed was by earlier to pay his respects. He and Mack seemed cool. I hinted around about Taz. His reaction? Seemed to me, he was fed up with Taz. Said he was starting to become more trouble than he was worth."

"They gonna have a problem when he disappears? I mean, just because he's not his Chapter President's favorite no more, doesn't mean the rest of his brothers don't care."

Cole shrugged. "To tell the truth, I don't give a fuck. It becomes a problem, we'll deal with it, won't we?"

"Damn straight," Green agreed with a grin, rubbing his palms together. "Wouldn't mind nailing a few more DK cuts to our wall. Something new to throw darts at."

A moment later, several more men walked in, but they weren't bikers. It was Jameson O'Rourke and his crew, and the man looked upset. He came to a stop, and the eyes of every brother in the room fell on him. He was quite the super star to this crew. The king of ink. And more than a few of his guys were in awe of being in the presence of such greatness.

O'Rourke's eyes scanned the room, until they fell on

Crystal, and then they lifted to Cole. "Thank God. She okay?"

"She's fine. One of my guys was hurt."

"The one called Wolf?" he surprised Cole by asking.

"Yeah." Cole frowned. "You know Wolf?"

"He came around last night just before she disappeared. I've been worried sick. I was about to file a police report when I caught wind of this."

"Caught wind of what?"

"Word on the street is the Evil Dead had a man in the hospital."

"News travels fast."

"Seems so," Jameson replied, his eyes again falling to Crystal.

Cole studied the man's expression and suddenly it slapped him in the face. This superstar, with his rock star bus and all his traveling sideshow, was fucking in love with Crystal. Well, Goddamn.

Cole extended his hand. "Cole Austin."

"Jameson O'Rourke."

Just then Crystal woke up, wiping a hand over her eyes. "Jameson? What are you doing here?"

"Been lookin' for you, Ace. You had me worried sick."

"I'm sorry. I…Wolf was hurt and…" She looked at Cole as if not sure how much to say.

Jameson's eyes also moved to him. "Mind if I talk to my employee alone?"

Cole gave him a hard look. "You can talk right here."

Jameson blew out a breath, obviously not used to anyone

not bending to kiss his feet. His eyes swung to Crystal. "Come on, Ace. You look beat. Let me get you out of here."

She got to her feet and approached him. "I can't leave Wolf."

Jameson's brows shot up. "You can't leave Wolf. The man who came to see you last night?"

She nodded.

His voice took on an edge. "The same guy who had you in tears the other day? The same guy who shredded your heart in Vegas?"

She nodded, looking embarrassed. "I love him."

He grabbed her by a forearm and held up her wrist, pushing her sleeve to her elbow. "You *love* him? The same guy you slit your wrists over?"

Cole stood shocked in place as he watched Crystal's eyes dart to him with shame and embarrassment.

"Jameson, please don't," she begged in a broken voice.

"Don't what? Don't try to stop you from throwing your life away for a guy who doesn't *give a damn?*"

Crash started to move toward the man, but Cole threw a fist up, hitting him in the chest and holding him back. Cole's eyes zeroed in on Crystal. "You want to explain that?"

When Crystal could do nothing but look up at him with big eyes pooling with tears, practically begging him to stop, to let it go, Jameson filled in the gaps.

"You never noticed? The bracelets she always wore to cover the scars? I finally talked her into letting me tattoo over them, but you can still feel the ridge of scar tissue. See for yourself if you think I'm lying." He glared at Cole.

Cole took her hand in his and gently ran his thumb across the inside of her wrist over the intricately beautiful tattooed cuffs. He felt the telltale ridge of scar tissue and his eyes lifted to hers. "Darlin', *why?*"

She whispered, "Please, Cole. Please don't make me talk about it."

He pulled her into his arms, and whispered, "Shit, babe. Why the fuck didn't you tell me?"

She clutched him tight, too overcome with emotion to speak, to do more than convulse with sobs.

Cole looked over her head at Jameson. "You want to give us a minute?"

A muscle in the man's jaw twitched, but he nodded and stepped back. Cole walked with his arm around Crystal, guiding her down the hall around the corner, where he pulled her to a stop. "Goddamn, Crystal. I know I don't know everything that's gone on, but this shit with you and Wolf has been messed up from the start."

She folded her arms tight around her, one hand coming up to wipe the tears from her cheeks.

"If you don't want to talk about it, I'm not going to make you."

"Thank you," she whispered.

"You know we all love you, don't you?"

She nodded, taking in a deep calming breath.

"So does that man out there."

She frowned at him. "Jameson?"

Cole nodded. "Yeah. Mr. Rock Star Tattoo God out there."

"You're crazy."

"Am I?" When she stayed quiet, he dropped a bomb on her. "You should go with him."

She looked up, confusion marring her face. "*What?* I can't leave Wolf."

"Yes. You can. And that's exactly what you're going to do."

"Cole—"

"Listen to me, Crystal. Go with O'Rourke. If Wolf loves you, if he wants a life with you, he'll come for you."

"But—"

"Crystal, Wolf's my brother, and I love him, but the man's got to step up sometime. If he doesn't now, he never will. I'm betting he will."

She didn't look convinced.

"Besides…" He grinned, trying to cheer her up. "You know Wolf's all about the chase. You run, he's gonna chase after you."

"He didn't last time I left."

"He will this time."

"I don't want to play games, Cole."

"This is not a game, darlin'. I'm bein' straight up with you now. You need to know you're worth it. *He* needs to know you're worth it. And by God, he needs to prove it."

Crystal looked down the hall in the direction of Wolf's room. "Just *leave* him? I don't think I can."

Cole leaned into her, putting a palm on the wall next to her head and got right in her face. "This is not up for debate. You're going. If Wolf's half the man I know he is, as soon as he's able to walk out of this hospital, he's gonna be coming for you, and when he does he's gonna haul your ass back to Cali."

"And if he doesn't?"

Cole straightened. "Then, sweetheart, you've got a man standing down that hall ready and willing to lay the world at your feet."

CHAPTER THIRTY

Wolf's eyes opened and moved around, taking in his surroundings. He was in a bed, wearing a hospital gown, an IV going into his arm. His eyes followed the line up to the bag hanging beside his bed. Monitors stood next to him, and then his eyes focused on the man sitting in the chair by the bed, flipping channels with the TV remote. Red Dog.

Wolf tried to move, and pain shot through him in a dozen places. He groaned. Christ that hurt. Then it all came flooding back. Taz and his knife… and Crystal.

Fuck. Was she okay? He tried to lift his arm.

"You dumb fuck, don't try to move. You'll tear your stitches," Dog growled, looking over.

Then suddenly Cole was there, standing in his peripheral vision at the foot of the bed. "So, you let a DK get the drop on you?"

"Where's Crystal? Is she okay?" He tried to sit up and grimaced against the searing pain in his gut and the lightheadedness that hit him.

"Take it easy, Brother. She's fine," Cole informed him.

"Who the fuck you think has been sitting next to your bed, you scary bastard?" Crash added as he came into view on the other side of the bed.

"Scary?" Wolf frowned, then reached up to gently touch the bandage on the side of his face, remembering. "Yeah, I guess so."

"You ain't gonna be a pretty boy no more. You got an ugly mug like the rest of us now," Red Dog teased coming to his feet.

Wolf's mind circled back, a little jumbled from the pain meds. "She's here?"

Crash and Red Dog exchanged a look with Cole, who explained, "She was. She had to leave. The traveling 'O'Rourke' show left town."

"She...she left with him?"

"Yeah, man. She left with him as soon as he showed up," Dog confirmed.

Crash looked across the bed at Dog. "Well, why don't you take Tiny Tim's crutch and beat him over the head with it."

"What? He *asked*."

Wolf lay back and stared at the ceiling as feelings of desolation washed over him.

"Look, Wolf—" Crash started, but Wolf cut him off.

"You guys mind leavin'? I'm kind of tired and my head's foggy."

Crash and Red Dog again looked at Cole, who jerked his

chin toward the door.

"You take care of yourself, Wolf. We'll be back in the morning." Crash patted Wolf's leg.

"Take care, man," Dog said. "By the way, you lucked out with some hot nurses. I'd insist on a sponge bath first chance you get."

Wolf nodded, his eyes still on the ceiling, but didn't even crack a smile at Dog's attempt at humor.

When Crash and Dog had left, Cole moved to the side of the bed, his hands resting on the metal side rail. "Before the law comes in for your statement, let's get your story straight."

Wolf nodded.

"Mack told 'em it was a botched robbery attempt. One guy in a ski mask."

"One guy. Gee, thanks for making me look like a pussy."

"Caught you unaware as you were taking a piss."

"How dignified."

"You fought over the knife."

"Where'd this fairy tale supposedly take place?"

"An alley behind that saloon on Main Street, round the corner from that t-shirt place."

"Wouldn't that leave a blood trail?"

"Crash used his t-shirt to staunch the flow of your blood. We dumped it and the knife in the alley. It's all good. Just don't change the story."

Wolf nodded, wincing as another wave of pain took him.

Cole's voice softened with regret. "This was all because of me, Wolf. Because of that beating I gave Taz in Reno."

Wolf looked over at him, taking in his tormented face, then back at the ceiling. "Don't beat yourself up about it, Cole. Taz was a sociopath."

Cole shook his head. "This was a message meant for me. He said as much."

Wolf frowned and looked back at Cole. "I may be a little fuzzy, but I *do* remember shooting the motherfucker. When the hell did you talk to him?"

"We went back after we loaded you off to the hospital. Crystal showed us where the campsite was, only he wasn't there."

"What the fuck do you mean he wasn't there?"

"He'd crawled off into the woods. Wasn't hard to find, just followed the blood trail." Cole attempted a grin. "Much better than breadcrumbs."

"And?"

"And before I emptied my clip into him, he told me it was all payback for Reno. *Apparently*, I'd fucked up his face."

That got a slight chuckle out of Wolf, which made him grimace in pain, his eyes closing. "Fuck that hurts. Don't make me laugh."

"Sorry."

"So, you saw the camp?"

"Yeah." Cole swallowed. "He was a sick motherfucker."

Wolf nodded. "It was a sick feeling, Cole. Being strung up in that tree, just hanging there like his personal piñata." He paused and looked over at his VP. "We've faced a lot of shit, haven't we?"

Cole nodded solemnly.

"But… Christ, Cole. I think that was the closest I ever came to checking out. I didn't think I was getting outta there alive."

He saw a muscle in Cole's jaw clench and knew this was an uncomfortable subject. Facing one's mortality wasn't easy for any man. Thinking you were the cause of another's near death was possibly worse. Wolf cleared his throat and caught Cole's attention. "Hey."

Cole's eyes, which had been staring at the bed, returned to him.

"It was Crystal that got us out of there. If it wasn't for her, I'd be dead."

"That's not the way she tells it."

Wolf frowned. "What do you mean?"

"She said you were the one who talked her through it. Got her to calm down enough to deal with it. Told her what to do."

Wolf looked at the ceiling, thinking about everything Crystal had done, everything she had endured to get them free. "I wanted her to go, save herself. But she wouldn't. She wouldn't leave me."

"You know she was never going to leave you."

Wolf looked over at him. "But she's gone now." *When I need her most.* Wolf left that part unspoken, but knowing Cole, he heard the silent words loud and clear.

Never one to hold back, Cole let him have it. "Yeah, she is. And whose fault is that?"

"Mine, I'm guessing."

"What goes around, comes around, Brother. I shouldn't need to tell you that."

"Well, I did take a blow to the head, so maybe I'm a little slow."

"You've never been slow, Wolf. Don't play fucking games with me."

Wolf frowned suddenly. "What day is it? How long have I been here?"

"It's Monday."

"You heading back?" Wolf knew they should have been gone yesterday.

"I'm not going anywhere until you're released."

"When's that supposed to be?"

"You tell me."

"Ha ha." Wolf closed his eyes, fatigue getting to him.

"Okay. How about a topic that's not funny? You know about Crystal's wrists?"

That got his eyes open. They darted to Cole's, and he swallowed. "I found out in Vegas."

Cole nodded, letting it drop. But then he twisted the knife. "I think Jameson has feelings for her."

"Oh, you two on a first name basis now?" Wolf grimaced against a wave of pain. Christ, he needed another shot of whatever the hell they'd been injecting into his IV.

"He'd give her a good life, Wolf."

"Shit, Cole." Wolf paused to lick his lips. He felt like he had a mouthful of cotton. "Kick a man when he's down, why don't you?"

"Just sayin'. Once you heal up and are out of that bed,

you need to pull your head out of your ass and figure out what the fuck you want. If it's Crystal, you better make your move before it's too late. If it's not, then you need to fucking let her go once and for all. Don't fuck up any chance at happiness she has. It's cruel to jerk her around like this. She deserves a hell of a lot better."

Wolf stubbornly stared at the ceiling again. "She does. The kind of life Jameson can give her apparently."

"What she deserves is to be loved. She deserves a man who's got the guts to give her that. She doesn't give a crap about some fancy life. If you haven't figured that out about her, you're dumber than I thought."

With that, Cole turned and stalked out. Wolf watched him go and felt the knife twist in his heart. Everything he said was the truth. All of it. Now he just needed to figure out just how brave he was. Brave enough to go after her or brave enough to live the rest of his life without her?

CHAPTER THIRTY-ONE

Wolf pulled up in front of the address and backed his bike in next to the line of four bikes parked with their back tires against the curb He set the kickstand down and took in the building. *Brothers Ink*. Jameson O'Rourke's place. It was two stories high, and he could see the man himself standing at a second floor plate glass window, looking down at him. Jameson lifted his chin, and Wolf returned the gesture, then headed inside.

The place was impressive. Sleek and modern. A reception counter stood across the entrance, tattoo stations lined behind it. No one stood at the counter. Wolf glanced around, but didn't see Crystal anywhere. One of the tattoo artists, who'd been busy sketching out a design, stood and approached the counter. He looked vaguely familiar from the shop in Sturgis. He was stocky, with a bald head, a thick beard and ten gauge onyx plugs in his ears.

"Can I help you?" the man rested his palms on the counter, his arms covered in ink.

"Is Crystal here?"

"Not at the moment."

"How about Jameson?"

"Do you have an appointment?"

Wolf took in the empty shop, and a grin pulled at his mouth. He shook his head as the man's eyes slid over his leather Evil Dead cut. "I think he's got time. Tell him Wolf wants to see him."

The man, who obviously was used to dealing with bikers, nodded once, then jerked his chin toward the seating area. "Take a seat. I'll tell him you're here."

Wolf just continued to stand, folding his own tattooed arms across his chest.

The man grinned, but turned to get Jameson.

As he stood waiting, Wolf couldn't help his gaze from traveling around the room. It was a classy set up. Since there were no customers at the moment, he assumed the four bikes outside must belong to the O'Rourke brothers.

Wolf didn't have long to wait. The guy returned and waggled two fingers at Wolf, indicating he come around the counter. Then he pointed to the open staircase in the back.

"Top of the stairs."

Wolf nodded and went up to find the entire top floor was an open-plan room, and all of it was Jameson's office. Framed sketches of some of his art lined the walls. A large modern glass desk sat at the front of the building.

Jameson stood near the window, one arm lifted high,

resting on the frame, the other held a rocks glass with about an inch of amber liquor in it. He downed it and looked over his shoulder.

"I wondered when you'd show up." He moved to sit in the chair behind the desk and nodded to one of the chairs in front of it. "Have a seat."

Wolf approached the desk. "I'll stand."

Jameson reached for a bottle and a second glass, sliding it toward Wolf and holding the bottle poised in the air. "Come on. Let's have a drink and discuss this like men."

Wolf ground his teeth together, but took a seat, leaning forward, his elbows resting on his knees.

Jameson poured a drink for Wolf and refilled his own. Lifting it, he toasted, "To Crystal."

Wolf wanted to throw the drink in his smug face, but found himself lifting the glass. "To Crystal." After he downed the shot, he glanced around the room looking for photos or any trace of her existence in his life. "Where is she, by the way?"

"First let's talk about why you're here."

"I think you know exactly why I'm fucking here."

The side of Jameson's mouth pulled up. "I suppose I do. What I'm not sure of is your intent."

"My intent?"

"What can you give her?"

Wolf looked around at the fancy office, knowing he couldn't compete with all this. But fuck if he was going to let that stop him. He stared down Jameson. "None of your fucking business."

"I'm making it my business."

Wolf let out a frustrated breath. Fuck, if convincing Crystal's boss was what he had to do to get to her, then he'd do it. He'd do whatever it took. "What do you want to know?"

"You've done nothing but cause her pain. What's different now?"

"I'm ready to give her what she wants."

"You think you know what she wants?"

"Yeah, I do."

"And what's that?"

"A white dress. A houseful of kids. Me. And I'm here to see that she gets it. All of it." He leaned back. "You looked surprised, O'Rourke. She didn't share those dreams with *you?*"

"So you think you know what she wants, but what about what she needs?"

"A man to hold her when she's sad, pick her up when she's down, and when she's cryin' to ask her 'whose ass are we kicking today, baby'?"

"That's pretty funny, when *you're* the one that's always making her cry. You've been the biggest cause of her tears."

"Yeah, well those days are fucking over."

"Right."

"If she's over me, there's no reason for you to stop me from talking to her, is there?"

"She still loves you. I know that. But that doesn't mean you can ever make her happy."

"Gonna damn well try."

Jameson stared at him, unmoving.

Wolf's brows rose, challenging. "You're not gonna keep me from her. You and I both know that."

Jameson leaned back in his chair, one hand running over his chin, his eyes on Wolf's face. "I was sorry to hear about what happened in Sturgis."

The change in topic threw Wolf for a moment, but he quickly recovered and bit out, "Yeah, I heard you came to the hospital."

Jameson nodded. "Crystal was a wreck."

"And that was my fault, right?"

"Didn't say that, but you do lead a dangerous life."

They stared each other down, and Wolf knew what he was thinking. "I can protect her, keep her safe."

"You both barely escaped with your lives."

"And the man who did it is dead."

"But he almost succeeded."

Wolf surged to his feet. He'd had enough. "Yeah. And I carry the scars to prove it, don't I?" He yanked his shirt up, revealing the ugly scars across his chest and ribs where Taz had slashed him. Revealing the fact that the scar on his face wasn't the only one he carried. He watched Jameson's eyes drop to take them in. Not with horror, but almost with a doctor's studied gaze...or maybe an artist's.

"I could help you with those."

Wolf let his shirt fall, the man's response taking him aback. "What?"

"I could cover those for you." He shrugged. "If you want. Unless you like having that reminder on your skin."

Wolf pointed to his face. "I've got a reminder staring me in the mirror every fucking day."

"That's a thin white scar, buried halfway into your beard," he said, almost dismissing it as if those facts somehow made it okay. "But the ones on your torso are much worse. The red raised scar tissue—"

"I know what they look like. I don't need you to describe them to me."

"So let me cover them. I do good work."

"So I've heard." Wolf's eyes narrowed. "Why?"

"Why am I good?"

"Why do you want to do this for me?"

Jameson considered him a long moment as if he was trying to figure that out himself. Finally, he replied, "Let's just say it's a slow day and leave it at that."

Bullshit. This was about Crystal. He wanted to do this for Crystal. Suddenly he felt like it was just another hurdle he had to jump. And Wolf had already resolved himself to the fact that he'd jump every hurdle God put in front of him to get her back. So if this was just another one, if this was some sort of fucked up hazing or test or gauntlet Jameson was throwing down, so be it.

"Fine. Let's get started."

The corner of Jameson's mouth pulled up. "I pick the designs."

"The scar on my ribs, I pick."

"All right. I'll give you that one," Jameson conceded. "You do know the ribs are one of the most painful areas to get worked on."

"Well, it's a good thing I lost sensation around the scar then, isn't it?"

***

A couple hours later, Wolf was still sitting in the chair as Jameson finished up the tattoo on his chest, having already completed the one on his ribs under his left arm. Jameson's brothers, whom he'd introduced as Liam, Max, and Rory, stood around them, their arms folded, their legs spread, watching their brother work.

They'd closed the shop for this, which had surprised Wolf, but then, nothing about this bunch would surprise him anymore. They'd taken to him like a pack of brothers meeting their sister's intended for the first time. Wolf wondered when the shotguns would come out.

Where the hell was Crystal, anyway? She hadn't made an appearance, and he'd been too stubborn to ask again after his first few times were rebuffed.

He'd find her. When he was done with these damn tattoos, he'd find her if he had to hunt her ass down.

He glanced down at the needle Jameson was wielding. He had to give the man credit. His work was phenomenal. The vibrant colors of the wolf's head were amazing, the detail unparalleled He'd captured his spirit that was for sure. He'd been half afraid the man would give him a piece of shit just as payback, but the man was an artist and obviously took his craft seriously.

The design on his ribs was just as amazing.

The buzzing clicked off as Jameson shut his machine down. "Finished."

His brothers stepped closer, examining the final product. They nodded their approval, but their eyes still bore into him coldly.

"Scars are totally gone. You can't even see them with the texture of the fur," Max remarked.

"I agree. You did wonders with the colorations, Jamie," Liam added.

Jameson snapped off the black sterile gloves, his eyes on Wolf. "I take it I don't have to explain tattoo care to you."

Wolf rolled his eyes. "I think I've got it down."

Jameson spun Wolf's chair around to face the mirror on the wall, giving him a better look at the finished product.

He sat up and leaned forward, his eyes watching in the mirror as the four men took in his full back Evil Dead tattoo. His eyes returned to the wolf on his chest. It was fierce and proud, and he couldn't have been happier with how it turned out. The men were right; the scars were completely obliterated by the design, as if they'd never been there.

He heard a door open and close in the back of the shop, and then Crystal's voice.

"What's going on, guys? I drove by and saw the closed sign, but the lights were all on. Aren't we open tonight?" She came around the corner from a back hallway and stopped dead, taking in the scene.

Wolf's eyes connected with hers in the mirror, and he watched the stunned expression on her face. Then her eyes dropped to the design on his chest, and her mouth parted.

Jameson's brothers stepped back as she came forward, almost as if her feet were moving her against her will, pulling her toward him.

Wolf sat there frozen, and then suddenly his feet were moving him unconsciously as well. He found himself standing, turning to face her.

They stood staring at each other for what seemed like forever. Then Wolf suddenly came to his senses and realized she was probably waiting for him to say something. He'd rehearsed this moment on the long ride here, going over his words again and again. But now as he stood in front of her, his mind was a blank.

"Crystal."

"What are you doing here?"

"I just rode 1200 miles to see you, and that's all you've got for me?"

Her eyes moved uncomfortably to Jameson, and she licked her lips, frowning. "You came to get work done? Here?"

"I came to see you." His eyes moved to the men, who obviously weren't going to give them any privacy, and then back to her. "Can we talk outside?"

Her eyes again dropped to the wolf on his chest. "Don't you need a bandage first?"

Jameson was already reaching for one. He pressed a large gauze square over Wolf's chest and taped it in place.

Wolf noticed Crystal's eyes taking in the bandage he already had taped under his armpit against his ribs, but she didn't ask. He shrugged into his flannel shirt, but didn't button it up. Then he put his cut on and followed her down the hall.

She stalked out the back door into the alley and stopped a few feet from the door. Wolf took in her rigid back. He looked up. Dusk had fallen, and a light rain had started up. She didn't care. She stood in it, letting the tiny droplets form a sparkling net of crystals on her hair. Finally she turned to face him.

"Why did you come?"

"I told you why. You."

"Me?"

He nodded.

She folded her arms and looked down the alley. "You drove 1200 miles for nothing then. I've got a great guy in there. One who won't hurt me."

"Then why are you standing out here in the rain with me?"

She kept her eyes averted, her arms folded, and her jaw tight. But he took solace in the fact that she didn't have an answer for that one. It meant he still had a shot. At least he hoped he did, she was still standing here listening.

But he could also see she was in full defensive mode, and he couldn't really blame her. He'd hurt her too many times. Still, he couldn't let that stop him. Not if any of this mattered. And it *did* matter. It mattered a hell of a lot. He'd come too far emotionally to give up now.

She huffed out an impatient breath. "What do you want, Wolf?"

"We'll get to what I want in a minute. First, I need to know what you want."

"What I want?"

"That future you had all planned out with the white picket fence and the four kids…"

"Six."

"Four."

"Whatever."

"Were you serious about that?"

She shrugged.

"What if I told you I want that, too?"

"I'm not sure I'd believe you. I'd think you were just saying that because you feel guilty about what happened in Sturgis. But that's no way to start a life together…based on you trying to make up for something. It has to be what you want."

"I do feel guilty about what happened in Sturgis. I probably will, 'til the day I die. But that's not what this is about."

"What is this about then?"

"I know what I want. I know it took me a fuck of a long time to figure it out. But it's you and all the rest of that dream of yours."

She shook her head, her eyes still staring down the alley, but he saw the emotion in them.

"Crystal, look at me please." She took her sweet time, but finally her eyes came to his. "I know what kind of life I lead, and I know that has never even been our biggest problem. I know the biggest obstacle has always been me pulling back, guarding my heart, pushing you away. I know I don't make it easy for you. I know I'm hard to love. I know all that, Crystal, all of it, and yet I'm still standing here asking you for another shot.

"I know you deserve better. I know that. Hell, I've probably crossed every line you've ever drawn in the sand, more than once. Hell, a dozen times. And yet by some fucking miracle of God you still love me."

"Do I?"

Wolf swallowed. Well hell, he hadn't expected her to make this easy, had he? "I wouldn't be standing here if I didn't believe in your love. I know you, Crystal. When you love, you love deep and strong, and I'm hoping *forever*. So here I am, asking you to give me one more shot. One last shot, Crystal. I swear to God, I won't let you down again."

"I'm supposed to just believe that? What's different this time?"

"I am," he didn't hesitate in answering.

"*You* are? How?"

"Because I finally pulled my head out of my ass. Is that what you want to hear?"

"Go on."

Shit, she really wasn't going to let him off easy. She'd have him down on his knees groveling in another minute. Fuck that. He still had some pride. In two steps he had her upper arms in his hands as he stood over her.

"I love you, Crystal. I always have. Through all of it, that's never wavered. And you've been the single stabilizing force in my life, the only true north on my fucked up compass. It's why I always come back to you. You are home to me."

She looked up at him with glassy eyes and whispered,

"It's not the coming home part that's so hard. It's the leaving part I can't take anymore."

"That's done. I'm done running, Crystal. I'm done being so afraid of failing you that I let that fear stop us from moving forward. I was never afraid of committing to you. I was afraid of not living up to your expectations."

"All I wanted was your love."

"You have it, sweetheart. You have my heart. You are my heart."

"But will it last? Will you change your mind in a month and want out?"

He pushed his unbuttoned shirt to the side and tore the bandage over, revealing her name scrawled across his ribs in scrolling cursive letters three-inches high.

"I'm betting on forever."

Her eyes fell to the tattoo.

"You're over my heart. Right where you've always been, Crystal. I love you. I always have."

Her eyes locked with his. "Jameson put that there?"

Wolf nodded.

"He never tattoos names. Never."

"He made an exception for this one."

Her eyes dropped to the beautiful scrollwork.

"You see a side of me no one else does, a side no one else ever will, a side no one understands but you. There will never be anyone else for me. No matter how long I live. Crystal, you're the love of my life, and you always will be."

"Wolf." Her voice was soft, trembling. "I'm afraid of being hurt again."

He took her face in his hands. "Baby, I know you are. And I want to promise you I'll never hurt you again. But I'm a guy, and guys have a tendency to fuck-up. So, I'm not gonna promise you I won't fuck-up. But I *can* promise you I will never walk out that door again. If you'll have me, I'm in it for life."

He stared down at her, waiting. Jesus Christ, he didn't know if he could bear it if she refused him now.

Her hands closed on his wrists, and she pulled away from him. "I can't."

He took a step back. "Baby, I know I fucked up—" He broke off when she remained silent, shaking her head. He swallowed as dread filled him. "It's done then? We're finished? I'm too late?"

He watched a tear roll down her cheek.

"If you want me to leave, I will. And I won't bother you again." He paused. "For what it's worth, Crystal, I'm sorry. For all of it." He turned and stalked back inside, through the shop, past the questioning looks from the O'Rourke's who glanced furtively toward the back door. He strode out the front door and down the steps to his bike.

He stood there a moment, his breathing heavy, his heart pounding and a sick feeling clawing at his gut. Jesus Christ, it was over. He couldn't believe it, couldn't wrap his head around it. She was done with him. Really and truly done with him.

He yanked on his gloves and strapped on his helmet, the whole time praying he'd hear the door behind him open, and her voice telling him to stop. But those sounds never came, so he threw his leg over his bike, lifted it up off its kickstand and fired it up. Then he roared off down the street.

***

Crystal stood motionless in the alley, his words replaying in her head as she turned over and over everything he'd just said, everything he'd just finally after all these years admitted to her. All the words she longed to hear for so long.

It wasn't until she heard the echoing rumble of his bike firing up out on the street that she snapped out of it. He was leaving!

She ran for the door and dashed through the shop. Two steps from pulling the front door open, she saw him through the plate-glass window as he pulled away from the curb to roar off down the street. She yanked the door open and stumbled down the stairs, dashing into the street as he turned the corner vanishing out of her sight.

Out of her life.

She stood there staring down the street, her heart pounding. He was gone. He was really gone this time.

The door opened behind her, and she turned with tears rolling down her face to see Jameson standing there.

"You love him, don't you?"

She nodded, whispering brokenly, "He's gone."

"It's not too late."

"Jameson, he's gone."

"We can still catch him." He held the keys to his bike up. "If you want him."

***

Wolf rode mindlessly, his brain on autopilot, his eyes

unseeing down the long stretch of endless highway rolling out before him.

He'd finally come to his senses, finally figured his life out only to find out it was too late. *He* was too late, and he had no one to blame but himself. He'd done this. He was the one who had squandered so many chances until there just weren't any left.

He couldn't blame her for not trusting him enough to believe the things he'd told her. But it still hurt like hell. It still tore his heart out. What was left for him now? He could only imagine a lonely life stretched ahead of him. Sure he had his brothers; he had the club. But they would never fill the empty hole in his life where Crystal used to be. Nothing would ever fill the void she'd left in his heart.

He couldn't even imagine trying again with someone else. What the hell would the point be? No other girl would ever be her. No one would ever be what she was to him.

She'd just sentenced him to a lifetime of hell, and he was guilty of every action that put him there. He'd brought it all down on himself.

The roar of a fast approaching Harley caught his ear, and his eyes checked his side mirror.

One bike, coming up hot.

It wasn't until it was almost upon him that he saw there was a passenger, a woman with long dark hair. Then his eyes focused in on the rider and flared wide when he recognized Jameson O'Rourke.

Wolf's hand let up on the throttle almost unconsciously, and then he was pulling over, coming to a stop on the gravel shoulder. He barely had time to drop the kickstand and throw his leg off the bike, before Crystal was off the back of Jameson's bike and running to him.

He caught her in his arms.

"Don't go," she muttered in his ear as he held her tight. Then she said the words he'd longed to hear and never thought he would again. "I love you, Wolf. Please don't go."

He pulled back, taking her face in his gloved hands and stared into her eyes. "Say it again."

"I love you. I love you, Wolf."

"Tell me you'll come home with me."

She nodded, her eyes pooling.

"Say it."

"Take me home, Wolf."

"If you ever try to run again, I won't let you," he warned as he took her in his arms again, holding her tight. He looked over her shoulder at Jameson.

The man smiled, and then fired up his bike and pulled out, making a U-turn back toward Grand Junction.

Wolf twisted his head, bringing his mouth to her ear and whispered, "Let's go home, baby."

EPILOGUE

Crystal—

Wolf was on the couch watching a football game. I sat down next to him and asked, "Who's playing?"

"Dallas and Denver. Game just started," he replied, not taking his eyes off the television.

"Hmm. My team and your team."

"My team's gonna whoop your team's ass," he guaranteed with a devilish look.

"Oh, really?"

"Yup. You can take that to the bank."

"Wanna bet?"

His eyes slowly moved from the game to me, and the corners of his mouth pulled up. "What did you have in mind, darlin'?"

"Hmm." I looked at the ceiling contemplating. "If you win, you get anything you want."

That got his attention, and he sat up a little straighter. "We talkin' sex, here, woman?"

I nodded with a smile.

"And if you win? What do you want, baby doll?"

I thought for a moment, and then shocked him by saying, "I want you to chase me through the house. I want you to be aggressive and dominant, and show me who's boss."

"Damn, girl." He shook his head amazed.

"What? Too much?"

"Hell, no. I'm in."

"So, you never said what *you* wanted."

He gave me a sly smile. "I didn't, did I? Maybe I'll just keep you wondering."

"Should I be worried?"

"I don't know. Should you?" He grinned and waggled his eyebrows. "Maybe we should make a side bet on the halftime score," he suggested.

"Hmm. That could keep it interesting. Such as?"

"Such as if my team is up at halftime, I get something."

"Like?"

"I get to spank your pretty little ass as many times as equal to their score."

"Spank me, huh?"

"And if your team is up, what do you want?"

"I'll just keep *you* wondering."

"Ahh. Should *I* be worried, darlin'?"

I just smiled.

***

"Fourteen-ten, Cowboys. Time to pay up, baby." He

pulled me on top of his lap, face down, slid his hand in the waistband of my shorts, and pulled them down. His hand smacked down on my cheek with a firm *crack*.

"Hey! What are you doing?"

Smack. Smack.

"Spankin' your ass, baby."

"You didn't say anything about being naked. Oww!"

Smack. Smack.

"It ain't a good spankin', if it ain't on a bare ass, baby doll. Now hold still or I'll lose count and have to start all over again." He continued smacking me on each cheek, watching them turn a rosy pink. "Damn, baby. I ever tell you, you've got a pretty ass?"

Smack. Smack.

I just moaned, my head down, my hands clenching the couch cushion.

"You okay, honey?" He rubbed his hand over my bottom, and then slid his fingers between my legs. Finding me wet, he rubbed rhythmically. "This is turning you on, isn't it, baby? You're all wet."

I moaned.

"You like it. Admit it."

Smack. Smack.

I moaned again, thrusting my ass higher.

"Say it."

Smack. Smack.

"Yes."

Smack. Smack. Smack. Then his fingers were back, delving inside me, rubbing me. "You're turning me on, baby.

Something fierce."

I moved against his hand. "Please, baby."

"You want something, honey?"

"You know I do."

"Well, since you took your whoopin' like such a good girl..."

I moaned as his fingers continued, bringing me to the edge and then over.

He leaned down and whispered in my ear, "Damn, baby. I love to watch you come."

***

When the game was over, Wolf flicked it off and threw the remote on the coffee table. "Damn, Broncos. I can't believe we blew that pass. He was wide open."

I just looked at him and smiled.

A grin spread across his face. "Oh, yeah. I've got a debt to settle up, don't I? How fast can you run, baby doll?"

"Do I get a head start?"

"Sure. One-two-three."

I squealed and leapt off the couch, heading around behind it.

Wolf jumped up, vaulted over it, and was two feet behind me. I darted around the dining room table. I could tell he was contemplating vaulting over it, but it held a crystal vase that was his grandma's. He stalked me, first to the right, then to the left.

"I can bide my time, baby. You know I like a good chase," he growled with a wicked smile.

I made a dash for the kitchen and got around to the other

side of the small dinette set in the breakfast nook. I faked to the right, to the left, to the right again. He stalked around until he was on the far side and I was near the hall. Then he smiled, reached out, and shoved the table out of his way.

I screamed and took off, running as fast as I could down the hall. He tackled me going up the stairs, catching me by the ankles. I fought and kicked, and managed to scramble free to dash up the stairs. He caught me again as I rounded the corner to the master bedroom, his body tackling me into the wall as his arms came up on either side of me, bracketing me in.

I was pushed face-first against the wall, his chest pressed up against my back. His breathing was heavy in my ears as he leaned his head in close. My heart was pounding. He slid his left arm around my neck until my chin was resting in the crook of his elbow. I slid my hands onto his arm, loving the feel of his muscles.

He pulled back on his arm, just enough to show me who was boss. Then he leaned down and whispered in my ear, taunting, "Now what're you gonna do, baby?"

My chest rose and fell with my quickened breath.

When I didn't respond, he tightened his arm just a bit and whispered, "Tell me."

I whispered back, "Submit."

"Mmm. I like the sound of that." His voice purred in my ear. "You're mine, woman. You understand? To do with as I please."

A shiver ran down my spine as a sexual thrill shot through me at his words. I answered breathlessly, "Yes."

He kissed my neck, nuzzling the soft skin below my ear. "Got your blood up, didn't it?" I taunted.

"You know it, darlin'. Was that your plan all along?"

I smiled. "Maybe."

He put a couple of inches between us, and out of the corner of my eye I could see his gaze rove down my back and over my ass. His right hand slid up my thigh, pushing the loose material of my running shorts aside, running his hand over my exposed cheek. He rubbed his jaw along the side of my head, his mouth hovering over my ear again as his hand slid around my hip bone, still inside the loose material. He pressed his palm against my pelvis and pulled me against him. "More than just my blood is up. Can you feel that, baby? I'm rock hard. Can you feel how much I want you?"

I nodded. "Tell me. Talk dirty to me."

His palm slid down, his fingers delving inside me. "You're so wet, baby. I can't wait to slide inside you. Bury myself all the way to the hilt. Feel you pulse around me, your hot wet pussy clenching around me."

I moaned.

"You're gonna give it to me. Anything I want." He spun me around and pushed me back against the wall. He took my hands in his, lacing our fingers together and held them pressed to the wall above my head. He brushed his lips over mine, just barely touching them. When I tried to deepen the kiss, he pulled back, letting me know he was in control, and we were doing this at his pace, not mine. His mouth brushed mine gently again and again, until I was crazy with need. When he had me writhing and moaning, he bent and scooped me up, tossing me over his shoulder like a sack of potatoes, and carried me down the hall to the bedroom. He kicked the door shut and dropped me on the bed.

I bounced once before he came down on top of me.

I stared up at him—this man I loved with such passion I couldn't even remember a time in my life when he wasn't in it. It was as if I hadn't really started to live until I'd met him. Now, every night I go to sleep with him lying next to me. Every morning I wake up with his arms around me.

He grinned down at me.

And I swear to God, that smile was all I'd ever need to be happy.

Wolf—

Crystal and I were in bed, she was admiring the new tattoos that covered my scars. She especially loved tracing with the tip of her finger the swirling cursive swoops of her name on the slash across my ribs just next to my heart. It had covered the wicked scar beneath well, as did the wolf tattoo on my chest.

I still have a scar on my face. No tattoo would ever cover that, and my beard only covered part of it. I looked up at the framed picture hanging above the bed. The picture Crystal had found. "Like the picture, babe."

It was a black and white photograph of a lion with a scar on its face and a saying below that read:

Never be ashamed of a scar.
It just means you were stronger than whatever tried to hurt
you.

"We both have scars now," she said. I took her hand and brought her palm to my cheek, pressing it against the scar on my face.

"Does this bother you?"

She shook her head at me, grinning. "That scar just makes you look even more badass and sexy."

"Ya think?"

"Definitely."

I glanced back up at the picture. "Big Cat...I can definitely relate. Guess you tamed this big cat."

It was ironic, I thought, as I considered that pacing cat inside me. It wasn't so restless anymore. In fact, it hardly paced at all. I smiled. Then I rolled over, taking Crystal to the mattress and coming down on top of her. I slid inside her.

"Again, Wolf?" Crystal asked, laughing up at me.

I grinned down at her. "Just getting started on those six kids you want."

"I don't want six kids, Wolf. I just said that to get a rise out of you."

I stared at her a stunned moment, then dropped my head and muttered, "Thank God."

Crystal shook with laughter under me, and swear to God, it was the sweetest feeling.

Wolf—
Eight months later...

Crystal and I went to visit Shannon in the hospital to see the baby she'd just delivered. As we walked in the hospital room, I could hear Shannon and Crash arguing about the baby's name.

"I am not naming my precious little girl Harley," Shannon argued in a no-nonsense voice.

"You're daddy's precious little princess, aren't you?" Crash cuddled the baby close as he stood holding her next to the hospital bed. "Tell Mommy to hush, Harley Jean. What does she know about a good biker chick name anyway?" He whispered against his newborn daughter's cherub cheek.

"Aw, isn't she precious?" Crystal cooed as she walked over to peek at her. She kissed Crash on the cheek, then moved to the bed to lean over and kiss Shannon. "You did good, Mama."

I slapped Crash on the shoulder. "Congratulations, Brother. She's beautiful."

"Oh look, Harley Jean, this is your Uncle Wolf."

I grinned down at the little bundle and reached a hand to tickle her belly with two fingers. She immediately lifted her tiny hand and grabbed my finger in her fist with a surprisingly tight grip that had me chuckling. "Well, good morning, Harley Jean. Aren't you a beauty?"

Crash tore his eyes from his daughter long enough to glare at me. "Really, Wolf? Already flirting with her?"

I grinned, enjoying his torment.

"I am not calling her Harley Jean, Crash," Shannon insisted from the bed.

"Harley Jean, don't listen to Mommy, she loves your name. She's just cranky because you gave her quite a workout. That and her nipples are sore as h—"

"Crash!"

He grinned and nuzzled his baby girl, whispering, "So go easy on 'em, okay, Princess?"

I watched Shannon cover her face embarrassingly, and then my gaze slid over to Crystal and our eyes connected and held, silent communication passing between us. I knew Crystal was already pregnant. It was something she'd shared with me just last night.

I winked, and damned if she didn't give me the most beautiful smile in return.

Maybe our story wasn't a fairy tale by anybody's stretch of the imagination, but that was okay, because we finally had our own happy ending.

And life was good. Life was very, very good.

The End

GHOST
PREVIEW TEASER...

Sturgis...

"Well, Goddamn. It's about fucking time!" Butcher muttered as he looked over Shades' shoulder. Shades, Griz, Boot, and Hammer all twisted, looking behind them.

Ghost roared back into the Evil Dead's Sturgis campsite with a girl on the back of his bike, her arms wrapped tight around him.

"Where the fuck have you been?" Shades growled to Ghost once he'd dismounted and stalked toward them. "You've been MIA for two Goddamn days. I've got half the club out lookin' for you!"

"It's a long story," Ghost bit out.

"We got time," Griz replied with a glare.

"And who the fuck is that?" Shades asked, lifting his chin toward the girl they were all now eyeing.

Ghost looked back over his shoulder to the girl he'd left

standing by his bike and muttered, "You ain't gonna believe it."

Evil Dead MC - California

San Jose Chapter

Mack—President
Cole—Vice President
Crash—Sergeant at Arms
Wolf
Red Dog
Green
Cajun
Shane
Jake

Evil Dead MC – Alabama

Birmingham Chapter

Butcher—President
Shades—Vice President
Ghost
Griz
Hammer
Heavy
Tater
JJ
Slick—Treasurer
Boot—Sergeant at Arms

12Gauge
Bulldog—Prior Vice President (deceased)

Gulf Coast Chapter

Moon—President
Rocker—Vice President
Case
Coop
Deez
Brick
Pipe

Evil Dead MC – Louisiana

New Orleans Chapter

Undertaker—President
Mooch—Vice President
Blood—Sergeant at Arms
Sandman
Marla
Grouch

Devil Kings MC (DKs) – California

Oakland Chapter

Big Ed—President

Taz—Sergeant at Arms
Pepper

Devil Kings MC (DKs) – Georgia

Atlanta Chapter

Growler—President
Rat—Vice President
Reno –Sergeant at Arms
Rusty
Reload
Bear
Quick

Death Heads MC – Florida, Texas

If you enjoyed WOLF, please post a review.
Thank you!
Nicole James

Also by Nicole James

The Evil Dead MC Series
OUTLAW
CRASH
SHADES
WOLF
GHOST

RUBY FALLS

Made in the USA
Middletown, DE
06 July 2016